SALVATION
LAKE

Also by G.M. Ford

Nameless Night
Threshold

Leo Waterman Series

Who In Hell Is Wanda Fuca?
Cast In Stone
The Bum's Rush
Slow Burn
Last Ditch
The Deader the Better
Thicker Than Water
Chump Change

Frank Corso Series

Fury
Black River
A Blind Eye
Red Tide
No Man's Land
Blown Away

SALVATION LAKE

A Leo Waterman Mystery

G.M. FORD

THOMAS & MERCER

Published by Thomas & Mercer, Seattle

www.apub.com

Amazon, the Amazon logo, and Thomas & Mercer are trademarks of Amazon.com, Inc., or its affiliates.

ISBN-13: 9781503936850
ISBN-10: 1503936856

Cover design by Kerrie Robertson Illustration Inc.

Chapter 1

Red Lopez was a spitter. When Red told a story, it was best to get yourself alee of something waterproof, lest you end up looking like you'd been run through the Elephant Car Wash.

"So we was comin' down Yesler," Red gushed. "Me and George and Ralphie."

Everyone had found cover, except the guy they called Frenchie, who was so tanked he probably thought it was raining inside the Eastlake Zoo.

"And you know, 'bout halfway down the hill, the Hotel Cairo there on the corner?"

Everybody nodded. Thus assured, Red went on.

"There's this big ol' black mutt laying there on the front step lickin' his nuts for all he's worth—I mean, just havin' a party with himself—and George looks over to me and says, 'Man, I wish I could do that.' And you know what Ralphie says?"

He threw a liquid leer around the bar. Having heard the story three or four thousand times previously, the cowering crowd was prepared.

"Ralphie looks over at George and says, 'I don't know, man . . . maybe you ought to try to pet him first.'"

The place came unglued. As they yukked it up, chairs chattered on the wooden floor, backs got slapped and then slapped again, somebody repeated the punch line *al castrato*, and another wave of unbridled merriment tsunamied about the room.

This was an easy crowd to amuse. It wasn't lost on them that their alcohol problems had more or less turned them into lepers, a fact which made them somewhat disinclined to make value judgments regarding one another's atrocious behaviors. Something about pots and kettles, I'd always supposed.

There were, however, limits to even this well-lubricated amiability, most of which revolved around the pressing need to stay liquored up at all times.

You didn't want to be stealing anybody's money. Not because they were much into money, but because money was the gateway to booze, which, for them, constituted the very nectar of survival.

And you particularly didn't want to be spilling anybody's drink, unless you were in a position to immediately replace it. So when Billy Bob Fung lost his balance and belly flopped across the table in the far corner, things got contentious in a hurry.

Even among the drunk and destitute, Billy Bob was considered a world-class sponger. While guys like George and Ralph and Harold supported their drinking habits on meager pensions and Social Security checks, Billy Bob supported his by showing up at the Zoo. No one could recall Billy Bob ever having bought a drink for himself, or, for that matter, for anybody else.

Billy Bob, the rickety pedestal table, and about three gallons of beer hit the floor simultaneously, sending a flotilla of peanut shells and a tidal wave of suds rolling across the floor like the Banzai Pipeline.

Needless to say, Large Marge, as the owner of said suds, was less than amused. She'd been around long enough to know that Billy Bob wasn't good for the spillage, and that what she'd imagined to be the makin's of a cozy afternoon buzz was presently seeping through the ancient floorboards.

"Goddamn you," she shouted as she hauled herself out of the chair. "Look what you done, you freakin' idiot."

I waited for the foamy wave to blow past my boots and then scrambled to my feet. After the yelling and finger-pointing died down, they'd work things out "in house," so to speak, a designation which, thank heaven, didn't include me. No . . . I just stopped by the Eastlake Zoo now and then, to buy the boys a couple of rounds and see how my old compadres were weathering the slings and arrows.

Harold Green, George Paris, and Ralph Batista were the last known survivors of my old man's political machine. For twenty-seven years, Big Bill Waterman had milked his seat on the city council for every dime it was worth, keeping a small army of functionaries hard at work, covering his tracks and laundering his ill-gotten gains.

When the big guy finally blew a heart valve and fell stone dead on University Street, the whole felonious facade had come tumbling down in what seemed an instant. Grand jury indictments fell from the sky like winter rain. The lucky ones just got fired. The less fortunate spent time as guests of the state, prior to joining their fallen comrades in the life *au naturel.*

The rest of the mob I'd inherited somewhere along the line. Kind of like I'd inherited my old man's money, when I turned forty-five. For a long time I'd been pissed off that my trust fund didn't find its way into my pocket a whole lot sooner. I got over it though. When I look at it now, I don't think any reasonable person could have concluded that I was the kind of guy who'd have invested the money wisely and then skulked back to his cubicle the following Monday morning. Not even close. They'd given me the money back then, I'd have blown it for sure. Turned out my old man was a pretty good judge of character after all.

Besides . . . being forced to earn a living while I waited for the family pile to fall my way was pretty much the reason I'd spent twenty years working as a private eye. Despite the nicks and cuts, the bruises and the bullet holes, there's no denying that the experience shaped my life in ways nothing else possibly could have. It's like my namesake Leo Tolstoy said: too much prosperity is bad for people, in the same manner that too many oats are bad for a horse.

I was sidling toward a quick exit stage left and reaching in my pocket for a twenty to throw onto the bar, figuring I'd replace the spilled beer and return this sylvan glade to its usual state of bucolic bliss. No such luck though.

A sudden movement in the corner of my eye pulled my head around. Billy Bob had struggled to his knees and, with the aid of a chair, was trying to force himself upright. I watched in horror as Marge snarled and drew back a size 14 work boot. The look in her bloodshot eyes left little doubt. She was gonna drop-kick Billy Bob's head into the next area code.

What saved Billy Bob from oblivion was that the chair he'd been using to lever himself upright suddenly skidded on the wet floor and went clattering off into the darkness, sending him face-planting back to the beery boards a nanosecond before the boot whizzed past his head like an angry comet.

George lunged out of his chair. "No, Margie," he croaked. "Don't . . ."

What transpired next would become the stuff of myth. Still oblivious to the fact that Marge was attempting to collapse his noggin, Billy Bob once again tried to regain his feet, only this time, when he reached out for support, the first thing his fingers came into contact with was Marge's skirt, which he promptly latched onto with both hands.

Whatever mechanical contrivance kept the skirt closed was never intended to withstand the weight of a grown man. Took about a half a second of tugging before Billy Bob's weight popped the fastener and the skirt settled onto the floor like a patchwork parachute, leaving Marge standing there in work boots and a pair of camouflage boxer shorts—Mossy Oak, if the label was to be believed.

I have no doubt she would have stomped him to jelly had she been able to free her boots from the skirt. As it was, however, she looked like she was dancing the tarantella as she struggled to free her feet from the encircling mound of fabric.

George was weaving across the floor like a deranged halfback, figuring he could scoot Billy Bob out of range before Marge was able to extricate herself. Instinctively I began to move in that direction too. No sense letting anybody get hurt here.

I was halfway across the floor when my feet had other ideas. Next thing I knew, I was staring at the tips of my cowboy boots, wondering how the hell they got all the way up to eye level, the answer to which, unfortunately, was not long in coming.

I landed flat on my ass, with all the grace of a cow flailing down an elevator shaft. Baboom. Every glass in the joint rattled. My spine felt flattened. I was sure I was paralyzed. And that was *before* I realized I'd landed in a huge puddle of beer and that, in addition to being crippled for life, I was now ball-dripping wet.

Like I said, this was an easily amused crowd. The place came unhinged again. Everybody pointing at me and whooping it up for all they were worth. Even Marge forgot her Billy Bob death wish and was laughing her ass off.

And then the strangest thing happened. Like a dream scene out of an old black-and-white movie. In the wink of an eye, everything went completely quiet. I mean it went from rattling-the-rafters laughter to total tombstone silence, like somebody'd flipped the "shut-up" switch.

I looked over at George. He was standing in the middle of the floor, weaving back and forth like he was dancing the fox-trot. His bleary eyes were fixated on something over by the bar. I pushed myself to my knees. I could feel my ass dripping beer back onto the floor. I winced and looked over at the bar.

And there she was. Standing at the corner stool, taking it all in. Her eyes bounced from Marge standing there in her drawers to me on the floor and back again.

"You kinda hadda be there," I said.

Her facial expression said she wasn't amused.

"I should have let Eagen have his way," Rebecca Duval said disgustedly. "He wanted to send a couple of uniforms down to haul you in as a material witness."

Rebecca Duval was the chief medical examiner of King County. In the sixth grade, she'd told me she was going to grow up, go to college, and become a pathologist. Swear to God. Looked me right in the eye and laid out her life for me. I, of course, was immediately smitten. We'd been more or less inseparable for twenty years or so, at which point she'd experienced a spasm of lucidity and decided she'd had enough of me and what she termed my *perpetually adolescent behavior.*

Unfortunately for all concerned, the new Mr. Wonderful turned out to be a devilishly handsome yacht salesman and drug runner named Brett Ward. A no-brain asshole who went down in a hail of bullets when he tried to rip off the wrong people. To this day, I get pissed off every time he crosses my mind.

The Eagen she mentioned—the one who wanted to have me arrested as a material witness—had to be Timothy Eagen of the Seattle Police Department. Last time I saw him he was a lieutenant. Probably a captain by now, but either way, he hated my big ass the way Ahab hated that whale.

I climbed carefully to my feet. I pretended not to notice the trickle of beer seeping from the seat of my pants. "Material witness to what?" I asked her.

She shrugged. "I'm not at liberty to say. You'll have to get that from SPD. It's their case. I was just going to be nice and give you a ride but"—she flicked her fingernails in my direction—"but . . . you know. Like this?" She shook her head. "There's no way you're getting in my car."

I opened my mouth to protest, but she headed me off at the pass.

"I'll meet you at the office," she said, and then walked away. Halfway down the bar, she read my mind, stopped, and turned back in my direction. "This isn't the time to channel your inner idiot, Leo. Just drive yourself down to the office and get this over with. Don't give Eagen an excuse to roust you. Nothing would please the man more."

She threw a disgusted hand in the air. "I'm not sure I could stand that much gaiety."

I watched her back recede until the front door opened and a bolt of pure white light assaulted my eyes, before the door swung closed. Click.

• • •

The King County Medical Examiner's Office occupies an entire city block up on the west side of Pill Hill. Nothing special, just a nondescript white office building that could have as easily been an insurance company. Rebecca had a plush corner office on the fifth floor, but her coat spent way more time there than she did. She spent her time down in the basement with the stiffs. You lived in King County and died violently or under any kind of suspicious circumstances, this was where you ended up, till they got things sorted out. Rebecca was the senior sorter-outer. Sorta.

They called them "examination rooms." Probably because it sounded better than "the room where they cut you to pieces and spread your guts all over the place."

They were expecting me. Margot the receptionist held up four manicured fingers as I dripped up the hall in her direction. Not wishing to chat, I leaned left and headed directly for the elevators. She toodled me good-bye.

Examination room four was way down at the end of the hall. The big one with the seating area for spectators on the other side of the Plexiglas window. Rebecca was seated at the desk, shuffling through some paperwork. Eagen and another guy, probably his driver, were slouched over a couple of metal folding chairs along the north wall.

Eagen was a skinny little turd with a salt-and-pepper comb-over pasted across his pate like a sleeping hamster. He pushed himself upright and shuffled over in my direction. The closer he got to me, the more amused he became.

"You piss yourself?" he asked with a grin.

"Yeah," I said. "I'm expecting the sphincter to go next."

"Always the smart-ass," he growled.

"It's a cross to bear."

"Gentlemen," Rebecca interrupted. "How about we dispense with the ribald pleasantries and get down to business." She got to her feet and started across the room.

The minute her back was turned, Eagen jabbed a bony finger in my direction. "I haven't forgotten about you, dirtbag. Don't you ever think I have. Not ever."

"Gosh and golly, I'll have to sleep with a night-light," I assured him.

A while back, I'd talked a friend of mine into helping me extricate Rebecca from the mess her late husband had gotten her into. Happened that Marty Gilbert, in addition to being a badass and one of my oldest chums, was also a lieutenant in the Seattle Police Department. Go figure. Paths not taken and all that rot.

We were up on Vancouver Island, turning over rocks, looking for Rebecca, when somebody decided the world would be a better place without us. They sent several hundred rounds of automatic weapon fire tearing through the little knotty pine cabin where we were spending the night. Marty took a bullet in the shoulder and came real close to bleeding out, right there on the floor. I'll never forget having to call his wife, Peg. I get the chills whenever it crosses my mind.

Eagen and most everybody else in the SPD held me personally responsible for Marty's plight, an indictment which, even I had to admit, was not altogether without merit. That Marty survived his injuries, took early retirement, and moved Peg and himself down to San Diego to be near the grandchildren didn't much matter to Marty's former colleagues on the SPD. As far as they were concerned, my status was, and would remain in perpetuity, lower than whale shit.

Corpses are big-time conversation stoppers. Something about dead bodies always reminds me that there's more to being alive than the sack of flesh and bones we walk around in. I know it sounds weird, but stiffs have always reminded me of junked cars. Like the once-beloved family station wagon, sitting out there in the field with the tires flat and weeds growing in the windows. To me, whatever spark, celestial or otherwise, animates a human being disappears back into the galaxy at the moment of death, leaving behind little more than the rusted shell of some broke-down Buick.

Two corpses? Well that's a whole 'nother matter, isn't it? Rebecca emerged from the darkness wheeling two stainless steel autopsy tables. From across the room, all I could see was two pair of feet moving my way, bright green toe tags flapping in the breeze like pennants. The pair on the left were pink and puffy and clean. The pair on the right were covered in rough calluses and the kind of dirt that doesn't wash off.

I could feel Eagen behind me as I stepped between the tables. What the two stiffs had in common was that Rebecca had worked her magic on both of them. They'd been sliced and diced from stem to stern, split down the middle like capons, and then sewn back together, with something akin to red fishing line. Other than that, they could easily have been from different planets.

Pink Feet was in his early forties. Couple inches over six feet. Hundred eighty pounds or so. Looked like he made it to the gym on a regular basis. Wavy black hair with a good cut. Well nourished. Looked like he'd had his chest waxed. All smooth and hairless. Mr. Metrosexual poster boy.

I picked up his hand. His flesh felt like chilled putty. His nails said he'd had a professional manicure in the not too distant past. For reasons I didn't understand, I patted the back of his lifeless hand several times, almost as if to, in some belated way, comfort him, then set the hand back on the table and turned to the other guy.

Everything about this guy screamed of hard living. His feet were hard and horny. He hadn't had a haircut this century. He could have been thirty; he could have been sixty. He'd been eroded by the torrents of life. Lots of sleeping outdoors. Lots of secondhand cigarettes. Maybe five feet ten, he couldn't have weighed more than a hundred thirty pounds soaking wet, which, from the look of him, was how he spent most of his time.

"Well?" Eagen said from behind me.

"Well what?"

"You know either of these guys?"

"Nope," I said. "Never seen either one of them before."

"Cliff," Eagen said.

I looked over my shoulder. Watched as Eagen's man rummaged around on the floor in the far corner for about five seconds, found what he was looking for, and then started across the room with whatever it was draped over his arm like a vestment.

The minute he hit the glare of the overheads, I knew what he was carrying. Hell, half the people in the Pacific Northwest could have told you too.

It was my father's overcoat. The one he bought in London, back when I was in high school. Forty square yards of the heaviest, ugliest tweed money could buy. Made by some famous British tailor, supposedly worth its weight in gold, it was quite possibly the least attractive piece of attire I have ever seen.

First time he wore it, everybody in his inner circle lost their minds. His secretary, his sisters, his cronies down at the courthouse. Everybody told him he couldn't possibly wear that atrocity in public. I remember my Aunt Jean telling him he looked like a bad motel carpet walking down the street. It fell on deaf ears though.

Either he'd paid so much for the coat that he was unwilling to part with it, or wearing it was just his way of telling them all to piss off, but he wore that damn coat for the rest of his life. Hell . . . he had it on the day he dropped dead coming out of the Fairmont Hotel.

"My father's coat," I said to nobody in particular.

"They were covered with it," Eagen said.

Cliff stood next to Eagen and held the coat by the shoulders, like I was going to slip it on or something. I reached out and folded the right side of the coat back. The label was still there. CROMBIE, SINCE 1865. HAND TAILORED FOR WILLIAM H. WATERMAN.

Somebody'd taken a knife and sawn off the bottom foot or so of the coat, a move which, considering the physical enormity of my old man, had probably been a safety measure. Here and there along the impromptu hem, thick tendrils of fabric hung down like fungal fringe.

"And you've never seen them before in your life?" Eagen prodded.

I looked over at the two guys again. Shook my head. "Nope," I said.

"When did you last see the coat?"

I thought about it. "Sixteen years ago. Coupla months after my father died," I said. "His sisters came over the house one Saturday, packed up all his personal stuff, and took it all down to Goodwill or to the parish or something like that."

"I'll need to talk to them," he said.

"You'll need to stage a séance, then. They've been dead for years."

He was about to start over with the questions. Cops like to do that. See if they can push you into making inconsistent statements so they can jump all over you like a trampoline. I wasn't up for playing that game, so I beat him to the punch.

"That all you needed?" I asked.

He clamped his jaws together hard enough to stamp license plates and flicked his eyes in Rebecca's direction. Like most everybody else in town, he knew about our prior relationship. He was a torn man. He really wanted to jerk me around, but wasn't at all sure he wanted to do it in front of her. To make matters worse, SPD, like many urban police departments, was, at the moment, under quite a bit of pressure to provide a kinder, gentler brand of law enforcement. The kind that doesn't look like Ferguson, Missouri, or Staten Island, New York.

Eagen opted for discretion. He nodded over at Cliff and the coat, then looked at Rebecca and raised an eyebrow. "You finished with the coat?" he asked.

"I've got everything I need," she said.

"It'll be in the North Precinct property room, if you need it again." She thanked him.

He snuck a glance at me that would have wilted kale, nodded at his toady again, and headed for the door. I knew he wouldn't make it.

When Cliff had pulled open the door and stepped into the hall, Eagen turned back my way. "This wasn't an invitation for you to get involved, Waterman."

"I understand," I said.

"I find you've got your nose stuck in this, I'll bury you so deep it'll take your fancy-ass lawyer a week to find you in the system."

"Got it," I said. I wanted to give him a big grin and a two-fingered salute, but restrained myself.

Rebecca and I stood silently and watched as the two cops walked past the Plexiglas window and disappeared from view.

"I'm impressed," she said, when they were gone.

"'Bout what?"

"Your discretion. I thought for sure you'd give him a raft of crap. And then he'd cuff you and stuff you in the back of a cruiser and poor Jed would have to go down and bail your butt out of jail for the ump-teenth time."

"Eagen's nobody to fool with," I said earnestly. "He knows how to play the game. Besides, I don't do that kind of work anymore. I'm retired."

"You were, more or less, *always* retired," she said.

Having traipsed beneath this conversational trellis before, I quickly changed the subject. "Where'd they find these guys anyway?" I asked.

"In the trunk of a Zipcar, over on Pontius," she said.

"Both of them?"

A nod.

"Together. Like in one trunk?"

Another nod.

"We know who they are?"

Shake of the head this time. "Not a stitch of ID on either of them, and neither of them comes up in the national IAFIS fingerprint data-base either."

I walked over and stood between them, looking from one to the other.

"Odd couple," I said.

"Very," she agreed.

"These two in the trunk of the same car is like finding Nancy Reagan and Charlie Manson in a shallow grave in Bakersfield."

She chuckled.

"What'd they die of?"

A scowl and another shake of the head. "No idea."

"Really?" I bordered on agape. This was the girl who always knew the answers to everything. I'd heard her assistants joke that she could determine cause of death from the coffee shop across the street. Not knowing must be killing *her*.

She shrugged disgustedly. "Everything I've done so far speaks of oxygen deprivation. But I can't find anything that might have caused it. It's like somebody put them in a big glass jar and screwed on the lid. Toxicology won't be in for a couple of days," she said. "Maybe we'll get something there."

She didn't think so. I could tell.

A strained silence spread over the room like an oil slick. Funny how difficult conversation had become for us. After twenty years together, you'd think we'd have a storehouse of anecdotes that would make conversing with one another easy, but somehow it hadn't worked out that way. Quite the opposite. Since we'd moved on from one another, all of our shared experiences didn't seem to matter anymore. We were more like strangers than strangers. Love's a funny thing, I guess.

I stood in the silent room as she wheeled the odd couple back from whence they'd come. We'd talked about maybe making a go of it again. Of putting all the crap behind us and seeing if some of the spark was still burning, but somehow it never came to pass. Neither of us seemed to be willing to take that first step. So when she reemerged from the darkness at the back of the room and asked, "How's Rachel?" I kind of came up short.

It was like she had some kind of radar. Rachel Thoms was the woman I'd been seeing for the past year or so. Up until a few months ago, anyway. I thought about saying "fine," and hoping like hell that would be the end of it. But no. She'd have seen through me in a heartbeat.

"Last time I heard from her, she was fine," I said instead.

No way she was going to ask me. She just stood there giving me the fish-eye.

"She's in Nashville," I said finally. "Down at Vanderbilt. Teaching undergraduate classes for a friend of hers who's having a baby."

"Love is strange," she said with a grimace.

"I don't believe that particular word ever came up," I said.

She started for the door. "Come on," she said. "I've got a floater waiting for me in room one. You can observe if you want."

"Think I'll pass," I said. "But hey . . . you think I could get a couple of postmortem head shots of those two?"

She gave me that look again. Wagged a finger at me.

"For my scrapbook," I threw in quickly.

She cocked an eyebrow. "You heard what the man said."

"Scout's honor."

She thought it over. "See Margot on your way out," she said finally.

She patted me on the shoulder and strode off down the corridor.

▪ ▪ ▪

By the time I got back to my car, I'd worked up a full chafe. Felt like somebody was sandpapering my inner thighs. The car's interior smelled like a bus station bathroom. I wrinkled my nose, winged the postmortem photos in the direction of the backseat, and reluctantly climbed in. The smell was overwhelming, so I rolled down all the windows and went roaring up Jefferson Street in a self-generated gale.

The skyline looked as if the city was under siege. Something like twenty construction cranes hovered over downtown like steel mantises. Entire city blocks were being razed. Anything lacking historical significance was pretty much destined to disappear overnight. We've got detours that lead directly to other detours without intermediate ground. Traffic moves at the speed of lava.

I ducked down off Capitol Hill, slid onto Denny, and started across the city at a crawl. On my right, South Lake Union bristled with the shards of progress. What had, five years ago, been the last of the down-town mom-and-pop business districts was nearly gone now. Everywhere you looked, plastic-shrouded, twelve-story pachyderms rose to fill the horizon. An overnight frenzy of building designed to fill the needs of the army of thirtysomething techno-geeks flooding our glacial shores these days. The hour of the hipster was upon us. God help us all.

While Rust Belt behemoths like Detroit fought for their very existence, Seattle had more money than it could spend. Fresh money, young money, Amazon money. You could see it in the artisan cheese, the German cars, the fancy eateries, the wine bars, and the herds of techies skittering among the food trucks at lunchtime.

I inched my way down Elliott, creeping along in a light rain, past the Pier 86 grain terminal and up onto the Magnolia Bridge. Built in 1930, the bridge looked like it belonged in Beirut. Seemed as if the thick, iridescent moss must be the only thing holding it together.

Like the rest of the city, my neighborhood was abuzz with transi-tion. The stolid folks who built the massive houses back at the turn of the twentieth century had long since passed away. Over time, their proud homes had passed from immediate family to distant relatives and finally to those who had no connection to the place at all. Folks who bought million-dollar houses so they could bulldoze them to the ground and build something else. Something newer. Something better.

Fifty years ago, my old man bought the house from a frozen fish magnate with eight kids and a gambling problem. A huge, ponderous Tudor, perched high on the north end of the bluff, staring out over Elliott Bay and Puget Sound like some disapproving dowager aunt.

I live in the downstairs of the house. A few years back I'd staged a major renovation of the ground floor. Updated everything. Got rid of my old man's office. Opened the space up quite a bit. Not quite *open concept*, but not the dark rabbit warren of rooms it used to be either. A couple times a year, the Maid Brigade goes upstairs and rearranges the dust. Other than that, I pretend the other two floors don't exist.

When I was a kid, the mail carriers had a key to the gate. They used to let themselves in, walk up the long driveway, and drop the mail through a brass chute in the front door. Somewhere in my mind's ear, I could still hear the clatter it made when it hit the slate floor every morning.

Nowadays, mail carriers have a union, and I've got a mailbox bolted to one of the stone pillars that supports the gate. I pulled over next to it and got out of the car. The rain had thickened, but, considering how I smelled, the icy downpour was more of a relief than a bother.

I stood by the mailbox, shuffling through the usual collection of utility bills and once-in-a-lifetime offers, when I heard the yelp. My first thought was that it was a puppy. I threw a glance across the street. What had always been a big green-and-white colonial belonging to the Moody family was gone now. Replaced by something made to look like it was from the mid-fifties. Mid-century modern I think they call it. Single story, flat roof, lots of glass, it looked like a light-blue junior high school. About as appropriate to its Northwest surroundings as a barnacle in a béarnaise sauce, but you know . . . different strokes and all that.

I'd watched it go up over the past seven or eight months but really hadn't paid a heck of a lot of attention. I'd also seen the couple whom I assumed were building it. Hadn't paid much attention to them either. Late thirties, drove matching silver Lexuses. Seemed like they came out once a week or so to stand around in the rain and check the progress of the house. He was always huddled under a huge blue-and-white golf umbrella, like if he got wet he'd melt into the pavement, whereas she used her baby-blue bumbershoot to shield the little white dog she always seemed to have tucked under her arm. A matter of priorities, I'd guessed.

We'd exchanged curt nods and a couple of halfhearted waves on occasion, but that's as far as it had gotten. Probably my fault. Not only am I not the most social of creatures, but my place is surrounded by an eight-foot stone wall, a holdover from my old man's time, a rather imposing barrier that makes it hard to show up on my front porch with a Bundt cake, even if you wanted to.

But there they were. Mr. and Mrs. Lexus. Standing there on their new fieldstone front walk screaming at each other like a couple of fishmongers. Above the hiss of the rain and the sound of my idling engine, I could hear the dog yapping like crazy, but couldn't quite make out what the Lexus twins were screaming at each other.

What I *was* sure of was that I didn't want to add to these people's embarrassment by standing there gawking at them, so I closed the mailbox and double-timed it for the car on tiptoes, hoping I could make my escape before either of them noticed I was there.

I threw the mail in the car window, grabbed the door handle, and started to lever myself up into the seat. From the corner of my eye, I caught the arc of his hand as it sliced through the rain and made contact with the side of her head.

She went down in a heap. The dog began to howl. I shouldered the car door back open and hopped out onto the pavement, at which point Mr. Lexus caught my movement in his peripheral vision, pointed a bony finger in my direction, and shouted something.

I didn't know what he said and didn't much give a shit. In a dozen strides, I was across the street and jogging up their driveway.

As I approached, Mr. Lexus set his umbrella on the hood of the car, took off his glasses, and set them next to the umbrella. Like he was getting ready for a little knuckle action. Without the glasses his face had a pinched, ascetic look to it.

"Get the fuck out of here," he said to me.

He was damn near my height, but skinny in that health club sort of way. A cross-trainer rather than a weight lifter. Unless we were going to start this thing with a wheat-grass enema and a road race, he didn't figure to give me much trouble.

"Get away from here," he said. "This is none of your damn—"

I ignored him and kept coming, using my bulk to shoulder him aside as I turned the corner and started for his wife, whose efforts to regain her feet were being hampered by a voluminous white terry-cloth bathrobe that seemed to be everywhere at once.

The moment I bent and offered her my hand, he leaped onto my back. I have no idea what in hell he thought he was doing. Under the circumstances, piggyback rides were pretty much out of the question. Or maybe he had watched too many mixed martial arts programs on TV and figured he was going to choke me unconscious or something. Either way, it wasn't the best idea he ever had.

I bent at the waist, reached over my shoulder, and peeled him off my back like a sweater. He landed on the stone walkway. The impact drove the breath from his lungs in a great, wet gust. The little dog began to worry him like a terrier tearing at a rat. He groaned, took a back-handed swipe at the snapping mutt, missed, and then tried to suck air, only to discover that his diaphragm was on vacation. His eyes got wide with panic. His face began to redden. He grabbed his throat, hiccupped a couple of times, and then rolled over onto his belly and began to retch.

I reached down and lifted the woman to her feet. She had an angry red blotch on her left cheek and difficulty maintaining her balance. I kept a hand on her shoulder until she stopped waving around in the breeze.

She was a good-looking woman. Everything the media told little girls they ought to be. Maybe five nine, with a thick head of what used to be called strawberry blonde hair and the kind of trim figure you get from never eating anything white.

She shrugged my hand from her shoulder and knelt down beside her hubby, who was still barking at ants down on the walkway.

"You okay?" I asked her.

She didn't answer me. "Richard," she whispered. "Richard."

I pulled my cell phone from my jacket pocket. "I'm going to call 911," I said.

She stopped rubbing the back of his neck and looked up at me.

"No," she said. "Please don't do that."

"He's got no right to put his hands on you."

She pushed herself to her feet, and, for the second time, I noticed how bad her balance was. Almost seemed like she was drunk. When she put a hand on my shoulder, I couldn't decide which of us she was trying to steady.

"He didn't mean it," she assured me.

"They never do," I said. "That's exactly why we need to call."

"No," she said again. "Please. Don't do that."

I didn't say anything. Just stood there and watched as she got down on her knees again and began to minister to her husband. I'd spent twenty years sticking my nose into other people's business for a living, and one of the things I'd learned is that there's a fine line between doing your civic duty and being a pain-in-the-ass busybody. Last thing on earth I wanted to be was one of those self-righteous twits with an unquenchable desire to tell other adults what to do. I mean, if I look over and you're about to step in front of a bus . . . yeah, I'm gonna stick out my arm. But other than that, presuming you're all growed up and haired over, as they say in Texas, as far as I'm concerned, you're pretty much on your own.

Hubby was up on his knees now. He twisted his neck and looked up at me. A line of green spittle still connected his lower lip to the pavement below. His narrow face was the color of an eggplant.

"Stay down," I advised him.

His lower lip quivered a couple of times, as if he had something to say. An awkward second passed before he thought better of it and simply turned his face away from me.

"Poco," his wife said. "Poco, come here." The hair ball gave hubby a wide berth as it skittered over in her direction. She reached down and scooped up the dog. And then her free hand was on my chest, pushing me backwards up the driveway.

"We'll be okay," she kept repeating in a soft voice as she nudged me backwards. The dog seemed to agree.

I let her move me all the way to the street, and then made one last plea. "You don't have to put up with that crap," I said.

Behind her, hubby had pushed himself to his feet and was staggering toward the front door. I watched as he wrenched it open, stumbled inside, and slammed the door. The whole glass front wall of the house undulated from the impact.

"It's okay," she said.

I reached out and put a finger on her damaged face. The dog started to growl.

"Just go," she said with a sigh.

So I went. Hesitatingly. Under protest. Turning back every couple steps. Noticing what a crooked, unsteady line she walked back to the house, and how she hesitated for a long moment before grabbing the handle and disappearing inside.

■   ■   ■

A hot shower had seldom felt better. By the time I'd scrubbed the stink off, found a set of clean clothes, and brewed up a cup of coffee, one of Jimmy Hallinan's On the Go Pro auto-detailing trucks was parked behind my rig out in the driveway, and one of his crews was crawling all over my ride.

Wasn't that long ago I'd have been out in the driveway cleaning the damn car myself. Not these days though. These days I'm a lot more likely to solve problems with folding money than with elbow grease.

My life of sloth started right after I moved back into the ancestral manse. Six weeks later, the place looked like it was inhabited by a troop of baboons. I was kicking stuff out of the way as I walked down the halls, and eating sandwiches off thrice-used paper plates. About the time I found myself staring down at the kitchen counter, trying to decide if that dark spot was a black olive and whether or not I was going to eat it, only to have it scurry off into the darkness, I knew something had to be done.

Housecleaning was first. An army of maids arrives on Tuesday mornings and gives the place the full monty. I drive over to Beth's Café for breakfast while they're thrashing about. By the time I get back, the place is spic-and-span and, with a little creative rationalization, I can pretend I had something to do with it.

I know people who just aren't content unless they're doing something. It's like they can't be left alone with themselves, or they'll go nuts. I don't have that problem. I'm perfectly happy doing nothing at all. Ask anybody.

Funny thing though . . . I've always felt a little bit guilty about throwing money at problems, which is weird, because guilt is not big on my "ways to feel" list. The life I've led doesn't much lend itself to second-guessing. If my family crest had a motto, it would be: "It seemed like a good idea at the time."

So, a couple hours later, when one of the car detailers knocked on my front door and told me my car was once again ready for human habitation, I stepped outside to grease some palms and further assuage my conscience.

I gave the car a quick once-over, inside and out. Looked and smelled great. The kid who'd come to the door told me he'd leave the plastic on the seats for a couple of days, if he was me. I said I would.

I thanked them all and gave each of them a twenty for a tip. As they turned and started walking toward the On the Go Pro truck, one of the Mexican guys turned to the guy beside him and said, "*Hombre extraño. Tener una imagen de ese chico predicador, al igual que.*"

"*Hijo de puta estaba muerto,*" the other guy said.

First guy nodded in agreement. "*Ambos estaban muerto.*"

I know just enough Spanish to be dangerous, but I was pretty sure a *predicador* was a preacher and was damn sure that *muerto* meant dead.

"Who was dead?" I asked.

Everybody stopped walking and turned back my way. I repeated the question.

"In the car," the guy who'd come to the door said.

When I didn't get the message, he walked back to my car, opened the door, and pulled something from the dashboard, then walked over and put the envelope containing Rebecca's postmortem photos in my hand.

"They was on the floor in back," he said.

"Did he say something about a preacher? *Un predicador.*"

He turned to the others and rattled off something in machine-gun Spanish. The other two took turns answering. It went on for a while. All of it in Spanish and coming by way too fast for me.

Door Guy translated. "They call him 'the Preacher' 'cause he's always talking about God and angels and hell and how we're all sinners and everything like that." He tapped his temple with his finger and nodded knowingly. Apparently, the consensus was that our boy the Preacher wasn't quite right in the *cabeza*.

"Who calls him the Preacher?" I asked.

Another rapid-fire discussion ensued. "The other people in the homeless camps," Door Guy said finally. "They say he's a crazy homeless guy. Lives around in the camps. Always drives people crazy after a while—you know, with all that God talk of his—so he has to move around a lot. Last time they seen him he was living under the freeway. You know . . . down a couple blocks south of Madison."

I tried a few more questions, but all I got was opus two. They were being polite but starting to get antsy. I guess twenty bucks doesn't buy what it used to.

I watched them back out of the driveway, music crankin', bumpin' so hard the sheet metal on the van shimmied like a stripper. I grinned, threw the photo envelope onto the passenger seat, and swung the car door closed. The rain had stopped, but a crystalline hiss lingered in the air. Boxcar clouds hurried across the western horizon, like they were scheduled to be somewhere else. To the east, out over the top of the house, the sky was bruised and broken. I stifled a shiver.

·   ·   ·

On any given night, there's something like nine or ten thousand homeless people in Seattle. Of that number, six thousand or so find a roof somewhere among the tent cities, the missions, and the shelters, which leaves about four thousand souls sleeping outdoors in a climate better suited to ducks than derelicts.

So, when I poked my head out the kitchen door the next morning and found myself staring at a steady, slanting rain, I had a pretty good idea how I was going to spend the day.

By two thirty, I'd worked up a full sweat tromping around beneath the maze of freeway ramps and intersection overpasses that form the southern border of the International District. Like I'd hoped, the rain had kept most of the denizens of the damp rolled up in their bedrolls, waiting for fairer skies. Not that it had done me any good.

I'd shown the Preacher's photo to a good fifty or sixty urban campers, none of whom had shown the slightest glimmer of recognition. I'd been cursed and growled at more times than I could count, outright threatened on two occasions, and, to put the icing on the cake, I'd just stepped in shit for the second time.

I was cursing under my breath, standing on one leg, using a broken piece of concrete to scrape the shit from the sole of my shoe. I rubbed the last of it off on the packed dirt and looked back down the incline. Half a dozen one- and two-man camps littered the barren hillside. Everything from ancient Sears tents to blue plastic lean-tos to nothing more than a pile of dirty cardboard. Trash everywhere. Three or four dogs wandering about. The wretched refuse of our teeming shore.

I decided I'd had enough. Whatever perverse curiosity my father's long-lost overcoat had instilled in me had been sorely diminished by my odyssey.

It had been years since I'd found myself in a place like this. Guys like George and Ralph and Harold had long since learned how to work the system to keep a roof over their heads. The people I'd met this morning weren't the old-time park bench bums of the past either. They were way younger, and way meaner. Waxen, hollow-eyed, and angry, these were the collateral damage of broken dreams and failed relationships and unspeakable sexual abuses. Kids who seemed to have fallen from grace without ever having attained it.

I looked around. Seemed like the best way out of here was to go up, toward the bottom of the roadway. That way I could peek out and see exactly where I was and decide which way to go from there.

I was angling across the face of the slope, working my way toward a chevron of light in the upper right-hand corner, when I noticed a little one-man camp set up directly beneath the underside of the pavement. Loud. Dirty. The low-rent district of the no-rent district.

I reversed field and moved in that direction. He'd dug out a terrace for himself. A place flat enough so he wouldn't roll off down the hill. That way he commanded the high ground, with six vertical feet of concrete covering his back. I was about halfway to the top when he heard me coming and sat up.

He was maybe seventeen. He had a knit cap pulled down so far over his ears nothing showed but an oval of face so dirty it looked like he was wearing a Lone Ranger mask.

"Ain't nothin' here for you, man," he said. He kept one hand hidden in his bedroll, making like he maybe had a weapon.

I showed him my palms. "No trouble," I said. "I just want you to look at a picture." I reached inside my coat. Above our heads, traffic roared like a hurricane.

He pushed himself up to his knees. Turned out he wasn't bluffing. He had a knife. One of those serrated bread knives you buy in supermarkets for a buck ninety-nine.

"I ain't lookin' at nothin'," he shouted at me.

I pulled out the photo, unfolded it, and faced it in his direction.

"You ever seen this guy?" I yelled.

He looked away. "Get out of here, man," he said.

I took two steps forward, waving the photo as I struggled up the steep bank.

He came bursting out of his nest like a scalded rat, slashing the knife back and forth, missing the front of my coat by about three inches, before turning tail and escaping back to the safety of his bedroll.

"Take it easy, man," I chanted. "Take it easy."

"I'll cut you," he yelled. "Don't think I won't."

I held up my hands in mock surrender. "You win, kid," I said. "I'm outta here." I watched his eyes flick over at my right hand, where I held the postmortem photo, flick back to my face, and then be drawn back to the photo almost against his will.

"Is that . . ." he started, but stopped.

"Is that what?" I asked.

"You know . . . like . . ."

"Like what?"

"Dead. That guy dead?"

"Yeah," I said. "Somebody found him in a car trunk up in South Lake Union."

He thought it over. "You a cop?" he asked after a minute.

"Nope."

"Then what's it to you?"

I told him about my father's overcoat.

"Biggest coat I ever seen," he said.

"My father was about the biggest dude anybody ever seen," I said.

"Bigger than you?"

"Way bigger."

He was duly impressed. He looked over at the picture again.

"Somebody off him?"

"Actually, they don't know what killed him. They're workin' on it."

"Wasn't a bad dude," he said. "If he'da just shut up once in a while."

"You know his name?"

He shook his head. "People call him the Preacher, 'cause he's always running his mouth about God and shit."

He walked over to a black plastic bag wedged under the roadway and started sliding it down the hill in my direction. "This here's his stuff. I told him I'd watch it for him 'till he come back, but I guess he won't be needin' it now."

"He say where he was going?" I tried.

"Just said he was gonna find the prophet of the Lord."

"Maybe he did," I said. I squatted down and untied the knot at the top of the bag. Above our heads, a sudden screech of tires filled the air in the second before the unmistakable sound of one car plowing into another reached us. Horns began to honk.

A cloud of mildew floated out of the bag. I pulled my head back. I'm not the squeamish type but, right at that moment, I'd have parted with serious money for a pair of latex gloves.

I held my breath and started pulling things out. It's all relative, I suppose, but I'm guessing you'd have to be down and out and homeless to understand why anything in that bag was worth toting around with you. I'm not altogether sure what freedom is, but it's sure as hell something more complicated than *nothing left to lose*.

One piece at a time, I unwadded everything and laid it out on the ground. Everything was damp and dirty and smelled of mold. An old wool blanket, army green. A pair of jeans with the seat blown out. A couple bath towels whose original color it was no longer possible to ascertain. The remnants of a bar of white soap. Two sweaters and a gray hoodie. Another black plastic bag with three holes cut in it. I was guessing he used it as a poncho when the weather went from bad to worse.

Finally, I turned the bag inside out and a couple pieces of paper and a piece of wood fell out onto the hillside. The papers turned out to be a pamphlet on personal hygiene from a local mega-church called Mount Zion Ministries and a folded-up picture of Jesus looking all blond and Swedish-like.

That was it. The sum of this man's life lying out on the ground and not one thing to tell me who he was, or even who he'd once been, as if poverty and degradation not only robbed a person of their dignity but of their identity as well. Almost like it didn't matter *who* they were anymore, 'cause they didn't own enough stuff to be listed among the living.

I used my toe to turn over the piece of wood. It was an award plaque. Or at least it had been once. I picked it up. Screwed to the bottom was a brass plate. The words MOST LIKELY TO SUCCEED were engraved into the metal. Above the words, the only thing that hadn't been scratched off was the number seven. The upper half looked as if it had once been a photograph of the recipient, likewise scraped to nothing.

I walked uphill and handed it to the kid. He ran his fingers over the face of it several times, and then handed it back.

"You think it was his?" he asked after a minute.

I shrugged, then sat down and held the ruined plaque in front of my face with both hands. This wasn't a casual scratch-out. Whoever had defaced it had spent a lot of time and energy doing it. They'd taken some sharp object and gouged all the way through the metal in places. I wondered what inner demons had fueled that much effort. Anger? Hate? Self-loathing? Something strong, for sure.

"Assuming it was his," I mused, looking around, "looks like he took one hell of a fall since he was voted most likely to anything."

The boy folded his arms across his skinny chest and sat rocking on his tailbone while he thought about it. "Ain't so far anymore," he said, finally.

"What's not far?"

"Ain't very far from top of the class to out on your ass," he said.

.   .   .

Took me thirty-five minutes to get back to South Plummer Street where I'd parked my car. Somewhere in my travels I'd passed completely under the freeway, so I had to walk all the way up to the overpass at Madison to get back to where I'd started.

As I'd trudged along, my mind kept wandering back to what the kid had said. About how it wasn't all that far from living in suburbia to living under a bridge. I kept wondering whether the American dream was dead, or if it had just morphed into something else while I was busy figuring out what wine went with what.

By the time I hopped up onto the plastic covering my car seats, I was bone tired and working my way to clinically depressed. I dropped the remains of the plaque on the passenger-side floor and fired her up. I told myself I was waiting for the heater to warm up, but mostly I just sat there looking out through the windshield, feeling like one of those Scandinavian detectives who spend most of their time staring out at dark water and brooding.

The dash clock read 4:10. The prospect of sitting in rush hour traffic held sufficient terror to snap me out of my stupor. I dropped the Chevy into gear and rolled down the hill. For once, my timing was perfect; I beat the thundering herd out of downtown and was heading north on Elliott in about ten minutes.

On my left, popping in and out of view between buildings, Puget Sound was ruffled with whitecaps. I fought the traffic lights past the exit for the Magnolia Bridge, all the way down to Dravus, so I could do a little shopping on the way home.

Shopping in my neighborhood meant going down to what had, for the past hundred years or so, been known as "the Village." A retro little collection of shops so super-white and squeaky clean you half expected Beaver Cleaver to come out of the sweet shoppe licking a cherry vanilla ice cream cone. Welcome to 1957.

I wheeled into the Metro Market parking lot and got out. I was running on autopilot, ruminating on the death of the middle class and income inequality in the twenty-first century, which probably explains why I didn't see her until we both reached for the same Sumo orange. Her hand landed on top of mine.

Funny how inadvertently touching another human being has become cause for terror. The whole zombie-pandemic thing, methinks. Our hands recoiled as if we'd touched a molten ingot. When I looked up, she was frowning into my face. Mrs. Lexus, my neighbor from across the street, wishing she was any other place on earth. The little white dog was riding on the fold-down area.

Dogs in supermarkets is one of those places where I've failed to evolve. Far as I'm concerned, any animal who considers toilet water to be an aperitif, or whose idea of hors d'oeuvres involves its own ass, ought to stay the hell outside.

I couldn't help myself. I laughed out loud.

"Talk about an awkward moment," I said.

To her credit, she had a sense of humor. She smiled in agreement.

"I'm not sure awkward quite covers it," she opined.

"Great oranges," I tried.

This time, she laughed.

I stuck out my hand. "Leo Waterman," I said.

She took it. "Janet Seigal," she said. "And everybody in the neighborhood knows who you are, Leo Waterman. You used to be a private eye. Your father was some kind of big muckety-muck in city government. Supposedly stole millions from the taxpayers."

"I prefer to think he was just more adept than most at doing business the way it was done back then."

"No revisionist history for you, eh?" she said with a twinkle.

"Things were different in my father's day. Everybody was in everybody else's pocket. It was the way they did business. They didn't look at it as corruption. They looked at it as greasing the skids."

"*La mordida*," she said.

"Exactly," I said with a grin. "Everybody gets a little bite."

Yesterday's events were hanging over us like a locomotive, but I wasn't going to bring it up unless she did. She did.

"About yesterday . . ." she began.

"I didn't mean to intrude," I mumbled.

"Yes you did," she said affably.

I opened my mouth, but she waved me off.

"And it was the right thing to do," she added. "But I just want you to know . . . You know, that kind of thing . . . I wouldn't want you to think . . ."

Suddenly, the amused expression slid from her face, and she was looking over my shoulder instead of into my eyes. Didn't take Sherlock Holmes to figure this one out.

I flicked a glance back over my shoulder, and there he was. The hubby—Richard, as I recalled—clutching a twelve-pack of bathroom tissue tight to his chest. As he moved our way, his back got stiffer and his stride more assertive, but it isn't easy to play the hard case while you're squeezing the Charmin.

Mr. Whipple walked around me and dumped his load into the shopping cart. He kept his eyes locked on mine, like we were about to have a fifth-grade staring contest.

"Can I help you with something?" he demanded.

"Probably not," I said.

"Well then?"

"Well then what?"

The air was thick as gravy. Wisely, Janet wanted no part of it. She swung the shopping cart in an arc and began walking toward the end of the aisle. I couldn't help but notice how hard she seemed to be leaning on the cart. Richard was backing away. He unfurled a bony finger and jabbed it in my direction. "You stay away from us," he said.

Janet and the cart disappeared around the end of the aisle. I lowered my voice.

"You hit her again and you'll need help wiping your ass," I promised.

He showed me a different finger and disappeared from view.

I took my time shopping, secretly hoping to cross his path again so's I could shove that finger up his ass, but, alas, it was not to be. By the time I collected some True North coffee and the makings for a mac and cheese, darkness had slithered over the bluff and the wind had bared its teeth.

■   ■   ■

First thing I used to tell prospective clients was not to hire me. That they'd be better off going to the cops. That modern police departments have resources available to them that no private agency, regardless of size, can hope to match.

But people don't hire private eyes because it makes sense. They hire them because they're desperate. Because they find themselves in a situation where they've tried everything reasonable and it hasn't worked, so they figure it's time to get crazy.

There's no excuse for me though. Not only did I know better, but I'd been warned to keep my nose out of it. Unfortunately, something inside me doesn't like being told what to do, so I figured I'd work off my rebellious streak by finding out whatever I could about the plaque. Maybe who manufactured it. Something like that.

Before I left the house, I'd surfed my way through Seattle's trophy and awards listings on the web, looking for those shops that had been around the longest, figuring the dead guy had to be under fifty, so the award must have been given in either 1987, 1997, or 2007. Wound up with five stores that had been around for at least twenty-plus years.

Problem was, although the companies may have been around for decades, the people presently working the stores had been around for about forty-five minutes.

The tattooed kid at Northwest Awards knew nothing from nothing. Athletic Awards in the U District was even worse. When I asked her for the store's address so I could GPS directions to Ballard Trophy and Awards, she had to find a piece of letterhead and read it to me. Sheeeesh.

The Ballard address was up north, damn near in Crown Hill. As I cut across North Fortieth Street, I experienced a moment of extreme clarity, wherein I decided that it would be sacrilege to be that close to Señor Moose at lunchtime and not suck down a couple Enchiladas de Puya, so, instead of turning right onto Eighth and getting about my business, I headed straight for the feedbag, grinning like an idiot and salivating like Pavlov's dog.

Four minutes later, as I rolled around the big bend on West Woodland, the Ballard Bridge came into sight. That's when a sign up ahead on the left suddenly jogged my memory. MOUNT ZION MINISTRIES, the black-and-white sign read. And it was a good thing it had a sign, too, because the rest of it was the least likely-looking church building I'd ever seen. Single story. The size of a grocery store. Three white doors out front, and not another aperture of any kind—no windows, no skylights, no nothing, just a solid black building with the sign on top. About as inviting as your average mausoleum, which probably explained why I'd been driving by it for years without ever really taking notice.

The guy behind me chirped his tires and then leaned on the horn as I jammed on my brakes, cut hard right into the driveway of a muffler shop, and slid to a halt.

I rummaged around on the passenger-side floor and came up with the Swedish Jesus picture and the personal hygiene pamphlet I'd found among the dead guy's things. *YOUR BODY AND YOU*. Mount Zion stamp down at the bottom of the back page.

Mount Zion had churches scattered all over the Seattle area. I'd figured they probably gave out thousands of *YOUR BODY AND YOU* pamphlets every year. Expecting anyone involved with the church to know anything that could help me identify the dead guy had seemed like a pipe dream, but now . . . you never know. Sometimes reality runs things right in front of your nose just to see if you're paying attention. So what the hell? I was here.

I eased myself back into the West Woodland Way traffic flow, staged a tire-squealing U-turn about a block on the other side of the bridge, and was standing in front of the church about two minutes later.

The only car in the lot was a white Range Rover. I sauntered down the length of the building and peered around the side, looking to see if there were any cars parked over there. Nothing there but one hell of a big parking lot. Coupla acres, anyway.

Seattle's a pricey town these days. Even in a semi-industrial area such as this, that much land, inside the city limits, was worth big-time folding money. Whatever Mount Zion's doctrine was, apparently poverty wasn't part of the program.

With those enchiladas dancing in my head, I made an executive decision that my time would be better spent with a full stomach than with an empty church. I was reaching for the car door when, from inside the building, a crashing sound stopped my hand in midair.

I walked over to the triple doors, thumbed down the latch, and gave it a yank. It swung open; I stepped inside. Took my eyes a minute to adjust.

The place was nearly empty. Wooden pews were stacked three high along the south wall. Up in front, along the edge of the stage, several nearly chest-high lines of folded metal chairs stretched completely across the building.

The sound I'd heard from the parking lot had been the front rank of folded-up chairs fanning out over the sanctuary floor like a deck of cards.

I watched in silence as two men appeared from behind the curtain and glared down at the mess.

The little guy caught sight of me first, cocked his head, then made his way to the stairs and started walking my way. Late twenties, early thirties, sporting rimless glasses and a case of early-onset hairlessness. One of those postmodern nebbishes who walks around with his cell phone faceup in his hand, staring at the screen, as if where he's going couldn't possibly be as interesting as where he's already been. He bellied right up to me and frowned up into my face. "Who are you with?" he demanded.

I made like I was checking the surrounding area. "At the moment . . . you."

He blinked once. "Is that supposed to be funny?"

"I hope not." I stuck out my hand. "Leo Waterman."

He ignored my hand. "You with Mount Zion?" he wanted to know.

I slid the handful of paper from my coat pocket and unfolded it.

"I found this among someone's belongings," I said, handing him *YOUR BODY AND YOU*. "I was wondering if there was any way to find out . . . you know . . . how he got this. Or maybe who gave it to him."

He never so much as glanced at the photo.

"This place look like it's open to you?" he sneered.

"I thought churches were open all the time," I said, holding my ground.

His partner was sauntering in our direction now. Looked like he was as wide as he was tall. Maybe six two or so, but real thick. Two seventy, at least. One of those bulked-up guys who puts on a layer of fat as he ages, but never loses the sheet of muscle beneath.

"What we got here, C-Man?" he asked.

"Some kinda nosey bastard," the little guy said.

"I was trying to get a line on this guy," I said, holding up the Preacher's likeness.

He plucked the photo from my fingers and brought it up in front of his face. I watched as his eyes slid around the image. His icy blue eyes were still running back and forth over the surface of the photograph as he reached out and handed it back to me.

He had a Malibu tan and enough gold teeth to cover the national debt.

His slicked-back hair was the color of dirty brass, and long over the ears.

He gave me a big shit-eater grin and extended a hand. "Brother Biggs," he announced.

I reflexively took it and then immediately wished I hadn't. He jammed his big paw all the way back into my grip and applied rock-crusher pressure. Took all I had not to sag at the knees. Instead, I matched him tooth for tooth and tried not to let on about the shooting pains racing up and down my arm.

"Leo Waterman," I said through clenched teeth.

"These holy rollers ain't in business no more," he said. "Me and the C-Man just lookin' after a few things for 'em. What's your angle here?"

"Just trying to get a line on that guy in the picture."

"What's it to you?" he asked.

"Curiosity."

"Killed a lot of kitties," he said, and then clapped his other hand in the middle of my back and began to steer me toward the door. I didn't resist, but I didn't help either. Didn't matter. Next thing I knew I was moving across the floor like I was on casters, and the little hairs all over my body were beginning to tingle.

Wasn't till he got me all the way outside that I finally got hip to what was going on with me. When you're as big as I am, it doesn't happen very often, so maybe that explains why I was so slow on the uptake: something inside of me was a little scared of this guy. I could feel it way down at the bottom of my innards. Some fundamental survival instinct was telling me that Brother Biggs could not only pound me to jelly, but that he almost certainly would relish the experience.

He pulled me in close and kept on crushing my hand until we reached my car. It was all I could do not to shake the cramp out. I could smell his breath mints as he pinned me with those ice-blue eyes. "Don't want to be seein' you around here anymore." He tapped me twice in the chest with his index finger. "I was you, I'd make it a point not to be runnin' into us again," he said. He looked over at the other guy. "Right, C-Man?"

The little guy looked up from his phone. "I was him, I'd make it my life's work."

At which point, they turned and began to walk away. Slowly, as a sign of disdain. I hopped into the driver's seat, started the car, and went rolling after them, pulling my phone from my pocket as I crunched across the gravel.

"Hey," I yelled out the window. They turned in unison. "Say cheese," I said as I snapped their picture through the car window.

Above the roar of the engine, I couldn't make out what either of them was yelling, but somehow I figured it wasn't Bible verses.

The day went downhill from there. Must have been fifteen people standing outside Señor Moose waiting for a lunch table. Forty, forty-five minutes, at least, I figured. I considered rustling up a parking space and getting in line anyway—you know, just to kind of spite myself—but just couldn't, on this day at least, bring myself to be quite that stupid, so the Enchiladas de Puya became the stuff of dreams, and I kept on driving, rolling up toward Crown Hill, up where you could still park in the street for free, and the city hadn't gotten around to putting in sidewalks they'd promised half a century before.

Lost in thought, I rolled up Twenty-Fourth in a daze, past the Buddhist temple and a big blue JESUS SAVES sign. I'd wasted a lot of time on this and wasn't one bit closer to finding out who anybody was than when I'd started. Worse yet, I was beginning to wonder why I was bothering with this thing. Which, of course, got me to thinking about my tenuous connection to my father, which, equally of course, started to take me places I'd visited often enough to know I didn't want to go back, so I snapped myself upright in the driver's seat, rolled my neck around in a circle, and turned the radio up loud. Santana. "Black Magic Woman." Could be worse.

.   .   .

I'm old enough to recognize those moments when the universe tells you to take a hike, that enough is enough and not to press your luck. Problem is, I'm apparently not smart enough to take advantage of the insight. Trust me. I've got the scars to prove it.

I pulled open the door of Ballard Trophy and Awards and walked in. Behind the counter an old man with a walrus mustache was polishing a bowling trophy.

He turned my way. "Help you?" he asked.

I reached into my coat pocket and pulled out the plaque. He turned it in his hands, looking at it from all directions, then brought it up to his face and sniffed it.

"*Schmatta*," he declared. Sensing that my Yiddish wasn't up to snuff, he helped me out. "Cheap crap. The kind of thing they don't even let you sell anymore. It supposedly emits some kind of gas into the atmosphere."

"Anything else?" I prompted.

He gave it a second look. "Looks a lot like the crap that used to come out of that factory down in Shelton." Shelton was a little town about eighty miles south of Seattle. "Used to turn 'em out by the tens of thousands. Tree huggers put 'em out of business years ago." He made a disgusted face. "Gotta be green, ya know."

"Any way to figure out who sold it?"

He shook his head. "Every shop in town sold 'em." He shrugged. "I was looking for whoever used to own this though . . ." He hesitated. "I'd start with the archdiocese."

"What archdiocese?"

"Of Seattle," he said. "You know—the Catholics! They used to buy these things by the truckload. Used 'em for just about everything. School awards, church awards. Athletic prizes. Knights of Columbus. Catholic women's charities. All of it."

■   ■   ■

The onshore flow was thick as cotton, and carrying enough water to make the wipers seem spastic. The lights in the fog-shrouded houses were soft and fuzzy as I crept up Magnolia Boulevard at about four miles an hour.

As I crawled past the Seigal house, I threw a quick glance in that direction. Between the floor-to-ceiling window and the front door, wedged back against the wall in the foggy darkness, I saw the orange glow of a cigarette. I braked to a stop. Squinted out the window, trying to make out the smoker. A sudden riffle in the fog told me that whoever it was had ducked around to the back of the house. I lifted my foot from the brake.

My front porch lights and the light over the garage come on automatically. Tonight they looked dim and distant as I eased into my driveway. I reached up and pushed the button on the garage door opener. I could hear it squeaking open, but couldn't make it out in the foggy gloom.

I eased through the yawning doorway and shut her down. I was feeling real uneasy, so I locked the car up tight and then locked it in the garage. Couldn't tell you the last time I did that.

The willies followed me into the house on tiptoe. I turned the thermostat to Caribbean, then went around flipping on lights until the place was ablaze, none of which seemed to lessen the sense of dread that shadowed me from room to room.

I opened the front door and used the remote to close the gate. The complete whiteout in the front yard made me feel clammy, like I was wrapped in wet felt. I closed the door, double-locked it, and then activated the security system, which I generally never turn on, because between the screaming of the alarm and the banks of halogen security lights, my neighbors tend to get seriously pissed off when it's tripped.

Last of all, I opened the hall closet and reached back into the darkness, behind the coats and boots and scarves, all the way to the corner. I pulled out my 12-gauge Mossberg Slugster shotgun. I grabbed the box of ammo from the upper shelf and fed five bright red shells into the magazine. Way I figured it, if I couldn't stop 'em with five of those cannonballs, I probably deserved whatever came next.

．　．　．

Anybody who believes that people can't levitate should have seen me at 2:47 A.M., when the security alarm went off. I lifted out of the seat like a friggin' moon rocket. Last I recalled, I'd just finished scarfing down the last of the previous night's mac and cheese and was ensconced in my favorite chair watching an episode of *True Detective* that I'd seen three or four times before. The one where Rust and Marty go to the tent revival.

The security buzzer was hammering nails in my ears, making it nearly impossible to collect my thoughts. I ran a hand over my face and scrambled to my feet. I was relieved to see the shotgun still resting in the corner. I reached over and grabbed it.

I held the Mossberg in my left hand as I started down the hall. My first instinct was to pull open the front door and confront whoever or whatever was out there. Instead, I turned right into the dark front parlor, slipped over to one of the front windows, got down on one knee, and peeked between the thick curtains.

The fog was mostly gone. In the harsh film noir light, a shimmering veneer of water clung to the upper reaches of the grass like a crystal tiara.

I stepped around the corner, found the switch inside the closet, and turned off the buzzer. Silence settled around me like new-fallen snow. Further fumbling produced a jacket and a big rubber flashlight.

I put the jacket on, slipped the security remote into the pocket, and, with the shotgun in one hand and the flashlight in the other, hustled toward the back door. On the way through the kitchen, I snatched my keys from the counter.

I held my breath as I opened the back door and duck-walked out onto the porch. I locked the kitchen door and then made my way to the far corner, where I could see in two directions at once. Nothing behind the house in the garage and garden area. Nothing to the south where the old orchard used to be either.

Under normal circumstances, I think I probably would have let it go at that. I'd have convinced myself a seagull or something wild must have landed on the lawn and set off the system, but I was feeling a little jumpy, so I pulled the remote from my jacket pocket, doused all the lights, and waited. Listened. Somewhere in the distance, a car alarm was bleating its plaintive cry. Went on for a full minute and then, mercifully, stopped.

Somebody whistled. I strained to hear. Voices? Maybe. I tiptoed down the back stairs and went around the house to the right. Walking on the grass so my shoes wouldn't make noise on the walkway, scanning the shrubbery for movement as I crept along. The voice again. And another whistle. The temperature was about fifty, but I was sweating like a racehorse.

I stayed in the grass as I made my way toward the gate. I was twenty feet away when I heard another rustle in the bushes. I stopped and dropped to one knee. And then the sound reached me again, louder this time.

Slowly, trying to keep the noise to a minimum, I pumped a shell into the chamber, then set the stock on the driveway while I rummaged around in my pockets for the remote. Sounded like somebody was moving between the shrubbery and the wall; I took a deep breath and then hit the red button on the remote.

The place lit up like a carnival. I jammed the shotgun stock into my shoulder and sighted down the barrel, then slipped my finger inside the trigger guard.

"You better come out of there," I shouted.

Nothing.

"I mean right now, motherfucker," I screamed.

And then he did. The Seigals' little yip-yap dog, Poco, or whatever the hell its name was, came trotting over to my side. Sat down right in front of my foot and looked up at me with big liquid eyes.

"I think maybe you've got a little too much gun there," a voice said.

Janet Seigal was standing outside the gate, wearing the same white bathrobe she'd been wearing the other night.

"Peashooter'd be too much gun for him," I groused.

I scooped the dog up in my free hand and wandered over to the gate, where I passed him through the bars to Janet.

"Sorry," she said. "He got out the front by mistake."

I waved her off. "Don't worry about it. I'm a little bit jumpy these days."

I cast a glance across the street. One of her garage doors was open. One of the his-and-hers Lexuses was gone.

She read my mind.

"We had a fight," she said. "That's how Poco got out." She gave a slight shrug.

There didn't seem to be anything to say, so I kept my mouth shut.

"Well . . . thanks for not blowing Poco to kingdom come," she said with a wan smile as she started away. I stood and watched as she took a couple of steps, lost her balance, and dropped to one knee. Poco jumped from her arms and began bouncing around her in a circle, yipping and yapping.

I opened the gate and started for her. By the time I'd gotten to her side, she'd wobbled up to her feet again. She made a disgusted face as she dusted her hands together.

"Not very clever, I'm afraid," she said.

"You okay?"

She heaved a giant sigh and caught my gaze with hers.

"I've been diagnosed with MS," she said. "Richard's having a hard time with it."

"Sorry to hear that," was the best I could do.

She scooped the dog up again. "Richard's the kind who likes everything planned right down to the smallest detail."

"Life's seldom so accommodating."

"Neither is Richard," she said as she started across the street.

I turned away, stepped back inside the gate, and closed it. I was reaching for the red button to shut off the lights when suddenly my body came to attention.

I'd been so focused on the noise in the bushes that I'd never looked behind me. Out on the lawn. Two sets of footprints. Instinctively, I began to move in that direction. In the harsh overhead light it was easy to see where their feet had kicked the water from the grass. Halfway down the west wall, a series of muddy scrapes showed where they'd climbed over and then slid down to the ground. A little further along, they'd propped the gardener's wheelbarrow against the wall and used it to boost themselves back over. Not exactly Ninja warriors, these two, whoever they were.

I leaned the shotgun against the wall, stepped up into the wheelbarrow, and chinned myself up to where I could see over the top. The flower bed that ran along the outside of the wall had been mushed flat by a tire. The muddy rut was beginning to fill with water. They must have climbed up on the vehicle and then dropped into the yard.

I grabbed the Mossberg and followed their tracks from the base of the wall out into the middle of the old orchard, where they'd tripped one of the motion sensors. The state of the grass suggested they'd stumbled around in a panic and then made a beeline back to the wall, grabbing the wheelbarrow on the way.

Despite the bumbling nature of the incursion, I decided to err on the side of caution. I locked the place up tight, turned the alarm system back on, and took the shotgun with me to bed.

■   ■   ■

The Archdiocese of Seattle was within easy walking distance of the medical examiner's office, so I parked in the ME's lot, where the parking enforcement guys would recognize my car and assume I was visiting with Rebecca. By the time I'd slapped myself into semiconsciousness and hoofed it over to holy ground, it was quarter to eleven.

While the archbishop himself was otherwise engaged in ecclesiastical enterprise, his secretary was at least willing to listen.

"What can we do for you?" she asked.

I pulled out the photo and the plaque and laid them on her desk. She looked them over, crossed herself, and then looked up at me. "Poor soul," she said.

"Yes, ma'am."

"What's his name?"

"That's what I'm trying to find out."

She picked up the plaque and turned it over in her hands.

"And you think this is one of ours?"

"Maybe," I said with a shrug.

"Are you a parishioner?"

"No," I confessed. The *I knew it* look on her face didn't bode well for my chances, so I played the only card I could think of. "But my Aunt Jean used to be real active over at Our Lady of Fatima in Magnolia."

"Jean?"

"Jean Pomeroy."

She sat back in the chair and folded her arms across her chest.

"Jean Waterman?"

"Yes, ma'am."

She gave me the gimlet eye. "That'd make you Big Bill's boy."

I nodded. "Leo," I said.

She looked me up and down. "The acorn doesn't fall far from the tree."

"He was a lot bigger tree," I said.

She picked the ruined plaque up from her desk and examined it again. Then looked back down at the postmortem photo and shook her head.

"I called a guy I know," I said. "Teaches over at Eastside Catholic. We played ball together a long time ago. He said he thought the archdiocese kept a full set of yearbooks for all the schools. That I might be able to save myself quite a bit of time and energy by coming over here rather than going to each school individually."

She got to her feet. "Your friend was right," she said. "Follow me."

She led me down one of those austere parish house hallways. All dark, carved wood and uncomfortable furniture. Pious portraits staring down from the gloom, in case you, even for a moment, forgot where you were.

She opened the second door on the left and stepped aside. The room was floor-to-ceiling books. One of those old-fashioned libraries with a ladder you could roll around the room on a brass rail. She pointed at the south wall.

"Those are the high schools," she said. "The red-and-white books are Holy Names Academy. The blue-and-whites are from Forest Ridge School of the Sacred Heart. Those are girls' schools, so it's a pretty good bet that poor soul didn't attend either of those." She pinned me with a gaze. "Put everything back where you found it," she said. "I'm getting too old for ladders."

■   ■   ■

I came upon him about an hour later. I'd already been through Archbishop Murphy, Eastside Catholic, and Bishop Blanchet high schools when suddenly there he was staring back at me from the "Class Prophecy" section of the Kennedy Catholic High School yearbook circa 1987. Most Likely to Succeed. Charles W. Stone. "Chuck" to his friends. Younger, cleaner, and back before the perils of existence had drained the hope from his eyes, but it was him all right.

Presuming he was about seventeen years old when he graduated from high school, that made him something like forty-five years old at the time of his death.

I was still sitting there, staring at his face, pondering the vagaries of existence, when my phone began to buzz in my pocket.

"Where are you?" Rebecca's voice demanded.

"Why?"

"Because the parking enforcement people just called to ask if you were up here visiting me. They're thinking about towing your car."

"You didn't let 'em, did you?"

"Not yet."

"I'll be right over. I've got something to tell you."

"So tell me. I've got meetings this afternoon."

"Not over the phone."

Click. Dial tone.

      ■   ■   ■

Rebecca smoothed the folds out of the Xerox copy of the yearbook page and set it on the desktop next to the postmortem photo.

"Yep," she said, after a minute. "That's him."

"Hard to believe he was ever that young."

"Hard to believe any of us were ever that young," she said.

She leaned back in her chair. "I wasn't going to tell you this . . ." she began.

"What?"

"The cops identified the other guy."

"Who?"

She pulled open the center drawer, extracted a yellow folder, and opened it. "Blaine Peterson." She read me an address in Medina, which was about as far removed from sleeping under a bridge as you could get in these parts. What living in Medina got you was the same zip code as Bill and Melinda Gates.

She read my mind. "That's all they told me," she said. "You gonna tell the cops about Mr. Stone here?"

"Nope."

"Eagen finds out you withheld information, he's going to be a very unhappy man."

"I know."

"You're not going to let this go, are you?"

"Nope."

"You really think figuring it all out is going to do something about the gulf you feel between you and your father?"

"Probably not." I lifted a hand and then let it drop to my side. "I don't know any more about my old man than everybody else in town knows. It wasn't like he had a public and a private persona. At home, he was the same guy everybody saw on TV."

"So, what? You're going to spend the rest of your days trying to find out who he was, and by extension who you are?"

"Jesus, I hope not."

■   ■   ■

Back in the day, Carl Cradduck had been one of America's most storied battlefield photographers. Two Pulitzer nominations. His work in *Time*, *Newsweek*, *Life*, and every other big-time photo rag of the era. He skated through five years in Vietnam without a scratch and was at the very top of his game when a piece of Bosnian shrapnel severed his spine in late September of 1993.

Paralyzed from the waist down and relegated to a wheelchair, Carl had parlayed his photographic expertise into a highly successful surveillance business. For the better part of two decades, Carl and his more mobile minions did all of my peeper work for me. You needed a glossy of the hubby humping Flossie, Carl was your guy.

Problem was, no-fault divorce was an even bigger buzz-kill for the surveillance industry than it was for the private eye trade. While I was willing to work for just about anybody, Carl had always hated big business and refused to work the industrial espionage angle and so, when the irreconcilable differences of marriage lost its commercial luster, Carl segued into the information business. Cradduck Data Retrieval specialized in skip tracing: finding felons, freeloaders, and deadbeat dads. He was the Duke of the Database. Unless you were planning to dig yourself a bunker somewhere in the wilds of Montana, Carl was going to find your ass, sooner rather than later.

He'd bought a little three-bedroom Craftsman over on Crown Hill a few years back and wired himself up to the world. Eleven monitors lined the north wall of what used to be the front parlor, each keeping track of something different.

I'd spent the drive over with Rebecca's voice ringing in my ears, trying like hell to conjure up a good reason why I was still pushing on with this thing, but even my finely honed capacity for denial and self-delusion wasn't up to the task, so I just chalked it up to bullheadedness and kept driving.

Carl asked the same question every time I walked in his door.

"What, are you playing at being a detective again?"

"I had some uninvited visitors last night."

"Any idea who?"

I shook my head. "That's why I'm here."

"You been working lately?"

"Nope."

I told him about my neighbor. About the two stiffs the cops found in the car trunk. My old man's coat. Putting a name on the homeless guy. The guy with the Medina address. The incursion into my yard last night. All of it.

He rolled back over to his bank of computers. "What's Mr. Medina's name again?" he asked.

I checked my notes. "Blaine Peterson. 11232 North East Twenty-Fourth Street."

He did a little typing, pushed a few buttons, and then sat back in his chair. Up on the overhead bank of screens, characters blinked and gamboled, whole screens slid by at warp speed, only to be replaced by another and then another and another, like some garish electronic dance working itself up to a frenzy.

"You bring your checkbook?" he asked.

"It's in the car," I said.

"Go get it."

■   ■   ■

One of the first things I learned as a private eye was that no matter how orderly and mundane people's lives may appear from the outside, they've all got secrets.

From the outside, Blaine Peterson looked like the very personification of the American dream. First in his high school class. Baseball and track star. Shipped off to Harvard, where he graduated magna cum laude, and then on to the University of Pennsylvania's Wharton School of Business for his MBA. Opted to come back home and go to work for Hindeman and Lowe, a Bellevue investment firm started by his grandfather. Made full partner in just under four years. Made his first million at twenty-nine. Married and divorced along the way. Parents still lived over on the Eastside, up on the plateau in Newcastle. Kinda guy could give an average fella an inferiority complex, and yet, somewhere along his well-scripted way, he'd come across someone who had stuffed him, stark naked, into the trunk of a rental car, alongside a demented homeless man, and then left them both on a dark city street to ferment. Go figure.

Chuck Stone was another matter. Him I recognized all too well. Maybe weller than I wanted. One of those unfocused souls who never quite found his niche in life. Graduated in the top half of his high school class. Bumped from college to college to college until he finally graduated from Seattle Central with an associate's degree in business marketing. Tried his hand at real estate, mortgage banking, car sales, and a number of other tough rackets, until 2006 when he too got divorced and then, within six months, completely dropped off the grid.

After that, as far as the world was concerned, Charles W. Stone ceased to exist, other than as a series of police reports, which, as I'd learned over the years, were pretty much par for the course after a guy hit rock bottom. Public drunkenness, unlawful trespass, urinating in public, drunk and disorderly, failure to appear on a charge of drunk and disorderly, resisting arrest, creating a public nuisance. The whole collection of infractions that just naturally came along with being broke and on the skids.

The best place to start was obviously Blaine Peterson, but that sure as hell wasn't going to happen. Not unless I was harboring a secret jail fetish. Since the cops had already ID'd him, it was safe to assume that they were hard at work on the question of how such an upstanding citizen ended up in a grimy car trunk. Guys like Peterson got their murders thoroughly investigated. Guys like Chuck Stone got a shrug and a toe tag.

I'd spent the past forty minutes sitting in a dusty morris chair in Carl's front parlor perusing the paperwork he'd printed for me. Last thing in Stone's file was a release from Harborview Hospital, dated December 30, 2007. He'd been involuntarily admitted two days before with a case of the delirium tremens and was sent on his way with a heart full of song and a pocket full of pills. That was it.

Neither man came up when Rebecca ran their fingerprints through the IAFIS system because Peterson had led such an upscale life that he'd never even had occasion to be fingerprinted, and because our friend Mr. Stone had committed the kind of nuisance infractions that, in an era of police budget cuts and staff reductions, weren't deemed important enough to get entered into the "known criminal" database.

The sunlight slanting between the curtains glinted on the blizzard of dust hanging in the air as I sat there giving myself a pep talk, telling myself I'd taken this as far as made any sense, that there was no place left to go.

"No fucking way," Carl growled from across the room.

"You say something?" I asked.

He held up a "just a minute" finger and went back to pushing computer keys. I walked across the room and stood behind him as he worked. He pointed over at the monitor on the right. "Charles Stone," he said. "Two thousand two. Goes to work for Lee Johnson Chevrolet over in Kirkland. Selling cars. The company perks include a small life insurance policy and a 401(k) plan." He went back to the keyboard. "Stone lists his wife as beneficiary of both. Theresa Calder Stone. Same address as his, up in Totem Lake."

"So? Isn't that what married guys do?"

More keyboard work. He pointed up at the center monitor. "Mr. Medina. Two thousand six. Gets married. Updates his survivorship information, and he and the new bride sign a prenuptial agreement." He looked back over his shoulder and grinned. He had a piece of yellow corn stuck in his teeth. I looked away.

"Guess who?"

"No."

"Theresa Calder."

"Naw."

"I'm tellin' ya."

"They were married to the same woman?" I threw a disbelieving hand in the air. "Tell me Area 51 is for real. Tell me Bill Clinton's joining the priesthood, but don't tell me those two guys were married to the same girl."

He showed the ceiling his palms. "What can I say? The Bible-thumpers always say the Lord works in mysterious ways," he said with a malicious grin.

I walked over to the bank of monitors and squinted up at the flocks of characters soaring around the screens, as if getting up close and personal would somehow change the facts. "What do we know about her?" I asked finally.

"Before she married the Stone guy . . . as far as I can see, she didn't exist. No birth certificate. No school records. No Social Security number. No driver's license. No nothing. It's like she just appeared from the ozone."

I opened my mouth to speak, but Carl waved me off. "That's a little exotic but not unheard of. People starting over with new identities, leaving the past behind, that sort of thing," he said. "What I haven't seen before—*ever*, and I mean *ever*—is how she disappears back off the grid as soon as she splits with Mr. Medina."

"What?"

"When she and Peterson split the sheets in April of two thousand eleven, she had all the bells and whistles of a Bellevue housewife: a year-old BMW, five credit cards, three gas cards, three debit cards—all the accouterments of well-to-do America."

He waved me over. On the screen attached to his wheelchair, a Washington driver's license. Theresa Calder. Grainy picture of a brunette with quite a bit more chin than she needed. Same Medina address as Blaine Peterson. Birth date that made her thirty-six in July.

Carl leaned my way. "Since the day they split, none of the cards have ever been used. I can't come up with a single transaction of any kind." He lifted his palms to the ceiling. "It's like she rose outta the primordial ooze, hung around for several years, and then sunk back into the swamp."

I wandered across the room as I tried to wrap my head around what he was telling me. People don't just appear out of nowhere. To live in America in the twenty-first century was to leave a paper trail a mile wide. Carl read my mind.

He pinned me with his gaze. "I don't like the way this one feels, Leo," he said. "And since this whole thing is just about Leo being Leo, and ain't nobody paying you to muck around in this, I'm thinking maybe you ought to take a rain check here."

I nodded in agreement, but Carl knew me too well.

"We're running blind here, my friend," Carl said. "I don't like it. When you're this far behind the curve, things have a tendency to go to shit in a heartbeat."

"Anything on where she might be now?" I asked.

Carl fixed me with his most baleful stare, then finally shook his head in disgust and went back to work. Twelve minutes passed before he sat back in his chair.

"Postal Service forwarded a stack of mail to a PO box at Port Gamble. That was almost two years ago. They tried again last year and the second stack came back." He shook his big, scraggly head. "I'll keep digging, but as of right now, that's it, man. The trail ends here."

"Port Gamble's pretty this time of year," I said.

Chapter 2

I grabbed a cup of battery acid coffee from the ferry snack bar and headed for the front of the boat. About the time the ferry *Spokane* got up to eighteen knots and the Canadian wind came roaring down Puget Sound, the crowd of rail-riders scurried for warmer climes, and I had the bow to myself.

Half hour later, I was bouncing down the ferry ramp into Kingston, crawling along with the rest of the ferry crowd, creeping from traffic light to traffic light on my way to Port Gamble, which was one of those terribly quaint places Seattleites always drag out-of-town visitors to. Founded in the mid-nineteenth century as a sawmill company town, Port Gamble consisted of a big mill down on the bay and an absolutely precious collection of late-Victorian houses built up on the bluff, replete with old-fashioned general store, curiosity shoppe, and ice cream parlor. Walt Disney would have loved the joint.

I'd been there often enough to know the post office was north of downtown, so I skipped the tourist traps, found a parking place half a block down from the post office, and moseyed on in. Looked like every post office everywhere, except smaller.

I headed over to the table in the corner and fondled some IRS tax forms while I checked out the lay of the land. The woman behind the counter was about sixty, long and lean and chattering away with a young blonde woman mailing a tall stack of packages.

I moved slowly along the wall of brass-faced post office boxes until I found number 2611, which turned out to be one of the big ones. The kind you could put packages in. I pulled my key ring from my coat pocket and had a look for anything that might fit into the lock. I was still at it when I heard the bell on the door tinkle. I turned my head and watched as the woman with the packages stepped out into the street. When I looked back, the woman behind the counter was directly across from me, looking at me through the little glass windows in the boxes.

"Help you with something?" she asked.

"I was . . ." I stammered. "I was supposed to pick up something from one of the boxes, but I think they gave me the wrong key."

"What box was that?"

"Twenty-six eleven," I said.

She stood for a moment, staring at me with an expression that looked a lot like pity, and then turned and walked back over to the service counter. I stood still for an awkward ten count and then followed her over. She was standing with her hands on her hips looking me over like a specimen jar.

"You musta been misinformed," she said.

"Yeah," was all I could come up with.

"You wanna tell me what you really want?"

"I'm looking for somebody," I blurted.

"What somebody is that?"

"Woman named Theresa Calder."

"What's she got to do with those people out there?" she asked.

"What people out where?"

"The Rectory."

"Like a church rectory?"

"That's what *some* folks call it."

"What do *you* call it?" I tried.

"I call it a damn cult, like most everybody who ain't a member does."

"Why a cult?" I asked.

"It's that damn Aaron Townsend guy."

"Who's that?"

She squinted at me. "Don't you read the papers?" she asked.

"Only if there's a score involved."

"You know . . . the whole Mount Zion thing."

"I know what Mount Zion is," I said hopefully.

"Two hundred acres on the Hood Canal. Used to be a scout camp. Since way back in the thirties. Till Townsend and those idiots who follow him bought it up and turned it into some kinda cult compound." She threw an angry hand into the air. "Wish he'd come round here one of these days. See how that *women gotta be subservient to their husbands* bullcrap of his floats down here with the regular folk."

"That's his message? That women got to do what they're told?"

Her voice began to rise. "Had him a *New York Times* bestseller." She made quotation marks in the air. "*The Christian Couple*, it was called. Said women belonged in the home, and oughta do whatever they was told."

She pulled a claw hammer out from under the counter and waved it in the air. "Let him come round here, I'll put a bend in him he won't never straighten out."

Somewhat taken aback, I asked, "How do I get out there?"

She was still muttering to herself as she slid the hammer back under the counter and pulled out a piece of yellow lined paper. I watched in silence as she sketched a makeshift map for me.

"Second right turn past Seabeck," she said as she finished up. "Keep your eyes open, it's easy to miss. Ways into the trees there's a big ol' gate. You can ring from there." She slid the map over to me and eyed me hard. "And you get an audience with Mr. Macho Townsend, you give 'im a good rap on the head for me."

I assured her that, should the gentleman and I cross paths, divine retribution would surely be forthcoming, then scooped up the map and backed out the door.

•   •   •

I spent the ride wondering why some people were inclined to surrender their lives to prophets and gurus, as if the responsibility for making their own decisions was simply too much for them to bear, and the only way they could go on living was to become pawns in their own games, willing to believe . . . in something, in anything, as long as the weight of personal choice was lifted from their sagging shoulders and placed elsewhere.

Like Ms. Post Office said, the road was easy to miss. I drove past it, caught it in the corner of my eye, U-turned and went back. Single-lane sand road, pointing straight as an arrow into the depths of the tangled coastal forest. About every third tree was festooned with a fresh No Trespassing sign.

The forest seemed to press in from all sides as I eased the car along. Just about the time I was starting to feel sweaty and claustrophobic, the rough track suddenly opened up into a wide man-made clearing. Big black gate down at the far end.

I tooled over to the gate and looked around. A concrete post inside the gate supported a speaker and a button. In my neighborhood they put the call buttons where you didn't have to get out of the car to buzz. I was guessing these guys wanted a good look at whoever was at their door, so they made it harder.

I left the car running and got out. My assumption proved correct. The trees closest to the gate on either side held surveillance cameras. Their little green eyes tracked me as I walked over and pushed the red button. Nothing, so I pushed it again.

The speaker crackled. "This here's private property," a disembodied voice said.

"I'm looking for Theresa Calder," I said.

"Gowan, get outa here."

"Theresa Calder," I said again.

"Ain't no one here by that name."

"The U.S. Postal Service sent her mail here. It didn't come back. So either she was here to get it, or somebody's been stealing U.S. mail. Which, as I'm sure you know, is a very serious—"

CLICK. Static. CLICK.

Apparently, my rapier-like banter had once again been wasted. I stood listening to the sound of the engine idling and the faint rustle of the wind, trying to decide what to do next. Going under, over, or around the gate probably wasn't going to end up anywhere I wanted to go. This was, after all, private property, and I'd been asked, in no uncertain terms, to get lost. Not much wiggle room there.

On the other hand, when it comes to doing what I'm told, I can be a bit of a dimwit. On more occasions than I'd prefer to remember, my propensity for pigheadedness had led me to venues I'd later regretted visiting.

Mercifully, circumstances prevented me from revealing my true colors. The hum of an engine pulled my attention back toward the gate. I watched as a familiar white Range Rover pulled into a turnout about fifty yards on the other side of the gate, coming to a stop with the driver's side facing in my direction. I was trying to detect movement behind the deeply tinted windows when the door opened and out stepped Brother Biggs.

As he ambled over to the gate, his partner, Mr. Peepers, came out from behind the Rover and followed along in his wake. "Well, if it ain't Mr. Waterman," Biggs said. "Seems like you the kind of asshole don't know good advice when he hears it."

I shrugged. "Could be," I said.

He walked over to the button and pushed it. As the gate began to roll aside, both of them stepped through the opening and walked my way.

That's when I made two mistakes in about three seconds. The first was assuming we were still at the talking stage of things. I'd imagined they were going to warn me off. Remind me I was on private property and tell me to be on my way. The second was in not noticing that Mr. Peepers had one hand out of sight and thus not seeing the spring-loaded sap he had secreted behind his back.

Without preamble, Biggs hauled off and tried to punch my lights out.

I moved my head and let his fist fly over my shoulder, then straight-armed him back a step and a half. "Take it easy, man," I said. "No need for—"

He bull-rushed me, spun me sideways so he could grab me from behind, clamped those big arms around me, and began to squeeze. The air spewed out of my lungs like a broken balloon. I dug my heels into the ground, bent my head forward, and then snapped it back as hard as I could. The sound of his nose exploding told me everything I needed to know. His arms slipped from my sides. I bumped him backwards and turned to face him. I could see I'd spread his nose from ear to ear. He roared like a lion, brought both hands to his flattened face, and stumbled back a step, where he dropped to one knee, staring cross-eyed and uncomprehending at the thick knots of blood running over his hands.

The sound of flesh in motion brought my eyes up. The billy hit me over my left eye. And then again in the forehead. Biggs was now trying to wrap his arms around my legs. I kicked back hard before he could lock his hands together and bring me to the ground. I heard a grunt in the same moment that Mr. Peepers head-butted me in the solar plexus, again driving the air from my lungs, sending me reeling back against the fender of my car, gasping for breath.

I regrouped and drove a solid right hand into the little guy's jaw. He collapsed in a heap, landing on top of Biggs. I slid along the fender of my car. At my feet Biggs was halfway to standing when I aimed a left hook at his jaw. He saw it coming and ducked his head. My hand connected with the top of his skull and simply exploded. His eyes rolled back in their sockets as he augered face-first into the ground.

I felt the door handle grind against my back and reached for it, only to find my left hand numb and totally useless. I groaned as bolts of pain shot down my arm, grabbed the handle with my good hand, pulled open the car door, and threw myself into the driver's seat.

Before I could slam the door, Peepers wedged himself into the opening, clawing at my face with outstretched fingers. I reached across my body, got hold of the inside door handle, and slammed it on his arms with all the force I could muster. He screamed like a panther and slid from sight.

I slammed the door and locked it. Threw the car into reverse, floored it, and went screaming backwards across the clearing. I looked up at the mirror just in time to see the woods coming at me like a freight train. I crimped the wheel hard right. The big car fought for traction in the sandy soil, began to drift toward the trees, then found sudden purchase and began to swing in a steep arc.

I stood on the brakes, slid to a halt, and dropped the car into drive. When I snuck a final furtive glance back toward the gate, both of them were standing.

I remember getting back to the paved road, turning left, and heading toward Port Gamble. After that, things got a little fuzzy. Next thing I can recall is seeing a sign for Salsbury Point Park and turning in.

I moved like the Mummy as I stiff-legged it from the car to the men's room. Everything ached. I cradled my left hand with my right as I shuffled across the grass and up the sidewalk. Mercifully, the john was empty.

I spent the next twenty minutes and every single paper towel in the dispenser trying to clean myself up. I had a carbuncle the size of a golf ball on my forehead, and a split in my upper lip you could have stuffed a dime into. My sternum ached from the head-butt and my kidneys felt as if they had been pureed. Worst of all, my left hand was turning purple and throbbed with every beat of my heart.

Wasn't till I crawled back into my car that I started wondering about the cops. Whether they were camped out somewhere along the highway, or waiting for me at the ferry terminal. Either way, I didn't have a leg to stand on. The Rectory folks were local and I wasn't. I'd clearly been trespassing on their property. I'd committed several counts

G.M. FORD

of assault. If they'd called the cops, I was going to spend a night or two in jail. I winced as I dropped the car into gear and started rolling for the highway.

My flight mechanism was screaming at me to put the pedal to the metal. Took all my willpower to drive at a grandmotherly pace. Fifteen clammy minutes later, I rolled back through Port Gamble, turned east at the big intersection, and headed for the Kingston ferry terminal. Halfway back, I passed a Washington State trooper going in the opposite direction. My eyes kept flicking back and forth between the road and the rearview, expecting the light bar to fire up at any second. When the cruiser finally faded into the distance and disappeared from view, I exhaled for what seemed like the first time in a week.

I stayed in my car for the ferry ride back to Edmonds. Just sat there, leaning against the window, listening to the throb of the big diesels and watching the black water slide by. By the time we docked and the crewman motioned me forward, I was crimped around the steering wheel like Quasimodo. Bumping up and over the ferry ramp pulled an involuntary moan from somewhere deep inside me.

Edmonds to downtown Seattle was less than twenty miles, but it seemed to take an hour. By the time I got there, I'd abandoned any illusions I may have harbored regarding self-medication. Band-Aids and Mercurochrome weren't going to get it done here, so I drove directly up to Harborview Hospital, parked the car a long block away, and wandered into the ER.

Harborview is the primary trauma center for the Pacific Northwest. If you've severed your aorta or extruded yourself through the windshield of a Karmann Ghia, Harborview is where they send you, so walk-ins with boo-boos can generally expect a pretty substantial wait time. Today was no exception.

By the time they'd gotten around to me, determined that although my hand wasn't broken, it might as well be, then forced all the bones back where they belonged and fixed them in place with a deep-blue soft cast, darkness and a steady drizzle had claimed the remainder of the day.

▪   ▪   ▪

I stayed in bed for three days. I guess you could say I was nursing my wounds, but, really, I spent most of the time going over the info I'd gotten from Carl and surfing the Internet, trying to catch up on the whys and wherefores of the Mount Zion church. And, believe me, there was a lot to catch up on.

Like most clusterfucks, Mount Zion had grown from humble roots. A young guy named Aaron Townsend started a Bible study group in Belltown on Tuesday nights. A group that, within a decade, had morphed into twenty-three branches in five states with thirteen thousand people showing up for Sunday services. Townsend appeared in *Northwest Travel & Life* magazine, preached at a Seahawks game, threw out the first pitch at a Mariners game, and founded a network of evangelical leaders who started hundreds of other churches.

Which was all the more amazing because Seattle is hardly a godly town. Yeah, we've got our share of coffee-social Lutherans and other true believers, but for most of the neck-bearded, tattooed hipsters traipsing around town in their jaunty hats and skinny jeans, Sunday services were far more likely to include chicken and waffles at their favorite brunch joint than those symbolic tapas offered at a standard house of worship.

But maybe that explains Mount Zion's appeal. Just as Pacific Northwesterners prefer to make their own software, airplanes, music, organic food, and political movements, they also prefer to make their own religions. They're freethinkers, anti-institution, and individualists, making them more inclined to participate in a Pilates class, hike a mountain, or even attend a Seahawks game to find spirituality rather than step inside a traditional church.

But, for reasons that may never be satisfactorily explained, Aaron Townsend's blue-jeans, down-home style drew them like lemmings to those icy Arctic cliffs. Unfortunately, as is all too often the case in cults of personality, the rise of the church proved directly proportional to the rise of Aaron Townsend's ego. By the time the first rumblings of discontent began, Townsend and his new wife, Alice, had written a nearly five-hundred-page tome humbly entitled *Real Belief*, a document which any number of conservative Christian scholars, not surprisingly, found sorely wanting in both piety and scholarship.

But, even with that, the dissension might well have ended there. It's not like churches don't have a long and bloody history of doctrinal disputes. But no. Emboldened by his meteoric rise, Townsend then began to hold forth on how marriages should be conducted. Early on my second day in bed, I downloaded a copy of Townsend's best seller, *The Christian Couple*, and spent most of the day working my way through it.

In a nutshell, what it says is that it is God's will that women are to be ruled over, controlled by, and dominated by men—particularly their husbands—in family, church, and civic life. Period, end o' story. Sorta like a "Grab your ankles, Agnes, it's the Lord's will" kind of thing.

Realizing that an unusual degree of compliance was going to be called for, Mount Zion Ministries began to make it more difficult to become a member. Simply showing up at services wasn't going to cover it. Becoming a full-fledged member—a process thunderously demanded, in Pastor Aaron Townsend's sermons—required months of classes and a careful study of *Real Belief*. To seal the deal, the prospective member had to formally agree to submit to the "authority" of the Mount Zion leadership, which included Townsend's macho interpretation of Christianity, one in which men are unquestioned heads of their households and "sissified church boys," as he called them, could feel free to get lost. He railed against mainstream Christians who imagined what he called an "androgynous Christ." Instead, he molded his doctrine on

manliness, sexual purity, and submission to authority: wives to husbands, husbands to pastors, and everyone to God.

Needless to say, not everyone was enamored with this somewhat tes-
ticular approach to religion. Almost immediately, rifts began to appear
in the social fabric. A full-scale *them* and *us* situation erupted. Those
unwilling to submit to church demands were ostracized and shunned
by members of the Mount Zion community.

Splinter groups soon formed. The chorus of protest rose to a roar.
And, not surprisingly, the church began to dissolve beneath the deluge.
Several church elders quit. A national "church planting" group called
Reach 36, cofounded by Aaron Townsend, removed Townsend and
Mount Zion Ministries from its membership rolls, while urging in a
letter that Townsend "step away" from his ministry and "seek guidance."

Which, interestingly enough, is exactly what he did. Calling it an
extended spiritual reconsideration, Townsend stepped away from the
church and went into self-imposed seclusion. Without its charismatic
pastor, the church immediately went into a death spiral. Attendance
and donations took a nosedive. All church memberships were sus-
pended. Petitioners were encouraged to seek their spiritual guidance
elsewhere. And the entity known as the Mount Zion Ministries was
quietly disbanded.

That was the end of February. As far as I could see, Mount Zion
Ministries didn't make the news again until April 6 of that same year,
when the *Seattle Daily Journal of Commerce* ominously noted that there
had been some serious holdup in the sale of Mount Zion's assets. The
following Monday, the *Seattle Times* broke the story. Front page of the
financial section.

Seems that several of the church's presumed holdings—including
the church building on West Woodland Way, the compound on the
peninsula where I'd gotten my ass kicked, and two unspecified private homes—had been donated not to Mount Zion Ministries, as had
always been presumed, but instead had been deeded directly to Aaron

Townsend himself. The resale value of the properties in question was estimated to be between twenty-three and twenty-eight million dollars.

Same day the story hit the papers, Aaron Townsend returned from his soul-searching odyssey like Caesar returning from Gaul. He arrived back in town with a hotshot law firm, which immediately began passing out restraining orders like they were breath mints. Townsend preached that night up in Mill Creek, to an SRO crowd, and was welcomed home with a prolonged standing ovation.

Four days later, the SPD found the naked bodies of Blaine Peterson and Chuck Stone wedged into the trunk of a rental car, covered with my old man's overcoat, which was, of course, the point where I'd stumbled into it.

As of yesterday, neither the elders of the church nor Aaron Townsend were making any public statements, although an anonymous elder was quoted as saying that Townsend was now claiming the property as his own. The unnamed elder wanted the public to know, however, that it wasn't about the money.

Funny thing was, after the better part of a week's work and after getting the shit kicked out of me, I hadn't dug up a single thing that took us any closer to solving the murders. Sure, I'd found out that both guys were once married to a "now you see her, now you don't" woman who'd called herself Theresa Calder, but what, if anything, that fact had to do with the price of eggs in Tibet was still anybody's guess.

The gate buzzer sounded and then again. I checked the bedside clock. 6:37. That would be Bite Squad, the food delivery service, bringing my dinner.

I rolled over and put my feet on the floor. I stopped at the hall closet long enough to collect a jacket and a Glock 9mm before stepping out the door. The wind was swirling in the tops of the trees as I made my way down the driveway. My body felt like it'd been threshed and baled. I opened the gate just far enough to grab the food package.

When I looked up, I noticed the Seigals out on their front walk again. The rush of the wind in the trees prevented me from catching anything being said, but if body language was any indication, their relationship was rapidly moving from bad to worse. I didn't like the look of it one bit. For a second I thought about wandering over, but just couldn't muster the gumption, so I closed the gate and headed back for the house.

.   .   .

Like its English namesake, the area they now call Newcastle had once been a giant coal mine. As the years passed, and suburban creep began to overtake Seattle, somebody noticed that if you got high enough up on the slag heap, you had a rather grand view of the Seattle skyline and then, of course, the property race was on. These days, it was an über-snooty golf club community. One of those places where the stone-fronted five-bedroom houses all looked the same and everybody drove a high-end SUV. Crime was limited to an occasional drive-by snubbing.

The family had buried Blaine Peterson day before yesterday. His parents lived in Newcastle, so I'd spent a few minutes online with what passes for a phonebook these days, and, for a mere $9.95, come up with their address, which, when I checked out the handy Google map, turned out to be along the sixth hole of the Golf Club at Newcastle. The body of water guarding the front of the sixth green was named Peterson Pond. These were charter members.

I had mixed emotions about today's agenda. First off, I felt shitty about showing up at the parents' house so soon after they'd put their son in the ground. I'd been kicking myself about it all morning. It was one of those places where *who you are* comes into contact with *who you're afraid you might actually be*. The story I was telling myself—and God knows I was good at doing that—said that the older and colder something like Blaine's death got, the harder it became to come up with any meaningful information. That was the story, anyway.

Secondly, I was still nervous about running into the cops. I had no doubt they were humping hard on the case. By now, there were probably multiple law enforcement agencies involved in the investigation. People with four-car garages generally got law enforcement's best efforts. The question was *where* they were working. What I knew for sure was that running into them was gonna ruin my day, but, as the now familiar story went, there was no way around that either. I didn't have so much as a starting place when it came to Chuck Stone, not a thread to pull or a stone to turn over, so it was either work the Blaine Peterson angle or give it up altogether.

I pulled my car to the curb and got out. Long, thin clouds raced across the bright blue sky like the vapor trails of the gods. The air was cooler up here. I bunched my collar about my neck as I walked up the driveway.

A dark-haired woman with thick eyebrows and a pink maid's uniform answered the door. She looked me over like I was the blue plate special.

"I'd like to see Mr. or Mrs. Peterson," I said.

She leaned out through the doorway and peered around me on both sides.

"Are you police?" she asked in an accent I couldn't quite pin down. Something Central European maybe.

I shook my head.

"Are they expecting you?" she asked.

I allowed that they weren't. She said, "Wait," and then double-bolted the door in my face. I could hear her heels clicking away.

A black Ford SUV rolled around the corner on my right, the clicking of its studded tires announcing its arrival. NEWCASTLE HEIGHTS SECURITY in gold letters emblazoned on the side. The sight of my car sitting in the street seemed to get their attention. The SUV slowed to a crawl. The side window slid down. I watched over my shoulder as they eased to a stop at the end of the driveway and the passenger door popped open. In the same second that a booted foot stepped out of the security car, the door behind me snapped open.

"Please come in," the maid said, stepping aside.

I was still stretching my neck and checking out the surroundings when, without a word, she turned and started walking away from me.

I followed her down a wide hall. Her uniform hissed and rustled as we clicked along. She stopped at an arched entranceway on her left and gestured with her arm that I should enter.

I gave her a big smile on the way by. She ignored me and quickly closed the door.

The minute I walked into the room, I knew exactly what the woman was doing. She had her son's whole life laid out before her in pictures. From cradle to grave, it was all there. Spread out over a dining-room table big enough to seat a football team. Glossies, albums, diplomas, yellowed newspaper articles under glass. All of it. She was circling the table, picking up one thing and then another, running her fingers over the surfaces of photographs and then setting them back on the table.

The room overflowed with cards and flowers, the air filled with the heady smell of dying vegetation. I stood still and watched as she moved slowly, lost in thought, along the far side of the table.

She was just a little thing. Five feet nothing in an expensive black two-piece suit and a pair of low heels. As I approached, she turned her tired eyes my way. She looked at me as if I might be the messenger she'd been waiting for. Someone from the Great Beyond who could finally straighten this nightmare out, once and for all. The anguish in her eyes made me wish like hell I could do it for her.

After a moment, she looked up. "Carlotta said . . ." she began, and then stopped, as if suddenly she wasn't certain what Carlotta had said.

"Sorry about your loss," was all I could think to say.

She reached out and picked up an eight-by-ten color photograph, studied it for a moment, and then turned it my way. One of those baseball team pictures with the boys in the front kneeling down holding baseball bats. Little guys in front, bigger guys in back. The Phillies. Somewhere in my attic, I had a very similar photo, only my team was the Astros. Things were simpler then. You either won or you lost. Nothing was ambivalent. Quite frankly, I liked it better that way.

I walked around the table and stood by her side. She pointed at the back row, second boy from the left. "That's Blaine," she said with a hitch in her voice. "He played third base."

"I played catcher," I said.

She looked me up and down. "You look like a catcher," she said.

I nodded in agreement.

She took a step sideways. Opened a white leather photo album. Blaine, ten years older, accepting a diploma. "Harvard," she said. "He was third in his class."

I stayed by her side as she moved on. Blaine wearing mouse ears way back when they went to Disneyland. Blaine and what I figured to be his father standing next to a huge marlin hanging by its tail, grinning like madmen beneath the bright Mexican sky. Skiing pictures. "Breckenridge," she offered with a wan smile.

Five minutes later, we'd crabbed our way to the head of the table, when she suddenly stopped and looked up at me as if she'd only just noticed I was there. "Did you say . . ." she began. Then answered her own question. "No," she said. "You didn't."

Figuring this for my chance, I said, "I'm looking for Theresa Calder."

She took in a short, shallow breath and looked down at the floor. "It broke his heart," she whispered. "I mean . . . just like that . . . completely out of the blue . . ." She threw a small, angry hand through the air. "Not even the courtesy . . . the common decency . . ." she sputtered and stopped.

For the first time since I'd been there, she moved quickly. Brushing a chair aside with her hip as she whirled around to the other side of the table and grabbed a thick photo album. OUR WEDDING was embossed on the cover.

By the time I reached her side, she'd cracked the album open and was frowning down at one of her son's wedding pictures. I peered over her shoulder. Blaine gleefully wedged between his parents. Theresa between what I imagined to be hers. Everybody spic-and-span and smiling for the camera. Just one big happy family.

"Where's her family from?" I asked.

"South America," she said. "They're missionaries somewhere out in the jungle. Said it took them nearly a week to get here." She looked up at me. "Like Blaine . . . she was their only child."

The front door slammed. A man's voice rose in the hall. She set the wedding album back onto the table and heaved a sigh. "Phillip," was all she said.

The dining-room door slammed open against the wall. He was tall and extremely thin, narrow lips, razor blade cheekbones, with a great shock of white hair bobbing around on his narrow head like a balloon. He pointed at me with a long bony finger. "Who are you?" he demanded.

I told him.

"You have no business here," he said.

"I'm looking for Theresa Calder."

My words stopped him in his tracks. He seemed to want to misunderstand.

"She sent you?"

"No, sir," I said. "I'm looking for her."

"Why? Why would you be looking for that . . . that . . ."

I didn't have an answer to the question, so I kept my mouth shut.

He angled in my direction. "That woman ruined my son's life," he rasped, his voice beginning to rise. "I wouldn't be surprised if she wasn't in some way responsible for . . . for what happened. Her and that so-called church of hers . . . that . . . He was obsessed with finding her. It ruined his life. Killed my boy."

He began jabbing his long finger into my chest.

"Without so much as a by-your-leave. Goddamnit! Gone," he shouted. "Cleaned out their accounts. Never even . . ."

He opened his mouth to continue his tirade, but nothing came out. I watched his eyes change from anger to confusion and then to fear. He brought a hand up to his sternum and clutched his own shirt, twisted it hard, and then looked down uncomprehendingly at what he was doing to himself. "Oh . . . oh . . ." He spit the syllables out like fish bones, and then his knees buckled and he dropped toward the floor.

I managed to get my good hand under his shoulder to brake the fall. As I gently laid him on his side, his whole body began to tremble violently. I watched as his eyes rolled back in his head, and his feet began to drum on the floor.

"Call 911," I said to his wife.

She just stood there, both hands clamped over her mouth, staring down at her husband in horror.

"Call 911," I yelled.

"Phillip," was all she said.

He began to vomit. I eased his head away from the widening puddle of puke on the floor and tried to quiet his spasms. When he finally stopped retching, I used two fingers to clear his mouth. His breath was coming in short, rattling gasps now. If anything, he was shaking more violently than he had been before. I cradled him in my arms, trying to keep his spasms from shaking him to pieces. My hand felt like somebody was jumping up and down on it. It was all I could do not to moan.

She was on the phone now, giving the dispatcher the address.

Took the aid car eight long minutes to arrive. By that time, his breath had gotten shorter, his spasms more uncontrolled. I rolled aside and let the medics do their thing.

I found a bathroom down the hall, splashed some cold water on my face, and washed the puke from my hands. By the time I got back, the docs had Phillip started on a couple of IVs, had wrapped him up like a mummy, and were wheeling him out the door at a fast trot.

Carlotta appeared in the doorway. "I'm going to drive Mees Peterson to the hospital," she announced. Took my addled brain a few seconds to realize that was my invitation to leave. I was bleary eyed, mouth-breathing, and numb all over as I started for the door.

.   .   .

Comes a time when a person needs to do a little soul-searching. No matter how I spun what had happened today, it still turned out that I should never have bothered those people. Not at a time like this. Probably not at all. Wasn't like I had a dog in the fight. None of these people meant anything to me, but, for selfish reasons, I decided to stick my face into their lives anyway, and why . . . because after forty-some years, I still couldn't put my finger on where I stood with my father, or because somebody told me to butt out, and I have this asinine aversion to being told what to do by authority figures.

The freeway was a parking lot, so I veered across five lanes and got off at the Seneca exit. City streets weren't moving either, but at least there was something to look at while I sat there breathing carbon monoxide fumes.

My nerves were shot. Seemed like it took two hours to get home from downtown. By the time I got down to Elliott, I was leaning on the horn and barking at other drivers, working my way up to a full-scale road rage hissy fit, so I calmed myself down and made an effort to find something positive in my surroundings.

The best I could manage was to notice that spring was late this year. It smelled like spring, but felt like winter. Here and there, in spots that got just a bit more sun than others, daffodils and primroses were beginning to show their colorful faces.

I didn't have a plan for when I got home. Didn't want one. I felt like crawling into bed, pulling the covers over my head, and not coming out for a week. At least, that way, I couldn't do any more damage to myself or others.

I didn't check the mail on the way in. I turned the phone off and dumped it on the kitchen counter. Anything anybody wanted was just going to have to wait. I grabbed a Stella Artois from the fridge and sat in front of the TV without turning it on.

I ran out of beer before I ran out of self-pity, so I started in on a big bottle of Stolichnaya I'd had in the freezer since the late eighties. An hour later, I remembered why it was that people drank. How the jagged edges of things got smoother. How "for sures" got to be "maybes," and "I's" got to be "theys."

I'd just about drowned my sense of shame when the self-defeating side of me decided he just had to know how Phillip Peterson was doing. I stumbled around a bit, remembered I'd left my phone in the kitchen, and lurched in to get it.

Took me about ten minutes to find out that, although Newcastle had its own medical clinic, anyone requiring serious attention was going to end up at Evergreen Hospital in Kirkland.

I asked for him by name. The switchboard connected me. It rang four times before somebody picked it up. "Meester Peterson's room," she said.

"It's me," I said.

"Excuse?"

"The guy from the house today." I heard Carlotta catch her breath and swallow. "How's he doing?" I asked.

"He die at four thirty," she said, and broke the connection.

I stood there for a long while, staring at the wall, phone dangling in my hand, until eventually I forgot I was supposed to be holding it, and it slipped from my fingers.

When I bent over to pick it up, I checked to see if it was broken. It wasn't. That's when I noticed all the calls and e-mails I'd been ignoring all afternoon. I pushed the button and dropped it into my pocket.

The calls would have to wait. I was in no shape to be chitchatting with anybody.

On my way back into the den, I sat down at my desk, hit the space bar on my iMac, and waited for the box to come alive. I sighed, and started to change my mind, to reach around the back and turn the damn thing off. That's when I noticed the e-mail from Carl.

I grabbed the mouse and double-clicked it. All caps across the top.

HEY ASSHOLE. YOU OUGHTA TRY ANSWERING YOUR FUCKING PHONE ONCE IN A WHILE. HERE'S THE REST OF YOUR INFO.

Two attachments down at the bottom. The attachment on the right was a list of the properties that had turned out to belong to Aaron Townsend rather than to the Mount Zion church. The attachment on the left sent me looking for another drink.

■   ■   ■

"The bitch chewed him up and spit him out," he said. "Poor bastard never had a chance."

His name was James Dunn. Five ten, ginger-colored hair, and a bit of a Philadelphia accent. He was the sales manager for Victory Motors, an outfit that specialized in restored American muscle cars. Years before, back in the period before Charles Stone had slipped into oblivion, they'd worked together at Lee Johnson Chevrolet in Kirkland. How Carl had found him was a mystery to me, but he had. And here I was. Telling myself I owed it to the recently departed Phillip Peterson to find out whatever I could about Theresa Calder.

We were wedged into his phone booth–sized office out next to the body shop, watching three guys pull the body off a purple '66 Dodge Charger.

"You knew her well?" I asked.

He shook his head. "Company picnics. The Christmas party. That sort of thing."

He thought about it for a second. "It wasn't like she wasn't comfortable around any of Chuck's old friends. You know—one of those women who marry a guy and want his life to start all over with her. Like nothing ever happened in his life before she came on the scene. You know what I mean? One of those honeys."

I said I did.

"You know those commercials where they say 'What happens in Vegas stays in Vegas'? Well this one followed old Chuck *all* the way home."

"That where he met her? Vegas?"

He nodded. "Chuck won a weekend for two in Vegas in a sales contest. Asked me if I wanted to go along." He threw a hand into the air. "I mean . . . why the hell not, you know? A free weekend in Vegas, who's gonna turn that shit down?" He leaned forward in his chair. "Second night we're there . . . we're in the Bellagio . . . I look up from the table and he's gone." He snapped his fingers. "Just like that," he said. "Thin fucking air. Poof."

He seemed to be rolling so I kept my mouth shut.

"Don't show up till noon the next day. Comes stumbling into the room, looking like he just won the lottery, and tells me that he's found the love of his life and is getting married." He shook his head. "I tried to tell him, man. You know: pussy's a renewable resource . . . don't be gettin' crazy here . . . there's probably forty more of 'em downstairs right now. But he didn't want to hear about it. Nope, man . . . this was the one. Said he'd already called home, got a few extra days off and was staying for a while." He shrugged. "That was it, man. He took a shower, changed his clothes, packed his shit, and left. Didn't show up back home at the store for a week."

"What then?"

"Then Chucky's a new man. No more goin' out for a few pops after work. Don't play on the softball team no more. Don't do a damn thing other than stay home and kiss her ass, which was just how she wanted it."

"When did you finally meet her?"

"First Christmas party."

"What did you think?"

He shrugged. "Not the best-looking broad I ever seen—kinda horsey lookin', if you ask me—but I mean, like, *seriously* put together." He chuckled. "I joked with Chuck, told him if he wasn't careful he was gonna end up with stretch marks on his lips."

He laughed again. "He didn't think it was funny though. Got all kind of pissed off."

"So what happened?"

He thought about it. "Hard to tell," he said finally. "I think she was some kind of Jesus freak. Got him involved in that kind of Holy Roller shit." He waved the idea off disgustedly. "And then what? Maybe two years in, Chuck starts coming unglued. Starts missing shifts. Showing up smelling like a distillery. Wearing the same suit for a week. That kind of shit. I mean, management was good about it, put up with a lot of shit for a long time, but you know, it just got to be too much, so they hadda let him go."

"And that was it?"

He shook his head. "Naw. So after they gave him his notice, couple weeks after that, I stopped by his place on my way to work one morning." He held up a cautionary hand. "You wouldn't friggin' believe it," he said. "He was being evicted, right then and there. Couple sheriff's deputies was frog-walkin' him out the door right as I pulled up. Place looked like that TV show *Hoarders*. I mean, like, there was shit everywhere."

"Where was she?"

"Long gone," he said. "Walked out a couple months before. Took everything that wasn't nailed down and left him for some stockbroker or something."

I was betting the so-called stockbroker was none other than Blaine Peterson.

"And that was the last you saw of him?"

He sat back in his chair. "Not quite," he said. "Somethin' like . . . maybe six months after that, I'm comin' out of the Lake City Fred Meyer and this bum asks me for spare change. I'm fumblin' around in my pockets trying to come up with a little something and I realize it's fucking Charlie. Crusty, dirty long hair, black dirt under his fingernails. I mean, man . . . it was terrible, so I said, 'Charlie, it's me, James.' Like, what can I . . . And he just turned and walked away from me, yellin' and screamin' about the Lord and Jesus and all that kinda shit. How he'd been cast out of the fold and stuff like that." He anticipated my next question. "Those were his exact words. Swear. Said he'd been cast from the fold into the pit." He went somewhere back in his mind and relived the moment. "Never seen him again," he said, finally. "Always felt a little guilty . . . you know, 'cause we was together in Vegas when he met that honey. Like maybe I should have stopped him or something."

"He made his own choices," I said, with a lot more conviction than I felt.

. . .

Seemed like no matter which way I turned, all roads led to Mount Zion Ministries and their wonder boy Aaron Townsend. That poor homeless bastard they called the Preacher left all his worldly goods with that kid, told him he was going in search of the prophet of the Lord, and never came back. Theresa Calder got Blaine Peterson mixed up in what his late father had called "that so-called church of hers," and he ended up composting in the trunk of a rental car. Seemed like having a few words with Aaron Townsend would be the next logical step, but, as is often the case, doing the logical thing was more easily said than done.

While the papers reported that Townsend was showing up at various churches to preach, exactly where he was staying was still an unknown. "In seclusion" seemed to be the agreed-upon phrase to describe his present domestic arrangements.

I figured he couldn't be making all these public appearances and staying out on the peninsula at the Rectory. It was just too big a pain in the ass getting back and forth on the ferry, so it had to be someplace here on the mainland. Common sense said he probably wasn't camping out in an abandoned church, which left those two other disputed properties Carl had identified as the most likely starting points.

One of them had a Shoreline address. The other was way out in unincorporated King County someplace, on a road I'd never heard of. In keeping with the story of my life, I thought about it for about three seconds and then opted for easy over hard.

Took me twenty minutes to drive to the address in Shoreline. Turned out to be an older neighborhood. The fresh, green tips of leaves were beginning to show on the branches, and the air smelled of turned earth. 14512 was the last of the old-time farms that used to dot this part of the county, the vast majority of which had long since been subdivided and cul-de-sac-ed out of existence.

The property sat way up above the road, with a rough stone wall holding the slope in place and a long-abandoned garage dug directly into the side of the hill.

I'd like to tell you how I parked down on the road and walked up in an attempt to be stealthy. I'd like to tell you that, but truth be told, that all-too-familiar white Range Rover was parked in the driveway, making rock star parking highly inadvisable.

The rutted track was just steep enough to remind me how many parts of my body still hurt. I was grunting and groaning along when the sound of raised voices brought me to a halt.

"I'm not telling you again," somebody shouted.

A woman's shrill voice rose above the trees, "Go on—get out of here!"

The Range Rover was between me and the voices. On my right an ancient orchard stood black and crook-knuckled against a slate-gray sky. On the left, a thick copse of tangled fir trees and brush, probably left in place by the original homesteaders to protect the house from the winter wind.

I ducked low and slid along the side of the car, then peeled off and slithered into the trees. Took all I had to force myself through the jungle of brambles and branches. Ten feet in, I had to get down on my knees and crawl.

About the time I ducked under a low-hanging branch, the tree voiced its displeasure by dumping about half a pound of dried fir needles down my neck.

As I scuttled forward, the voices began to rise. The air was suddenly filled with adrenaline and acrimony. I rested on my elbows and wondered how it was I'd somehow morphed into an engine of conflict. Seemed like no matter where I went something bad was just about to happen. Like, all of a sudden, I'd become the Typhoid Mary of hard feelings or something.

I got down on my belly and crawled the last ten feet. By the time my head popped out the far side, the situation was really beginning to unravel. First thing my eyes were drawn to was Brother Biggs, standing directly behind the Range Rover, his arms folded across his thick chest, flashing a grin bigger than the grille of a '57 Chevy, despite the half a mile of surgical tape holding his nose to his face.

Up on the front porch, a young couple stood shoulder to shoulder. Tall blonds, both of them, early thirties, trying to present a united front, but looking scared as hell.

"Gonna tell ya one more time," Biggs said. "We are the owner's duly authorized agents. We have given you the required seventy-two hours' notice to vacate the premises." He unfolded his arms and waved a handful of legal papers at them. "Now get your personal things together and get on up the road."

They held their ground. "Pastor Highsmith told us—" the young man began.

Brother Biggs heaved a sigh. "Pastor Highsmith can flat-out kiss my ass," he said.

"We're not leaving," the woman blurted.

Biggs ambled across the ten feet of gravel that separated them, mounted the stairs until he was nose-to-nose with the pair, and then put on his most unctuous grin.

"Oh . . . you leavin' all right, missy. Only question is how," he said.

With a speed not normally associated with a man his size, he snatched the blue drawstring purse from under her arm.

She started forward. "Don't you dare . . ."

He stiff-armed her back. She bounced off the door with a dull thud. He tossed the purse to his partner. "See iffn you can't find some car keys in there," he told him.

Peepers got down on one knee and dumped everything out of the purse.

"Right here," he said, dangling a set of keys from his fingers.

"Bring their car around," he said, nodding at the detached garage.

She was screaming now. "You can't do this. You have no right . . ."

The young man tried to force his way past Biggs on the stairway. Biggs swept him aside like he was a moth, sending him cartwheeling down into an untended flower bed, bristling with the remains of last year's roses. A high-pitched moan rose from the kid's throat.

"Martin!" the young woman cried as she hurried toward her partner.

At that point, things seemed to go into fast-forward. The sound of popping gravel announced the approach of a lime-green Ford Fiesta.

Peepers wheeled the little car out onto the lawn, slid it to a halt in front of the Range Rover, and got out, leaving the engine running.

"Martin," she cried again as she knelt by his side.

By the time she'd managed to wrestle Martin into a sitting position, Brother Biggs had scooped up the contents of her purse, jammed everything back inside, and was headed in their direction. "Let's go," was all he said.

The sight of Biggs coming her way set her rocket off but good. She came roaring out of the flower bed like a moon shot. Red faced, screaming at the top of her lungs, talons extended. A low groan escaped my chest as Biggs backhanded her hard enough to turn her in a half circle, then grabbed her by the hair and lifted her completely off the ground.

The terrible keening sound she made was equal parts rage and agony as Biggs carried her flailing body over to the car and crammed her into the driver's seat. She rocked spastically in the seat, hugging herself and sobbing hysterically. Biggs dropped her purse into her lap, kicked the door shut, and started back for the house.

Martin had staged a partial recovery. He was on his feet, waving like a willow in a windstorm, when Biggs grabbed him by the throat with one hand and by the crotch with the other. And suddenly Martin was bug-eyed and frozen, his mouth wide open, screaming silently at the dark afternoon sky.

I thought about jumping out and trying to put a stop to this. Mercifully, I never got the chance.

"Open that damn car door," Biggs yelled.

I began to crab backwards out of the thicket. I peeked around the edge of the foliage just in time to see Brother Biggs hurl Martin into the backseat like a javelin. I winced at the sound of his head hitting the other door. Peepers folded Martin's legs up and slammed the door while Biggs walked to the driver's side.

"Drive," Biggs growled.

He didn't have to tell her twice.

I took off running, staying low across the grass all the way down to the stone wall. The three-foot drop to road level looked like ten stories. I took a deep breath and stepped off. My feet hit at the same moment that the little Ford's front tires bounced onto the pavement with a screech. I groaned from the impact as I watched her floor it, fishtail twice, and then straighten the car out. Some blind urge told me to follow, so I hoisted myself up into the driver's seat and started after them.

She drove all the way to Holman Road, up by the north border of the city, before she pulled into a QFC parking lot, got out, and leaned into the backseat.

I backed into a parking space in front of Vera's Nail Palace and waited. She ministered to Martin for the better part of ten minutes before climbing back in and heading toward Ballard.

I stayed about five cars back as we wound uphill on Holman and started down the other side. Right before Holman miraculously changed into Fifteenth Avenue NW, she put on her turn signal and eased into an empty parking lot. The sign out front read NORTH SEATTLE CHURCH OF THE HOLY SAVIOR. PASTOR RODGER HIGHSMITH. And then, under that, a long list of times for services, Sunday schools, and weekday Bible study groups.

The curb was bumper to bumper, so I had to drive a full two blocks past the church before I could pull over and park. By the time I'd limped back uphill to the church's driveway, she'd already rallied the faithful. Three men and a woman surrounded the car, leaning in from all directions at once.

I mamboed across the street and watched the proceedings from behind a red Audi as two of the guys leaned in and lifted Martin out of the car. His neck was loose like a bobblehead doll's and his legs were like spaghetti as they helped him up the stairs.

Shepherding over the proceedings was a tall guy with a turned-around collar and a silver streak running through his curly black hair. Pastor Highsmith, I was guessing.

I leaned on the Audi and watched as the church's big double doors swung shut.

. . .

Whoever pointed out that there was a leisure class at both ends of the social spectrum had been right on the money. The Eastlake Zoo was packed with folks for whom fifty bucks constituted a serious piece of pocket change, but when I asked, "Who wants to make fifty bucks?" nobody so much as flinched.

The jukebox was blaring "Land of a Thousand Dances." Billy Bob Fung was doing the funky chicken over in the corner with Red Lopez and Crazy Shirley.

Na, na na na na, na na na na, na na na, na na na . . .

George Paris leered at me over his beer. "Doin' what?" he asked.

"Just sitting on your ass and listening to some guy talk."

"What guy?"

"Guy namea Aaron Townsend."

"The preacher guy?"

"Yep."

"I don't do preachers," he said.

I went for the coup de grace. "You don't even have to clean up."

Now he was really wary. "How's that?"

"The paper says the Downtown Gospel Mission is taking a bunch of folks to hear him preach tonight. You're tight with those guys. I'm betting you can talk your way into going along for the ride."

"If you're so interested in what this guy's got to say, how come you ain't going?"

"They've already had the pleasure of my acquaintance," I said.

George almost smiled. "Looks like you come out with the worst of it too."

"But a temporary setback," I assured him.

He thought it over.

"I ain't goin' alone."

I looked around. "Where's Harold?" I asked.

"Doin' thirty," George said disgustedly. "Failure to appear."

"Ralphie?"

"He'll be out on Thursday," George assured me.

That was the merry-go-round for these guys. They'd get busted for something stupid, like pissing in public; they'd get a ticket and a court date and then not show up for court, which was a considerably more serious offense than alfresco weasel draining; and then they'd end up serving thirty days for failure to appear.

Na, na na na na, na na na na, na na na, na na na . . .

George was wavering, so I went for the throat. I reached up and tapped Nearly Normal Norman on the shoulder. Norman was immense. Six seven or so. Somewhere in the neighborhood of three and a half tons. Not only that, but even a cursory glance into his deep blue eyes made it frighteningly clear that the big fella wasn't watching the same cable network as the rest of us.

He turned my way. "Leo," he said with a lopsided grin.

"Wanna make fifty bucks?" I asked.

"How'm I gonna do that?"

"Go over to Fremont with Georgie tonight and listen to a guy preach."

His face grew grave. He shook his big head. "No preachers, no churches, Leo. The Lord gave up on me a long time ago. Far as He's concerned I'm persona au gratin."

I told him I understood and patted him on the shoulder. My options were limited. I was thinking I might have struck out, when Large Marge came striding into the bar.

"Marge," I called. She looked my way. I beckoned her over.

"Noooo," George hissed from behind me. I ignored him. "Don't, Leo. For God's sake . . ." he whispered.

Marge plopped herself down in the empty chair. I ran it by her. Before I'd finished talking, she was bobbing her head up and down. "Sure . . . why not," she said. She broke into a wide grin. "I've been tryin' to get Georgie here into a church for years."

George was squirming in the seat and staring up into the mezzanine.

"He's just shy is all," she added with a wink.

When she reached across the table and tickled him under the chin, George began making noises like a gored animal.

She got to her feet. "What time?" she asked.

"He'll meet you at Downtown Gospel at six thirty," I said quickly.

"Well then, I better get home and lather up," she allowed. She took a step toward the door, stopped, and then turned back our way. "Less'n you want to come along, Georgie. We could work up a fine froth, we could."

George began making those animal noises again.

Marge grinned and headed for the door.

George kept his face averted until he heard the front door close.

"What the hell's the matter with you?" he demanded.

I ignored him. "I want to know what Townsend says. How the audience feels about him. Talk to people. What I really want to know is whether anybody's got any idea where he's staying while he's in town. You know the drill. Find out whatever you can."

"That woman's been trying to jump my bones for years."

"What are you . . . holding out for marriage?"

"Not funny, Leo."

I got to my feet and dropped a crisp new twenty on the table. "Incidental expenses," I said. "I'll catch up with you guys sometime tomorrow."

George grunted.

I slid my phone across the table. "Call the mission," I said.

Na, na na na na . . .

▪ ▫ ▪

I was parked three doors down from the Church of the Redeemer when the mission bus pulled up out front at about ten to seven. If ever there was a group who could use a bit of redemption, it was the festering flock that stumbled off that bus.

Being around the destitute always gave me the same eerie feeling. When you've made as many mistakes as I have, you can't help but wonder how many more bad decisions it would have taken to put you in *their* shoes. Not many, I suspect. Not many at all.

I don't send these guys out on their own anymore. Not since Buddy Knox was tortured and killed down in Tacoma, while conducting what I'd imagined to be a routine stakeout. That monumental misjudgment took a divot out of my soul that's never gonna heal, so these days, if they go . . . I go. It's as simple as that.

Besides . . . maybe I could get lucky and follow Aaron Townsend to wherever he was holed up. It wasn't as easy as they made it seem on TV, but what the hell, why not give it a whirl.

The evening onshore breeze began to massage the trees. Gently at first, like a lover, then gradually rising in intensity. As the trees began to sway like ghostly dancers, the rain arrived at its leisure. One drop here and one drop there. Big, wet spit-gobs of water falling piecemeal from the sky, clanking onto car hoods and canvas awnings like cosmic conga drums.

Lightning flashed in the western sky about two seconds before an explosion of thunder sucked all the oxygen from the air. I pulled in a metallic breath and checked my watch. 7:35. I reached for the radio just as the heavens opened and a torrent of rain tumbled from the sky. Sounded like an army of monkeys was hammering on the car as I fiddled with the knob, hoping to find something familiar on the airwaves.

For me, the radio had been the unwelcome harbinger of middle age. Seemed like one day I was the hippest guy around, and then, all of a sudden, there was nothing on the radio I recognized anymore. Every time I heard a song I knew the words to, it was on the "oldies" channel. Like the passing of time had turned the world inside out and shaken me to the ground like a loose stone.

I was still fiddling with the dial, trying to reclaim my lost youth, when the rain disappeared as quickly as it had come. I snapped on the wipers just in time to catch sight of a pair of pedestrians coming down the sidewalk toward the church.

Even with his black curls plastered to his head, the bright silver streak in Pastor Highsmith's hair was clearly visible. The woman whom I'd assumed to be Mrs. Highsmith was locked onto his arm like a barnacle. Unless I was mistaken, this was a Pastor Posse, come to do battle with the former prophet of righteousness.

As the Highsmiths mounted the front stairs, I popped open the car door and stepped into the street. The last of the rain was dripping from the bare branches. The sound of trickling water filled the air.

When Pastor Highsmith yanked open the church door, I could hear Aaron Townsend's brash baritone coming over the PA system. "We owe the Lord . . ." his voice boomed. The door swung shut.

Before I could cross the street, the church doors were flung back with a bang. The sodden air suddenly overflowed with raised voices. Bible verses being quoted at high volume, curses being cast, invectives hurled, as the whole surging mass of humanity began to flow down the church steps like a Slinky. The Highsmiths were trying to hold their ground, but were being forced down the stairs backwards by the surging mass of bodies boiling out of the building.

I ducked into a nook beside the stairs. Half a minute later, the Highsmiths were backed up against the row of cars parked in front of the church.

Mrs. Highsmith looked to be in a full panic. Her eyes rolled in her head like a spooked horse's as a heavyset woman stepped up and began bellowing into her face, waving a Bible like a hammer, mashing Mrs. Highsmith hard into the side of a car as she filled the air with equal parts spittle and invective.

I took two steps forward, shouldered the big woman aside, bent my good arm around Mrs. Highsmith's waist, and pulled her out of there. I set her on the sidewalk and waded back in for her husband.

By this time saner heads were beginning to prevail. It had occurred to some of the assembled multitude that perhaps a church was an inappropriate venue for the sort of mean-spirited, threatening behavior presently being exhibited by a number of their more excitable brethren.

As a pair of burly parishioners sought to shield Pastor Highsmith from the seething mob, I slipped into the gap, grabbed Highsmith by the elbow, and began to pull him to safety. He jerked his arm away and began to scan the crowd. "Maryanne," he called. "Maryanne."

"Your wife's over here," I shouted above the din.

He looked at me in stunned disbelief, then caught sight of his wife over my shoulder and began to sidestep in her direction. That's when I heard the sirens for the first time. Two, maybe three sirens coming this way.

"I'm thinkin' maybe we ought to get out of here," I said to them.

"I . . ." he stammered. "We didn't . . . I only wanted to . . ."

"Where's your car?" I asked.

"We Ubered," his wife said.

I took her by the arm. "My car's over here," I said. "Probably best we're not here when the cops arrive."

Pastor Highsmith was still grousing about how he never intended something like this to happen as we pulled away from the curb.

I looked at him in the rearview mirror. He was sweaty and slack jawed.

"Where to?" I asked.

"Crown Hill," his wife said.

I knew where we were going but didn't let on.

"What was *that* all about?" I tried.

"That man has no right to preach," Highsmith said.

I turned right onto Thirty-Ninth. "Bunch of folks back there at the church seemed to think he did." I used the mirror to watch his neck get stiffer.

"He's been removed from the rolls. He's no longer affiliated."

"I didn't realize you had to be affiliated," I quipped. "Was Jesus affiliated?"

That one pissed him off, I could tell.

"His thugs assaulted two of my parishioners. Put a young man in the hospital. I wanted those people to know who it was they were listening to."

"Maybe bearding the lion in his den wasn't such a good idea," his wife said.

"There was no other way," he said stubbornly. "The whole Salvation Lake thing was a disaster."

"Salvation Lake?" I said.

"It's where Townsend and his family stay," his wife said. "The church council sent a delegation out there to serve him with disaffiliation papers." She patted her husband's shoulder again. "He had them all arrested."

"He needed to be confronted in public," Highsmith insisted.

I worked up my best "gee whiz" tone. "Salvation Lake. Where's that?"

"They're all living in a fool's paradise if they think Aaron Townsend is going to fade quietly into the background. I told them that then and I'm telling them that now. Now that there's a lot of money involved . . ." He picked up on the bitterness creeping into his voice and stopped himself.

I thought about asking again, but decided against it. Pastor Highsmith was in full "I told them so" mode and not likely to take kindly to geography questions, so I kept driving, running up Holman Road and down onto Fifteenth for the second time today.

"The driveway's right up on the right," Mrs. Highsmith said.

I pulled in and braked to a stop. The churchyard was dark. The reverend was still muttering under his breath when he got out of the car and marched off. Mrs. Highsmith reached over the seat and put a hand on my arm.

"Thank you, Mr. . . ."

"Waterman," I said. "Leo Waterman."

"Thank you for being such a Good Samaritan," she said. "My husband thanks you too. He's just a bit upset tonight." She patted my arm. "We need more people in this world like you, Leo."

Took every bit of willpower I owned not to tell her how wrong she was. Instead, I forced a dented smile onto my lips, and watched in silence as she followed her husband into the darkness.

■   ■   ■

"There's no such fucking lake," Carl insisted. "No body of water called Salvation Lake is within a hundred miles of here. Period. End o' story."

"Who's in charge of lakes?" I asked.

"Whadda you mean by *in charge*?"

I shrugged. "You know . . . like *responsible for*."

Carl thought it over. "Department of Ecology, I'm guessing."

"Maybe they'd know."

"Not at ten o'clock at night, they won't."

"Can't you like . . ."

He sneered at me. "Just hack my way in?"

"Yeah."

"No," he growled. "That's dorky TV shit."

Before I could come up with something else, he waved a bony finger in my face. "And, I was you, Fearless Fosdick, I'd spend a lot less time trying to find out where this guy lives, and a lot more time worrying about those two assholes who keep trying to rearrange your face."

"Why's that?"

"'Cause those two are a real piece of work. I looked up this Biggs guy. Brother Biggs," he intoned.

"What's his first name?"

"That *is* his first name. Brother Biggs. No middle name. No known parents. Twenty-nine. A lifetime foster child. Broke a guy's neck in a bar fight. Got sent to Walla Walla when he was eighteen, where he ended up doing an extra three and change for assaulting a female staff member. Listed as 'unmanageable' by the Washington state prison system. Spent his last two years in solitary. Pretty much the worst of the worst."

He started flipping through a pile of paperwork. Handed me a mug shot of the little guy with glasses. "That the other one?"

I said it was.

"Chauncey Bostick," he said. "Thirty years old. Born God knows where. Mother Wanda May Bostick gave him up to the state of Washington when he was three. Father unknown. What is known is that Chauncey likes to shoot people. Killed a childhood friend in a so-called hunting accident, when he was fourteen. Then did two stints for aggravated assault involving a firearm back in the nineties. Pretty much clean since then, except for a couple of beefs he beat in court, claiming self-defense.

"Biggs and Bostick met when they were both in the same Spanaway foster home. A local do-gooder name of Nathaniel Tuttle took both of 'em in and tried to make men of them, but by that time they were so far down the wrong path, there was no turning them around. All they did was drive him nuts. Spent half his time getting them out of the slammer, until they finally did him a favor and ran away together."

Carl brought out a red file folder marked "Peterson" and flipped it open. "Which brings us to the honey," he began. "Theresa Calder. Took the Peterson kid for the better part of four hundred gs on her way out the door. Last record I could find of her was when she transferred the dough from the Bellevue Square branch of Washington Mutual to the Shinhan Bank of South Korea."

"What's in South Korea?" I wondered out loud.

"She was," Carl said. "The only way you can open a bank account in South Korea is in person. You have to show up with your alien registration card and your passport."

I was still turning that over in my head when I looked down and saw that Carl had printed up the Google map of the Peterson home in Newcastle. Nestled there on the sixth hole fairway, hard by the banks of Peterson Pond.

An unaccustomed spasm of lucidity flashed across my consciousness.

"What if it's private?" I asked.

"What if what's private?"

"The lake. Salvation Lake. What if it's a private lake?"

.   .   .

Something about gated communities gives me the willies. Maybe it's that Frost poem from high school, where he says that before he'd build a wall, he'd be damn sure what he was walling in and what he was walling out. That sentiment was pretty much the same feeling I got every once in a while when I closed the gate at my house. That moment when it occurred to me that "they" might already *be* inside and all I'd just accomplished was to have locked myself in with them.

I'd followed the Google directions to something called Retribution Road, way the hell out behind Duvall.

I'd driven by the clearing twice before I noticed the half-dozen gray four-by-fours sticking up out of the ground like broken teeth. I pulled up to the rusted chain, got out, and then waded off into the underbrush.

Looked to me like somebody'd clear-cut about four acres. Judging from the size of the undergrowth, maybe ten years ago, something like that. What had once been a Douglas fir forest had been chainsawed into a twisted morass of scrubby oak, pasture grass, and browned-over thistles.

An old roadside sign lay facedown on the ground in front of the posts. I reached down, grabbed the edge with my one good hand, and heaved upward. It came off the ground about a foot and then stopped. Not only was it way bigger than I'd imagined, but it was all twisted up in the grown-over vegetation.

I rested it on my foot, got myself a better grip, and gave it the full monty. It rose grudgingly, tearing the long grass as it rose, and slowly showed its face to the sunlight for the first time in years.

I leaned it against the rotting four-by-fours and stepped back. The sign was too mud-caked to read, so I walked back to the car, found the hand brush I use to sweep French fries out from under the seats, and started back.

Took me a full five minutes to brush the dirt and grime from the sign. Again I stepped back for a look. Heavenly rays of sunshine, falling from an azure sky, bathing a bucolic forest setting in the Lord's pure white light.

Ascension Acres in big, puffy white letters. A Gated Christian Community in black beneath. On one side it read: Come Home to the Lord. On the other: A Little Taste of Heaven. Down beneath: Sinless Living in a Country Club Setting.

In the center, a picture of a redbrick Georgian mansion, about the size of a Safeway. Visit Our Sales Office. Prequalified Buyers Only. And a big black arrow pointing west from the sign.

On the bottom, a rendering of what looked like an antebellum mansion. Fluted columns and all. OPENING SOON. MODEL HOME. SEE WHAT THE LORD HAS IN STORE FOR YOU!

As I was picking my way back to the car, I stumbled over a hummock of plowed ground. Intrigued, I climbed atop the nearest stump and looked around. From this higher vantage point, I could see that somebody had, at some time in the past, bulldozed a series of roads, fanning out from here like the spokes of a wagon wheel. Each leading to your own little mansion of glory.

I got back in my car and followed the arrow. About half a mile up the road, a muddy track branched off to the left before disappearing into the trees at an angle. No signs, no gate, no nothing. I was about to drive on when I noticed that the rainwater in the ruts was muddy, telling me somebody had driven this way in the not too distant past.

I'm a slow learner, but I'd already had my ass kicked once and wasn't about to be driving myself into another hornet's nest if I could help it, so I rounded up the postmortem photos I'd been carrying around for a week, locked the car, and started hoofing it up the track, keeping one foot in front of the other on the grassy berm, trying like hell to keep my shoes out of the mud.

The woods were indeed dark and deep. I was several hundred yards in when I heard the voice. High-pitched. Plaintive. A child shouting something, I thought.

I had my eyes locked on the grassy medium, doing my famous tightrope routine, when the voice pulled my head up.

"Buster," the voice cried. "Buster."

And there he was, running directly at me. A golden retriever puppy. All fluffy blond hair, black nose, and pink tongue of him, loping along the grass.

I stuffed the envelope under my arm, reached out with my good hand, and scooped him up. I held him against my chest as I wire-walked down the berm. He licked my face and squirmed.

And then the girl came galloping into view. Seven or eight. Dark brown hair. Tall for her age. She skidded to a halt at first sight of me, then turned, as if to run.

"This your dog?" I asked.

She nodded but didn't say anything.

"His name Buster?"

Another nod. "He ran away," she said.

"Puppies are like that," I said. "Curious. Always want to see what's over the next hill." I held him out. "Here."

She took me in with her brown eyes for a moment, and then stepped over and took Buster from my hand.

"What's your name?" I asked.

"Lila."

"I'm Leo," I said, offering my hand.

"I'm not supposed to talk to strangers," she said.

"But I'm a friend of Buster's."

She laughed. "Did you come to see my daddy?"

"Depends on who your daddy is," I said.

"Lots of men come to see my daddy. He preaches the Gospel."

"Then he's the one I came to see."

"Come on," she said.

We walked up the road together. The sky was beginning to spit rain.

"Shouldn't you be in school?" I asked as we strolled along.

"I'm homeschooled," she said. "Momma is my teacher."

"You like that?"

She shrugged, kissed the puppy on top of his head, and lowered her voice. "She's not really my mom. My real mom is in heaven."

"I'm sorry to hear that," I mumbled.

"Me too," she said with a sigh.

As we rounded yet another muddy bend, the house suddenly came into view. Same Georgian house that was painted on the Ascension Acres sign. Truth in advertising.

Always seemed to me that every house has a personality. My gloomy old Tudor seemed to whisper about scheduled eye gougings and last week's bungled beheading. This one here spoke of jodhpurs and red jackets and packs of eager hounds thrashing about the countryside in search of a wily fox. All teatime and tallyho, you know.

"Lila," a man's voice called.

Aaron Townsend was about forty yards away, walking in our direction. Lila took off running, babbling all the way. "This is Leo, Daddy, Leo found Buster after Buster ran away from me, I kept calling him but he wouldn't stop and I was calling and calling and then Leo gave him back to me and then we"—Townsend threw an arm around Lila's shoulder and pulled her close—"and we were walking up the road and . . ."

He was a very handsome guy with thick dark hair that seemed to repel the rain. Quite a bit shorter than either his voice or his reputation had led me to imagine. Maybe five eight or so, but well built in a subcompact sort of way.

I walked over and stuck out my hand. "Leo Waterman."

He ignored my offer of a hand. "Didn't you see the signs?"

"I . . . uh . . . I was . . ." I stammered.

"This is private property," he said. "I'll have to ask you to leave."

Lila ducked out from under his arm. "But he found Buster," she chirped.

He pinned me with an Old Testament gaze. Lila began pulling on his leg.

He swallowed his anger. "Thank you for rounding up Buster. That dog seems to have a mind of his own."

I was sorely tempted to say "Unlike your parishioners," but instead went with, "I was hoping I could ask you a couple of questions."

"Please, Daddy. He's nice. He found Buster," Lila whined.

He held my gaze for about two seconds longer than polite company demands.

"Leo Waterman. Any relation to Big Bill Waterman?" he asked.

"He was my father."

Mercifully, the heavens intervened, and I was spared the usual historical repartee regarding my old man. A sudden volley of rain raked the yard like grapeshot. I ducked my head and brought a hand up to keep the rain out of my ear.

"Come out of the weather," another voice called.

What I figured had to be the new Mrs. Townsend stood in the doorway, beckoning for us to come her way.

Aaron Townsend heaved a resigned sigh. "Come on," he said grudgingly.

I winced a thank-you, ducked my shoulder into the wind, and followed him up the front walk. The new Mrs. Townsend was an absolute stunner. A blonde bombshell, put together in that opulent fifties kind of way. Dressed to the nines, heels, pearls, and all, on a rainy weekday afternoon. To complete the illusion, the house smelled of cookies. Almost too good to be true, I thought as I wiped my feet.

She produced a bath towel and wrapped it around Buster. "Alice Townsend," she said by way of introduction. "Come into the kitchen," she said, scrubbing the dog as she walked away. "I've got something in the oven." The noise she made walking will be welded into my psyche till they put me under the sod.

I shook the rain from my shoulders and my blood supply back to where it belonged and then followed along.

We could have played soccer in the kitchen. Two of every appliance and a kitchen table big enough for a rugby team. Several dozen chocolate chip cookies were cooling on the counters. Alice set Buster on the floor. He clattered off with Lila hot on his heels.

"Let me take your coat," Aaron Townsend said.

I held up a restraining hand. "I can't stay," I said.

Over his shoulder, Lila was trying to pick Buster up, but he was having none of it. Mrs. Townsend was removing another tray of cookies from the oven.

"What happened to Ascension Acres?" I asked.

He stifled a grin. "It never got off the ground," he said.

I did it for him. "I guess I walked into that one, didn't I?"

He made an expansive gesture with his hands. "This is all there ever was. They used it as a model home and as the sales office."

I couldn't resist. "How come it never took wing?"

"One of my parishioners from years ago . . . his name was Nate Tuttle. This was his brainchild. Nate was a pious man but not the most practical of people."

"How'd you end up with it? He leave it to you?"

"Actually . . . he left the property to Alice before he passed last year," Townsend said. "Alice was always bringing him food and inviting him to holidays. Nate didn't have anybody. We were as close to family as he had. I think it gave him joy to leave it to Alice."

The explanation sounded canned to me. Like he'd said the words plenty of times before. I wanted to keep him talking, so I changed the subject.

"Where's Salvation Lake?" I asked.

He indicated I should follow and walked to the rear of the kitchen. He pointed out the window. "There she is," he said. "Salvation Lake."

And indeed it was. Three acres or so of weedy man-made lake, with a little wooden jetty jutting out into the water. "Nate named everything on the property for something biblical. Salvation Lake. Retribution Road. Heavenly Haven. Everything."

Before I could manufacture another segue, he asked, "So . . . what is it I can do for you, Mr. Waterman?"

I threw my eyes Lila's way. Townsend picked up on it.

"Lila," he called. "Why don't you take Buster out to the garage and give him some food and water."

"Yes, Daddy," she said from around a cookie. "Come on . . . Come on, Buster . . ."

She skipped from the room with Buster gamboling along in hot pursuit.

I pulled the envelope out from under my arm and walked over to the table.

"Without going into all the whys and wherefores of the thing," I began, "what I want to know is whether you know who either of these men are."

I pulled both postmortem photos from the envelope and when I smoothed them out on the table, I had to stifle a chuckle. Each photo had a little sticker in the corner that read Cradduck Data Retrieval. You put something in Carl's hands and it came back to you with one of those stickers on it somewhere.

Mrs. Townsend was drying her hands with a dish towel as she leaned in close. The scent of her suddenly filled the air. I heard the breath catch in her throat at the sight of the grisly pictures.

"They're . . . I mean . . . they're . . ."

"Yes," I said. "They are."

"Never seen either of them," Aaron Townsend said.

"Poor souls," Alice Townsend said.

"Why would you think we might know these men?"

"I thought they might be parishioners," I said.

"I'm afraid not," Townsend said.

I slid the photos from the table and put them away. "Well then . . ." I said. "I'm sorry to have intruded on you. Please accept my apologies."

I started to leave. Aaron Townsend put a hand on my back and helped me toward the door. "Mr. Waterman," his wife called. When I turned she was wrapping half a dozen cookies up in tinfoil. "Take these for your ride back."

I walked over and took the package from her hand. "Thanks," I said. "I . . ."

And then the words froze in my throat. Behind her, on the second shelf of a huge mahogany china cabinet, stood their wedding picture.

On the left, Aaron Townsend and what, from the eyes, had to be his father, each with an arm around a much younger Lila. On the right, Alice and her parents. Alice's parents I'd seen before. Lately. Those were the same smiling faces I'd seen at the Peterson house. Only then, the faces were in Blaine Peterson's wedding picture. They'd been Theresa Calder's parents. I felt as if my brains might be leaking out my ears.

"Thanks for the cookies," I mumbled.

"Thanks for rescuing Buster," she said as she slid yet another rack of cookies out of the oven.

Aaron Townsend offered me a ride back to my car. I told him I wanted to get some air. We shook hands in the doorway. I don't remember the walk back to the car.

. . .

"They sure as hell don't look like each other," Carl said. "I mean . . . look at the anvil chin on the Calder broad. She could be Jay Leno in drag."

Laid out on the table in front of him were the driver's license photo of Theresa Calder and the family photo on the back of *Real Belief*. Lila in between Aaron and Alice Townsend. All warm light and fuzzy sweaters.

"The rev's old lady's a knockout though," he said. "That broad could raise the dead . . . among other things." He squinted up at me. "You're sure? Same parents in both wedding pictures?"

"I'm sure."

"Not sisters? Or stepsisters, some shit like that?"

I told him what Mrs. Peterson said about Theresa being an only child. "And that South American missionary parents stuff . . ." I was shaking my head. "I mean . . . now that nobody's having a heart attack in my lap, what's the chance of that crap being true?"

Carl nodded. "Real convenient, if you don't wanna be found," he said.

"Too friggin' convenient," I said.

"You know the rev's wife's maiden name?"

I shrugged. "No idea, but they had a big public wedding at the Bellevue Mount Zion church," I said. "Musta been in the papers."

Carl began pushing buttons. Screens began to roll and blink as sheets of information floated across the monitors.

"Maiden name . . . Alice Brooks," Carl said after a moment. "Parents . . . Tom and Annette Brooks . . . Huánuco, Peru."

"That South American shit again."

"How old you think she is?"

"Thirty-something."

Carl went back to pounding on his keyboard.

"There's sixty-three Alice Brookses born between nineteen seventy-five and nineteen eighty-five."

"How many with parents Tom and Annette?"

"Can't tell," he said. "I'd have to search each of them individually and even then not all the parents are going to be on record."

"Alice Townsend have a Washington driver's license?"

"Let's see."

A Washington driver's license appeared on one of the overhead screens.

"That's her," I said.

Carl shook his head in mock disbelief. "Anybody looks that damn good in a driver's license picture gotta be some sweet piece." He banged a final key and sat back in his chair. He pointed at the screen. "Issued four years ago last week," Carl said. "About six months before she married Aaron Townsend. An initial."

"Initial what?"

"Initial Washington driver's license, rather than a renewal."

"Didn't she have to turn in her old license?"

"That's how it usually works," he said and went back to pushing buttons. Carl barked out a short, dry laugh. "It figured," he muttered.

"No previous driving history," I ventured.

"You got it."

"So what did she use for ID?"

"Birth certificate." He sat back, folded his arms across his chest, and waited as the screens did their thing. "Born Alice Anne Brooks. Nineteen eighty, Bakersfield, California. Mercy Hospital Southwest. Five pounds seven ounces. Parents, Thomas J. Brooks and Annette no middle name Rivera."

"Can we—" I began.

Carl held up a gnarled hand. "You're gonna love this," he said as he went back to pushing buttons. A woman's haggard face appeared on the screen, with a number under it. Clark County Police Department, Number 139830. July 7, 2009.

"Who's that?"

"Alice Brooks."

"Well that's not even close to—"

Carl pointed at the vital statistics. "Five foot three," he said. He tapped the mouse and Alice Townsend's driver's license came up.

"Five foot nine," I read out loud.

"Helluva late-life growth spurt."

Carl pointed at the screen on the far right. "Alice Brooks was reported missing in April of twenty ten." Several of the upper screens suddenly filled with data. "She's got a rap sheet as long as your arm," Carl said. "Coupla minor fraud beefs, but mostly solicitation."

"You don't say."

"Yep. Five foot three Alice Brooks is a missing Vegas hooker."

"Who reported her missing?"

"Doesn't say," Carl said. "You know the drill, Leo. Missing hookers don't exactly give the boys in blue an urge to work hard."

"There's got to be some way . . ."

The front door opened. Charity walked in, carrying a white Styrofoam food container. Not Charity the virtue, but a dreadlocked Jamaican guy who worked as Carl's part-time caretaker. Charity was also an underground IT specialist. Carl had never gotten specific about it, but I got the impression Charity specialized in things reputable geeks frowned upon.

"Hey Leo, mon. How's you been?"

"Fair to middlin'," I said.

He looked over at Carl. "Got soma Pam's jerk chicken for you, mon." He waved the container enticingly and then headed for the kitchen.

I turned to Carl. "What if—"

Carl cut me off. "You come up with any bright ideas, you know where to find me. Right now, I'm gonna have a little bite to eat."

As he rolled off toward the kitchen, I thanked him, and headed outside to my car.

I hopped into the driver's seat and sat there for a moment, trying to remember if I'd ever put this much energy into a case and come up with less useful information. On the passenger seat lay the tinfoil packet of cookies. As I started to reach for some sweet solace, my hand stopped in midair, and I smiled for the first time in a week.

∎   ∎   ∎

"Can I borrow an evidence bag?" I asked.

Rebecca arched an eyebrow at me. "You ask that of all the girls?" she inquired as she reached down, opened a desk drawer, and produced a one-gallon Ziploc.

Using the tips of my fingers, I wiggled the package out of my jacket pocket and laid it on her desk.

"What's that?" she wanted to know.

"Cookies," I said. "Chocolate chip."

The eyebrow got higher. "Maybe you ought to fill me in."

So I did.

"What does this have to do with the two guys in the trunk?" she asked.

"Both of them were, at one time, married to Theresa Calder."

That stopped her for a minute. "And you're sure it was the same set of parents in the wedding photos?"

"Positive. The mom was wearing the same dress in both pictures."

"Weird."

"No kidding."

"Sisters?"

"No way."

"What, then?"

"Not a clue. You figure out what killed them?"

"Nope," she said. She checked the clock on the wall. Ten to five. "I've got a staff meeting in ten minutes. What do you want from me?"

"I want you to send that piece of aluminum foil there through IAFIS. See what comes up." The Integrated Automated Fingerprint Identification System contained more than seventy million sets of fingerprints. If you weren't in their files, you'd never been arrested, never applied for a teaching certificate or a government license of any kind, never served in the armed forces. The list went on and on. Wasn't going to be long before everybody on the planet was going to be on file.

"There's going to be two sets of prints," I said. "One is going to be mine. The other is from the woman called Alice Townsend."

"Aaron Townsend's wife?"

"The very same."

She took a moment to digest the information. "As I recall, your prints are already on file."

"Regrettably."

She thought it over. "What's in it for me?"

"The cookies."

"Why don't you sic Carl on her?"

"Already did. On both her and Theresa Calder. Theresa has no past history prior to marrying Charles Stone. Apparently, she just appears out of the ozone, marries one guy, divorces him, marries another guy, and then walks out on him too. The same day Theresa Calder walked out on Blaine Peterson, she transferred a substantial pile of money out of the country and then, as far as we can tell, disappeared from the face of the earth."

"Out of the country where?"

"South Korea."

The brow again. "Plastic surgery capital of the universe."

"Plastic surgery, I get. But Theresa Calder had a jaw like a linebacker. Could they do anything with that?"

"If you had enough cash, they could make you into a nine-year-old Hindu boy."

I tried not to work up an image of that. "Which brings us to the other one. Alice Townsend. Maiden name supposedly Brooks. Lots of past history, none of which actually belongs to *our* Alice, but lots of history. The real Alice Brooks *is* or *was* a Vegas hooker who went missing in two thousand and ten. Half a foot shorter and I've seen her picture. It's not Theresa Calder, and it's not Alice Townsend."

"I'll put a rush flag on it. Call me tomorrow."

I watched in silence as she pulled a dissection kit from her top drawer and, using a pair of forceps, unfolded the package sufficiently to free the cookies, then dropped the foil into the evidence bag and sealed it.

She got to her feet. "I've gotta go." She swept all the cookies but one onto a paper towel and into her top drawer. Took a big bite of the remaining cookie. Her eyes narrowed with delight.

"These are great," she pronounced.

．　．　．

I was halfway back home before I figured out what was gnawing at my gut. It was Aaron Townsend, or more specifically, how different he'd turned out to be from what I'd imagined. Everything I'd heard had led me to expect some wild-eyed despot, spouting hellfire and damnation, treating his browbeaten wife like an indentured servant.

The love and cookies act could have been conjured for my benefit, but I didn't think so. The affection I'd seen among the three of them had been genuine. What I saw was a nice guy with a nice family, and as unlikely as it seemed, I actually liked him. I couldn't help thinking that there was probably a lesson for me in there someplace.

Technically speaking, the days were supposed to be getting longer, but you'd never have known it from this afternoon. Out over Puget Sound, steel wool clouds squeezed the horizon flat, leaving nothing but a narrow band of uncertain light to keep the rumor of daylight alive.

It hadn't been a particularly arduous day, but I was full-scale whipped. I require a certain amount of gratification in order to function effectively. Futility wears me out in a hurry. I left the car in the driveway. On my way inside, I glanced out at the gate. Somehow, I couldn't bring myself to roll it closed.

Wouldn't have mattered anyway. Poco's small enough to wiggle between the bars. He was standing in the drive, out by the street. No sign of Janet. Poco made a feint for the street, stopped and came back my way, and then yelped at me twice.

I felt like I was in one of those old Lassie TV programs, where the dog comes running into the barnyard, barks twice, and little Timmy miraculously discerns that Granny Smith has crashed her Buick into Franklin Creek and is about to drown.

I heaved a sigh and started walking in his direction. "What's going on, little fella?" I said as I ambled closer. He dodged left again, out into the street. I followed along. I was halfway to the Morrison house next door to mine when I noticed a hint of color down by the bottom of their carefully tended hedge. I walked over.

Janet Seigal was sitting on the ground next to their driveway. Her yellow raincoat and matching boots made her look like the Morton Salt girl. She heard me coming and turned her face away.

"You okay?" I asked.

She managed an unconvincing nod, but didn't say anything. Poco climbed into her lap.

I held out a hand to help her up, but she ignored it.

"You don't want the Morrisons to find you camped out in their driveway, do you?"

She looked at me for the first time. She'd been crying.

"Did he . . . ?"

She waved me off. "No . . . nothing like that. I stepped in a hole while I was walking Poco."

I offered my hand again. She set Poco on the ground and took me up on my offer. I pulled her to her feet. She ran the backs of her hands over her tears. Poco bounced around her feet as she straightened herself out inside the raincoat.

"You always seem to show up when things are at their worst," she said, steadying herself on my arm.

I flexed my muscles and grinned. "Captain Magnolia to the rescue."

She looked at me like I was speaking Turkish.

My attempt at levity having tanked, I segued back to serious.

"Really . . . can I help you in some way?"

She shook her head. "You've already been too kind."

"What's going on?" I asked.

I didn't think she was going to tell me, but before we ever got to that point, the squeal of tires tore a hole through the air. And then again, in the nanosecond before Richard's Lexus roared into view, zigzagging up the hill at about twice the legal limit.

"Oh great," she whispered under her breath.

We watched as Richard pulled the wheel hard left and went screeching into their driveway. The car came to a shuddering stop about three inches from the garage door.

Ten seconds passed before Richard came lurching out of the car, looking like he was learning to ice-skate. He tried to kick the car door closed but missed, sending him pinwheeling to the ground. "Fuck," he screamed. And then again. We watched as he used the fender to lever himself upright.

Janet's fingers dug into my arm as Richard finally noticed us standing across the street. He blinked, ran a hand over his face, and stumbled out from behind the car.

"I'm not interrupting anything, am I?" he shouted.

"Richard—" Janet began.

"Don't talk to me, you fucking whore," he bellowed. He started our way, his face strawberry red, his gait uneven.

Janet felt me twitch. "Please," she said. "He's just drunk."

I'd already made up my mind. If he got this far, drunk or sober, bad hand or no bad hand, I was going to kick his ass, for no better reason than I really wanted to.

He tripped over the curb, sending him stumbling closer. About the time he negotiated the street and was fifteen feet away, I said, "You probably ought to just stop where you are."

"And why should I do that?" he slurred.

"Because if you get within arm's reach I'm going to slap the shit out of you."

He kept coming.

"Oh you think so?" he smirked.

"Yep," I said. "I do."

He stopped, unsteady on his feet, waving around like a palm tree in a hurricane, then reached into his jacket pocket, rummaged around for a second or two, and pulled out a small silver automatic. "Gonna bitch slap me now, asshole?" he demanded.

"Yep," I said. "And maybe stick that popgun up your ass while I'm at it."

"You think I don't know what's going on?" he bellowed.

"There's nothing going on," Janet said.

"I'm not blind," he blurted. "Standin' over here in the dark playin' grab ass. I see what's going on."

"Your wife fell down. I helped her up. That's it."

He pointed the gun in our direction, waving it around like a conductor's baton, as he struggled to maintain his balance.

Janet Seigal stepped in front of me. "Stop it, Richard. Just stop it."

"You fucking cripple whore," he shouted and then turned his attention to me.

"You like cripples? That your thing? Like to prop 'em up and—"

That was as far as he got. Whatever common sense I had went out the window right then and there. I stepped around Janet and lunged for him.

Fortunately for all concerned, his reflexes were just about shot. I was nearly on his shirtfront before he started to raise the gun. I grabbed his wrist and pushed his gun hand straight up. BANG. A flat report fractured the silence.

I kneed him in the crotch with everything I had. He let out a deep, shuddering groan, bent at the waist, and began to crumple. I kneed him again, just for good measure.

As he began to collapse, my hands slid up his arm until gravity pulled the automatic from his hand and left it in mine. I had a strong urge to kick him in the face a couple of times, but resisted. "Hooooooo. Hooooooo," he groaned as he rocked back and forth on the grass, holding his crotch with both hands.

I snapped the magazine out of the gun and then jacked the one in the chamber out onto the ground. Then walked over and dropped the magazine and the little automatic into Janet Seigal's raincoat pocket.

That's when I noticed the car out in the street. Wilson Harvey, my neighbor from three doors down, was sitting there in his Cadillac Escalade taking it all in like it was a movie. When he saw me glaring at him, he took the hint and drove off.

Janet opened her mouth to speak, but I cut her off. "I was you, I'd throw that peashooter in the Sound," I said. "We're way past the Richard's-just-an-asshole stage of things. Somebody's going to get hurt here." Her cheek was beginning to quiver, but I kept talking. "I was you, I'd call the cops and charge him with aggravated assault with a deadly weapon. Might be an introduction to the criminal justice system is just what he needs to get himself straight." She wanted to say something, but I wasn't in the mood for listening. "Treating him like a spoiled seven-year-old doesn't seem to be working. It's time to try something else. But I'm gonna leave that to you."

Richard was on his hands and knees now, scrabbling across the pavement at tortoise speed.

"He's going to leave me," she said.

"Are you kidding me?"

"I heard him talking to his lawyer."

"Best thing he could do for you," I said quickly. "Take him for his shirt. This is a community property state. Judges here are real hard-nosed on spousal abuse. By the time the state gets through with him he won't have a pot to piss in or a window to throw it out of."

"Invalids aren't part of Richard's life plan," she said.

"He points a gun at me again, and he's not going to need a life plan."

. . .

She wanted to meet at Vito's. Made me feel like I'd somehow come full circle. Back in the sixties and seventies, Vito's had been the social center for Seattle's movers and shakers. Most of my old man's nefarious day-to-day activities were conducted within the friendly confines of Vito's Madison Grill. Vito's was the kind of joint where the walls have ears.

I stifled a chuckle as I walked in the door. It had been closed for a while and had changed hands a couple of times since 2008, when a couple of gang members staged a full-scale gun battle in the lounge, but otherwise it looked just like it always had . . . dark, dank, and dirty. The kind of place where you kept expecting to see Luca Brasi and a mackerel holding court in one of the studded Naugahyde booths.

Rebecca had commandeered a booth along the front wall. She'd changed out of her scrubs and was hiding under a silk head scarf and a pair of sunglasses the size of hubcaps. All very Melina Mercouri, 1963.

I slid in opposite her. "You develop a sudden urge for bad Italian food?" I asked.

"What I developed was a sudden urge for deniability," she said in a low voice.

"How so?"

She reached down into her purse and pulled out a manila envelope with an FBI logo adorning the flap. She slid it across the table at me. And then leaned in close.

"When I sent your Mrs. Townsend's aluminum foil to IAFIS, I used Sue Orris's name." She waved a finger in my face. "Which, as it turns out, was one of the best ideas I ever had."

"How so?"

"Before this ever got back to me, she had three private party queries and a response request from the Las Vegas PD."

"Sue gonna be all right with this?"

"Sue quit last month. Married an Arab guy. Renounced her Christian past. Changed her name to something three feet long and Arabic. Moved to Qatar and is presently aboard his yacht on a world cruise. I've been checking her computer to make sure we didn't have any loose ends."

I picked up the envelope. "They get a match?"

"I didn't open it."

"Really?"

"I'm an officer of the court. Anybody asks me about that IAFIS request I need to be able to say I have no idea who sent it or what the response, if any, might have contained."

"I understand," I said.

She got to her feet. "Be careful," she said.

"Aren't I always?"

Her eyes rolled behind the shades. I sat and listened to the sound of her heels clicking on the floor, until the door opened and closed and all I could hear was Jimmy Roselli singing "Am I Blue?"

The prints belonged to somebody named Tuesday Jo Hollister. Born 1980, in Elko, Nevada. Orphaned at six. Raised by her grandmother. By the time she was sixteen, she'd also been known as Betty Blew, Cherry Pie, Martha Sweet, and about a dozen other equally clever monikers. Nine prostitution busts before she graduated to extortion at twenty. Did seventeen months for being part of a ring that was rolling tourists in their hotel rooms. But it was the last notation on the page that grabbed my eye. Anyone with any information concerning her whereabouts should contact Detective Sergeant Roscoe Templeton of the Las Vegas PD. An 800 number.

A mug shot peeped out from under the paperwork. I picked it up. She was just a kid in the picture, but already angry with the world. Same face as Theresa Calder. A little thinner, several bright blue streaks in her hair, but that same lantern jaw.

I gathered up the paperwork, threw some money on the table, and headed home to pack.

■   ■   ■

Sergeant Roscoe Templeton kept me cooling my heels in the squad room for forty-five minutes before inviting me into his office, so by the time I planted my butt in the battered wooden chair, I'll admit to being a bit testy.

"You wanna tell me where you got those fingerprints?" he said to me, before I even sat down.

"Depends," I said, settling in.

"On what?"

"On what *you* tell *me*."

He sat there and stared at me like he couldn't believe I'd said that. Cops get that way. You walk around carrying a gun on one hip and the power of the state on the other and you just naturally get to thinking your shit don't stink.

"She wanted for anything?" I asked.

"Depends on what you mean by wanted," he hedged.

"Warrants. You know . . . criminal charges. The kind of stuff they pay you for."

Long pause. "Not that I know of," he said finally.

The spring in his chair creaked and he leaned back and took me in again. Typical cop. Pouchy from all the free lunches, with a head of salt-and-pepper hair so thick it must have taken a weed whacker to cut it.

"You used to be some kind of private eye," he said.

The disdainful half smile on his lips said it all.

"A while back."

"So . . . what's your interest in Tuesday Jo Hollister?"

"Curiosity."

He gave me another of those long cop stares. Like he was deciding whether or not to have me fed to feral swine. A minute passed, then, inexplicably, his face began to soften. Looked to me like he realized he had nothing he could really threaten me with and figured I'd been around the block often enough to know it.

"I always had a soft spot for that girl," he said. "Anybody ever got dealt a bad hand in this life, it was that poor kid."

"How so?"

"I mean, she was still a toddler when her parents . . ." He rolled his eyes. "A couple of the dumbest skagheads on earth . . . decide to cheat some half-ass Mexican drug dealer out of two ounces of heroin."

"I take it he was miffed."

"I'd have to look it up to get the exact figure, but, between the two of them, I believe he shot them something like forty-one times." He was shaking his head. "Kid got sent to live with her grandma, way the hell out in the middle of nowhere by Dixie Valley." He threw a disgusted hand in the air. "One day, when she was about fourteen, she just hitch-hiked off and never went back."

He got to his feet and walked over to the file cabinet in the corner. I watched as he fingered his way through the contents, found the one he was looking for, and pulled it out. "I was a Clark County deputy in those days," he said as he motored back across the floor. "Everybody drew jailor duty once or twice a week. That's how I got to know her. I took her under my wing, you might say. Kept the bull dykes off her. Made it plain that messing with her was the same as messing with me."

He plopped back into his seat, flopped open the folder, and began to read.

"She was fifteen when she first got popped for solicitation," he began. He looked up at me. "As I'm sure you're aware, Mr. Waterman, here in Las Vegas, peddling your ass is quite the cottage industry; we got more hookers than Seattle's got seagulls."

"There *is* a rumor to that effect," I allowed.

"Girl always handled it with class. Never addicted to anything. No greaseball pimps. No screaming, no hollering, no makin' life hard on the staff, just took her medicine and waited for the bail money to arrive. If it didn't, she did her time like a trooper and then went right back out onto the street. Ain't like she had a hell of a lot of life choices, if you catch my drift. Hardly ever been to school. Taught herself to read and write while doing time in the county lockup. All that little girl had was a body like Marilyn Monroe and an intense desire to make her miserable life a little better." He waved a hand in the air. "No matter what it took."

He slid the folder at me. "You can read the rest of it for yourself. Most of it's pretty standard fertilizer." He kept his hand on the folder, until I looked up. "It's what's *not* in there that might get somebody killed."

"What's that?"

"The thing with the Castiglione family."

"What thing?"

He took a deep breath and started talking. "She was still running the same scam, just doing it better. She'd bring some square back to a room someplace, ball his brains out, and then all of a sudden a couple more skells would break down the door, screaming the girl was under-age, threaten the poor slob with rape charges, be screaming about thirty years in prison—you know, the usual brand of bull."

"Take him for every dime he could muster," I filled in.

"'Cept for one night . . ." Templeton began. "She workin' with a boyfriend by then, kid namea Kerry Collins. Word gets around there's a john over at the Golden Spur askin' around, sayin' he likes 'em real young. Offerin' five grand for something all fresh and dewy." The expression on his face told me he wasn't comfortable talking about it.

He went on anyway. "Make a long story short, Tuesday and the Collins kid try to run their usual number on him, but the kid's not your usual john. He turned out to be Frank Castiglione's nephew from Philly."

He could tell the name meant nothing to me. "One of the old Vegas families. Owned the Golden Spur, had a big hand in linen service, owned most of the dry cleaners in the city. That sort of thing." He held up a hand. "Here's the good part. From what I hear . . . the Philly kid wanted to cut holes in the girl and then fuck her in the holes."

My jaw must have been hanging open.

"Yeah. I know," Templeton went on. "Some fucking people."

"Anyway . . . she's bleeding all over the joint, screaming bloody murder; hotel security shows up and gets things under control; she wants the cops, but security convinces her they'll take care of it, which is, of course, a crock of shit, 'cause the family owns the hotel and they ain't about to be making trouble for one of their own, no matter what kind of sick motherfucker he might be.

"But she won't go away about it. Goes to the cops, goes to legal aid, goes to the DA, makes so goddamn much noise the cops got no choice but to charge the Philly kid with aggravated assault, which is the point where Frank Castiglione completely loses his dumbass dago mind. Frank decides he's had enough of this big-mouth whore and her boyfriend showin' no respect for his family. Sends one of his old-time button men out to shut them up. Guy namea Boris DelMonte. Coupla days later a pair of off-duty county mounties are out in the back of a lumberyard in Henderson, looking for lumber to build a picnic table, when they walk in on Boris nailing the Collins kid to a sheet of three-quarter-inch plywood with a nail gun. I mean, they catch his big hairy ass red-handed."

He shrugged. "Kid's dead. Boris's got three prior felony convictions, which in this state means you're spending the rest of your days up at Ely sweatin' bullets, so Boris does the only thing he can—he rolls over on Frank Castiglione. Guess he figured he was dead either way. The off-duty cops testify, Tuesday Jo testifies. Frank, who's about seventy-five at the time, pulls fifteen to life for conspiracy to commit murder. Worse yet, the family loses its gaming license. Probably costs them fifty million a year."

"And the girl?" I asked.

Snapped his fingers. "Disappears," he said. He pinned me with a gaze. "I only left the case open because I was hoping someday somebody'd find her remains out in the desert someplace and maybe I could put her in the ground. You know, decent-like. Until I got that IAFIS query, never even occurred to me she might be alive." He made a rude noise with his lips. "Boris didn't last a week in prison. Had a little accident. Tripped and fell three stories down the cellblock. Frank popped a brain aneurysm about two years later."

He put his hands on the desk and leaned down into my face. "I'd like to be able to tell you this was just between us, but it ain't."

"It's clean on my end," I said.

He choked out a short, dry laugh. "The second that IAFIS request saw the light of day, the Castiglione family knew about it. Trust me on this. This is a connected town. Everybody's in everyone else's pocket. They ain't the players they used to be, but they ain't chopped liver either. They know you're with me right now. They know where you're stayin'."

"I'm not staying anywhere," I said.

"Good. Keep it that way. Whenever you get done here, you get yourself back on a plane to Seattle, 'cause none of these goombas can hold a job, but they sure as hell can hold a grudge. It's in the blood, I think." He tapped my forearm with a thick finger. "They ain't gonna forget about this . . . now or ever. They're gonna be lookin' for that girl until every one of them's in meatball heaven. You keep that in mind."

I said I would.

He picked up the file. "You can take this down to interview room three. Give it to the duty sergeant when you're done."

He stood up.

"You didn't ask me if she was still alive," I said.

"That's 'cause I don't want to know," he said. "I'm five months from retirement. Last thing I need is for a couple of those greaseballs to show up at my back door."

He walked over and opened his office door.

I picked up the file and took the hint.

I was halfway down the hall when he called, "Hey."

I stopped and walked back.

He checked the corridor. "They're gonna want to find out what you know, Waterman. Here . . . Seattle . . . wherever. They're gonna come for you."

"I can take care of myself," I assured him.

. . .

Tuesday Jo's file was pretty much as advertised. Sad. According to her parole officer at the time, she'd been in the process of moving up to the escort service level of the business when the thing with the Castiglione family hit the fan.

When you figured in the dates, Charlie Stone in Vegas showed up the same week Tuesday developed a sudden need to leave town. A girl with her skill set would have had little trouble enrapturing a horny, half-drunk car salesman, and, truth be told, marriage not only got her out of Vegas but was a significant step up the social ladder as well.

Things didn't get interesting until I got to the "KNOWN ASSOCIATES" section. She'd started out working the pedophile angle. She'd dress up in pigtails and Mary Jane shoes and let some slimeball drag her back to a roach motel way off the strip, give him a little bit of action, and then, just about the time the guy figured he was gonna get his knob polished, the door would burst open and her parents would come rolling in. "Oh God, what have you done to our baby? We're calling the police." The whole nine yards. The same sex scam hustlers had been running for a couple thousand years now.

It was the pair playing Mom and Dad who got my attention. Margery Tildon and Franco Rollins. A pair of lifetime low-life grifters with rap sheets from here to eternity, both of whom were presently doing short time in Arizona for grand larceny. I'd seen the faces before. Twice. In both sets of wedding pictures.

The rest of it was pretty run of the mill. I stayed at it for an hour or so and then returned the file to the desk sergeant.

Walking out the front door onto MLK Boulevard was like walking into a blast furnace. Musta been two hundred degrees in the shade as I picked my way through the parking lot, trying to recall the color of my rental car. If it hadn't been for the fob that let me blow the horn, I'd probably still be out there looking for it.

The steering wheel was so hot I had to crank the air up full blast and sit there long enough for it to cool down. How people lived in this heat was a mystery to me.

I flipped on the GPS and plotted a route back to McCarran International Airport. Fifteen minutes later, I'd turned off Interstate 15 onto Wayne Newton Boulevard and took the big loop back under the freeway. I was humming "Danke Schoen" as I nosed into the underpass and very nearly rear-ended a green Cadillac that was stopped in the deep shade. My heart was still dancing in my chest when I felt another car tap my rear bumper.

A glance in the mirror told me everything I needed to know. Black Lincoln Town Car. All four doors open. Four guys in bad suits jumping out. I slammed the transmission into reverse and floored it; the sounds of broken glass and fractured metal suddenly tore through the air, as angry voices rose toward the ceiling and clouds of smoke billowed from the rental car's tires. One of the guys in the Lincoln got in the way of a slamming door and went down in a heap.

I jammed it into drive and blasted the car in front just as my driver's window exploded, showering me with a crystal wave of safety glass. I crimped the wheel all the way to the left and put the pedal to the metal. Something thumped into the headrest as the rental car shuddered for a moment, then ripped the rear bumper off the Cadillac as I tried to shoulder my way past.

The guy behind the wheel of the Cadillac smoked the tires, crumpling the passenger door and grinding me into the concrete wall. The rental car screamed as the rough wall peeled the paint from the driver's side. The engine was beginning to knock; smoke was roiling out from under the hood.

Just as I shuddered to a complete stop, the passenger-side window evaporated. I lashed out with a foot as a hand reached for the door handle.

"Goddamnit," I heard somebody shout.

A forearm was thrown across my throat. I tried to scream but couldn't force anything out. I heard the metallic sound of the seat belt unlatching in the second before I was dragged from the seat. The pavement drove the air from my lungs.

After that, it was pretty much assholes and elbows. They were on me like a pack of rats. Within thirty seconds, they'd rolled me over and bundled my hands together behind my back with a pair of plastic flex-cuffs.

As I was lifted from the ground, somebody pulled a bag over my head. Last thing I remember seeing was the Lincoln pulling up next to me and the trunk bouncing open.

After that, I think maybe I passed out. When I came around, took me a minute to figure out I was in the trunk of a moving car. I was lying on my side, sweating buckets and starting to cramp up. Scared shitless didn't begin to cover it. I'd been afraid before. Lots of times, but never like this, never to the point where I was totally convinced that my moment here on earth had come and gone. That I wasn't going to make it home from this one. The only reason I wasn't dead already was that they wanted to ask me questions. Soon as that was over, they were going to pull my plug and then leave me out in the desert somewhere. I had no doubt about it. I was seeing vultures.

Terror fueled me. I nearly popped a temple vein trying to break the cuffs on my wrists, but that injection-molded nylon would have held an elephant. All I accomplished was to reduce myself to a sweating ball of agony.

I stopped struggling and tried to compose myself. I swallowed a whimper and started to feel around with my manacled hands. The hand I'd injured on Brother Biggs's head sent splinters of pain running up my arm, but I kept at it anyway.

There was no carpet, just stamped metal. I pulled my knees up as far as I was able and tried to scrunch myself around in a half circle. Made it about halfway around before getting stuck. My hands dropped into the indentation where the spare tire had once been.

I put my feet up against the inside of the fender and pushed myself in that direction. I kept pushing until my knees dropped into the spare tire cavity. I was panting like a terrier. Never been so hot in my life. I wanted to stop. To rest. But didn't dare.

Sliding my knees into the cavity allowed me to pull my knees beneath myself. Took every ounce of strength I possessed to force myself into the kneeling position. The inside of the trunk lid pressed hard against the back of my neck. I began to move my head forward and back, up and down. The bag on my head was moving slowly, an inch at a time. I groaned and kept at it.

After what seemed like an hour, the bag finally dropped free and I could see. I was facing backwards, on my knees out in the middle of the trunk, bent at the waist with my back against the inside of the trunk lid.

I tried to straighten my back but felt the trunk lid pressing me down. I took several deep breaths, and then began to heave upward with all the power my back could muster. I felt the trunk lid buckle outward a bit and redoubled my efforts. In the second before I ran out of strength, the trunk latch broke and the lid flopped open, bringing a great rush of sunlight and air flowing into the trunk cavity.

That was when the Lincoln's driver noticed the trunk was open and slammed on the brakes. I watched in mouth-breather amazement as the guy in the car behind us failed to get stopped in time and rear-ended the Lincoln, sending me slamming back into the trunk lid.

I pulled one foot down under me and launched myself out of the trunk, landing in the middle of the hood of the car behind. Another metal-crunching jolt sent me bouncing up onto the car's roof.

I looked around. We were on a four-lane street, in between what seemed like endless strip malls. Cars on both sides of the divider were pulling over. People getting out to see what this idiot was doing sitting on the roof of a car.

Before I could fully collect my wits, the Lincoln roared off up the street, trunk lid wagging up and down like a tongue. When I looked away from the Lincoln, I was surrounded by gawkers. "You okay, buddy?" somebody asked.

"No," I said. "I think somebody better call the cops."

* * *

Sergeant Roscoe Templeton waited for the emergency room personnel to complete their examination and pronounce me bruised but unbroken before he started with the sarcasm.

"Nice to see how you could take care of yourself," he said.

I was feeling pretty contrite and considerably past the snappy rejoinder stage of things, so all I said was, "I fucked up."

Roscoe smirked. "While I'm pretty sure it wasn't the first time, it damn near was the last."

"Not just today," I said, buttoning my shirt. "I made a bad misjudgment. Sticking my nose into something that was none of my business. It's a bad habit of mine and now I've put other people in jeopardy. I'm gonna have to figure out how to fix this."

"I've got a few suggestions," he said.

"I'm all ears," I assured him.

"We rescued your travel bag from the rental car, which means they may or may not know who you are and where you came from. They know where the IAFIS query came from, so Seattle's going to be at the top of their look list."

I nodded and pulled on a boot. "What about the guys who snatched me?"

He made a disgusted face. "Plates on both cars were stolen. Both cars wiped clean, and even if we could put names on them, they'd be alibied up the ass." He spread his hands in resignation. "It's going nowhere."

I nodded again.

"If this Susan Orris is a friend of yours . . ." he began.

I waved him off. "They're not going to find her," I said.

"You're sure?"

"Positive."

He nodded toward the door. "I've got two uniforms outside. They're going to take you to the airport and put you on a plane. I suggest you fly somewhere other than Seattle. Who knows, it might give the Castiglione clan pause to wonder and gain you a little time."

"Can I use your phone?" I asked.

Chapter 3

It was fifty degrees and raining sideways when I climbed into Carl's van at Portland International Airport. Before I approached, I'd circled the short-term parking lot twice, nice and slow, making sure we didn't have any unwanted company.

Carl's Mercedes van was eighty grand worth of handicapped conversion paradise. I pulled open the door, dropped my bag over the seat, and buckled myself in.

"You need anything else? Other than being picked up at an airport two hundred miles from home," Carl asked. "Open heart surgery? A colonoscopy? Just say the word."

"I really screwed up this time," I said.

"You mean as opposed to all the other times."

"For real, this time."

Nothing Carl liked better than busting my chops, but something in my manner brought him up short.

"You're serious."

I checked my watch. "About five hours ago, I came as close to getting my ass killed as I ever have in my life."

"You wanna tell me about it?"

"Let's get out of here first," I said.

Carl dropped the van into drive and headed for the tollbooth.

I kept my head on a swivel as we exited the lot and headed east toward the freeway.

"You expecting company?" Carl asked.

"Maybe," I said. "We probably ought to do a few cut-outs on the way back. Just to make sure we don't have any unwanted visitors."

We rode the next twenty minutes in silence. Wasn't till we were driving over the Columbia River that Carl asked, "Anything special I'm supposed to be keeping an eye out for?"

"Why don't we take the next exit and see if anybody gets off with us."

He stared at the side of my head for a long moment. "You're really jumpy," he said as he took the exit ramp.

I pointed at the Chevron gas station coming up on the right. "Let's turn around there," I said.

"You wanna tell me what's goin' on?" he asked as we eased around the pumps.

A plumbing supply truck ground past us, and then a battered eighteen-wheeler full of sawdust. Satisfied we weren't being followed, I said, "Let's go. I'll tell you on the way."

We pulled off the interstate three more times in the hour it took me to tell the story. He just sat there and listened.

"What are you gonna do?" he asked when I'd finally finished.

"I've gotta fix it," I said.

"You got a plan?"

"Not yet."

"You gonna tell the Townsend broad?"

"Don't see how I can avoid it."

"Me neither."

"But I'd like to have some sort of plan in place before I do."

"So's you won't have to walk up and say, 'Oh by the way, Mrs. Townsend—or Calder or Hollister or whoever the hell you are—just for my own amusement, I seem to have stirred up your past to the point where there's going to be people showing up to kill you, pretty soon here.'"

I winced. "She's got a good thing going for herself," I said. "She's not recognizable as Theresa Calder. As long as I don't lead them to her, she should be fine."

"You think they can find you?"

"Probably," I said. "I rented a car in my own name."

"And they know where the IAFIS inquiry came from?"

"Right . . . which puts Rebecca into the equation too."

We were cruising through the southern outskirts of Olympia. An hour from home. "Remember where this all started?" Carl asked.

"The two guys in the car trunk under my old man's coat."

"You any closer to finding out who offed them than you were when you started?"

"Not as far as I can tell."

"And those two bozos—Biggs and his buddy."

"Chauncey Bostick," I filled in.

"Where do they fit into this?"

"No idea."

We rode another twenty miles in silence. Just south of Tacoma now.

"She's gotta die," I said finally.

Carl looked horrified. "Rebecca?"

"Theresa Calder has to be dead and buried."

"There is no Theresa Calder."

"That's gonna make it harder."

. . .

I had Carl leave me off down the street from my house. I waited until he drove off and then tiptoed along the north side of the Morrisons' yard, staying close to the giant boxwood hedge that separated our properties.

I used to do this when I was a kid, sneaking out of the house to meet Rebecca, after my curfew. Either the gap between the Morrisons' hedge and my stone wall had somehow gotten smaller, or I'd gotten quite a bit bigger.

I forced myself through the tangle of branches, threw my bag over the wall, and then, with great difficulty, climbed on top and jumped.

I landed with a resounding thud, and then fell forward onto my face. Some things improve with age. Jumping from high places wasn't one of them. Had to sit there in the wet grass for a few seconds getting my senses back together before walking around to the side of the house, where a pair of old-fashioned cellar doors angled out from the house like buckteeth.

I couldn't remember the last time anybody'd opened these doors, but I remembered where we used to hide the key. It was still there, under the one-eared ceramic rabbit head—dirt-clogged and rusty, but still there.

Took me a couple of minutes to clean up the lock and key, but eventually I got the right-hand door to open and slid down the concrete ramp into the cellar.

I chained the cellar doors from the inside and headed right for the front of the house. I crept up the stairs, let myself into the front hallway, and opened the closet. The 12-gauge Mossberg Slugster was in the back corner where I left it. I gave it a quick check. Still had a full load. My pulse rate slackened.

Me and Mr. Mossberg searched the whole house. Upstairs and down. Attic included. Looked in closets and under beds. Inside ancient cedar chests. Checked all door and window locks. Satisfied that I was alone, I turned off all the lights, activated the security system, and closed the gate.

Feeling better lasted for about thirty seconds. First thing I saw when I walked into my TV room was the phone light blinking. The old phone that had, at one time, belonged to my father. The phone I only keep because some asshole invented a scam called "bundling" wherein companies get you to use services you don't actually need or want so that you can get the stuff you *really* want cheaper. Whoever thought that shit up ought to get the Nobel Prize.

Thing was, I hadn't made or received a call on that phone for at least five years. Worse yet, barring a wrong number, I could only think of three people who *had* that number, and I'd just spent three hours in a van with one of them, so it probably wasn't him. I leaned the shotgun against the couch and reached for the phone.

The receiver felt humongous in my hand, like I was talking into a swim fin. I pushed the button. Tom Waits singing about waltzing Matilda. CLICK. I felt cold all over. It was Rebecca going to a lot of trouble not to be traced. We used to do this a lot, way back when. Back when her mother made it as difficult as possible for us to see each other. We had a set of signals that told us where to meet and when. "Wasted and wounded. Ain't what the moon did. Got what I paid for now" meant: call me as soon as you get this. Ring twice and then hang up. If I don't immediately call you back, meet me in the parking lot of the Blue Moon Tavern as soon as you can get here. He's not much of a talker, but I took Mr. Mossberg along with me anyway.

.   .   .

She opened the laptop and pushed a few buttons. She was pretending not to notice the shotgun. A fuzzy closed-circuit tape began to play across the screen. Margot, the medical examiner's office receptionist. Two guys in ski parkas standing in front of her desk.

"Ms. Orris is no longer with us," Margot was saying.

"We'll be needing to talk to her," one of them said.

"Afraid I can't help you." Margot managed an insincere smile.

"You got a forwarding address?" the other one asked.

"That would be confidential information. State law forbids—"

"Who's in charge here?" the first guy asked.

"Dr. Rebecca Duval."

"We'd like a word wit her."

"I'm afraid Dr. Duval is at a luncheon."

"Listen—"

Margot cut him off. "Besides which, sir, you'd most definitely need to make an appointment if you wished to see Dr. Duval."

Rebecca pushed a button. The video disappeared.

"They came by the lobby twice yesterday," she said.

I opened my mouth to say something, but she waved me off. "They were sitting in my office when I got to work this morning."

"I screwed up big time," I said.

She snapped the laptop shut and sat back in the seat. "Who are those guys?"

"A couple of leg-breakers from Las Vegas."

"I had to call security to get rid of them."

"You got time for a long story?" I asked.

"Sounds like I better."

I laid it out for her. Usually she's got a thousand questions, and stops to correct my grammar a couple of times along the way, but not tonight. Tonight she just sat there and listened, until I stopped talking.

"What are we going to do?" she asked when I'd finished.

"I'm not sure," I admitted.

"Does Alice Townsend know?"

"Not yet," I said.

"You're going to have to tell her."

"Sorry I got you into this."

"Don't flatter yourself, Leo. I make my own decisions." She looked over and pinned me with her steeliest gaze. "You know . . . if this was just the two of us involved here, I'd think very seriously about going into the office tomorrow and admitting what I did. They wouldn't fire me. Most I'd get would be a reprimand and a suspension. But . . ." She shook her head. "I couldn't live with myself if anything happened to Alice Townsend because of something we did."

A long silence ensued.

"Theresa Calder has to die," she said finally.

"Great minds think alike."

She stuffed the laptop down between the seats and started the car. "You going to get out, or are you going home with me?"

"I didn't realize I had a choice."

"Things change," she said as she dropped the transmission into drive. "Besides, we're partners in crime now. Something good may as well come out of it."

.   .   .

"Did the sex used to be that good?" I asked.

"Not even close."

"I guess abstinence doth indeed make the heart grow fondler."

She laughed and settled deeper into my shoulder. "You're a man of means these days, Leo. Money changes everything."

"From what I understand that was pretty much Tuesday Jo's opinion."

"You can't blame a girl for trying to improve her station in life. She married her way up the social ladder, like Jackie Onassis and any number of other swell types. She just started on a lower rung. Finding yourself a good meal ticket is a major part of the American dream." She waved a hand. "The white picket fence and the orthodontist."

"Such a romantic."

She made a rude noise with her lips.

"You given any thought to what we're going to do?"

She nodded. "We need a body."

"What?"

"A body turning up would explain the IAFIS request, and put them off Alice's scent for good. We'll also need a chain of paperwork to move it through the Health and Safety Code."

"I'm still back at *we need a body*."

"Female. Caucasian. Between twenty-five and forty. Partially decomposed would be best. Decomposition makes getting an accurate age more art than science. A floater would be good, as long as it's not too far along. The crabs get the fingers pretty early on."

"I'm guessing we can't count on Amazon here."

"Probably not."

"You perchance got one you can spare?"

"Not at the moment. Right now the only John Doe I've got in the bins is a male African American the size of a small car."

"When they bring you a John Doe, how long do you give it before you . . . you know . . . do whatever you do with them?"

"Depends," she said. "The younger they are, the longer I wait. Anyone with usable prints we send to IAFIS. That generally takes a week or so to get an answer. After that, we cremate about ninety-nine percent of them and spread their ashes on Puget Sound."

"And the other one percent?"

"We bury them."

"Who decides which?"

"I do," she said. "Usually I only bury people who are never identified. In case . . . you know . . . something comes up later. But sometimes, especially with kids, I bury them, even if we know who they are. It just seems more respectful."

She kissed me on the cheek and got out of bed. I watched her marvelous ass disappear into the closet. A moment later she reappeared, wearing a deep blue silk *yukata* covered with wide-eyed carp. "I told Margot I'd be in by one o'clock. I've got some toaster waffles in the fridge. You interested?"

"I'd nibble six or eight."

"Soon as I get to the office, I'll check with all the other coroners and medical examiners in the area. We've got a computer network that allows us to check each other's inventories and missing persons reports. That way I can see if anybody has a Jane Doe who might work for our purposes."

"And they'll just ship one over."

"Sure. All I've got to do is tell them I may know who it is and want to have a look, then the transportation and final disposition costs come out of my budget and not theirs, and they do their happy dance."

"Even death is a matter of money," I said.

She smiled. "I'll see you in the kitchen," she said and padded out of the room.

Took me a couple minutes of crawling around the floor to find my clothes and another couple to get dressed. By the time I made it downstairs to the kitchen, four Eggos had come popping out of the toaster.

Rebecca forked them onto a paper plate, pulled a bottle of real maple syrup out of the pantry, and handed both to me. "I'm out of butter," she announced.

We were both chewing away contentedly when she asked, "You figured out how you're going to tell Alice Townsend what's going on?"

I swallowed and said, "Not sure. Somehow I need to get to her without going out to her house. There's no way for the parka brothers to find her unless I lead them there, and there's no way I'm gonna take a chance of doing that."

"He's speaking at Downtown Baptist tonight," she said around a mouthful of waffles.

"You sure?"

"SPD's making a big deal of it. Calling out the storm troopers. They're determined not to have the kind of mob scene they had the other night in Fremont."

"I was there. It got ugly in a big hurry."

She frowned. "He deserves it. He's lucky every woman in town doesn't go down there, drag him out in the street, and kick his ass."

I waved my fork. "You know . . . I've met the guy, and I'm not sure he actually believes any of that male domination stuff. He's sure as hell not living *his* life from that perspective. I think maybe he just says that crazy stuff to put people in the pews."

"Is that better or worse?"

"I'm not sure."

She got to her feet, threw the paper plate in the garbage and the fork in the sink.

"I've got to jump in the shower."

"I'll Uber home," I said.

"Do you realize you just made a noun into an intransitive verb?"

I wiped my mouth. "Story of my life," I said.

.   .   .

It was the lions and the Christians all over again, with pretty much the same results.

True to their word, the SPD was out in force. They'd formed a skirmish line all the way around the Downtown Baptist Church. Regular cops immediately behind the barrier, backed up by SWAT officers stationed at strategic intervals along the line.

I'd showed up an hour or so early and lucked into a curbside parking spot in the 1100 block of Tenth Avenue, right behind the church's day-care center. From the look of it, tonight's lecture was by invitation only. Everybody who started up the steps was being checked against some kind of list. Most were issued a blue badge and then ushered inside; a couple were sent packing. One guy was frog-walked back down the stairs and unceremoniously stuffed into a police cruiser.

On the other side of the yellow tape, seemed like every women's organization in the city had a bone to pick with Aaron Townsend. The LGBT community was particularly strident in their dissent. The National Organization for Women was a bit more staid, but just as adamant, as were the Washington Women's Foundation, the Refugee Women's Alliance, and what I was estimating to be three or four hundred other folks of indeterminate gender and political affiliation.

When the big white tour bus stopped in the middle of Harvard Avenue, things looked like they were beginning to get interesting, so I got out of my car and leaned against the fender for a better view.

A moment after the bus door swung open with a hiss, Pastor and Mrs. Highsmith stepped out into the street, followed by a veritable herd of pastors and their significant others. I was guessing that what we had here were the pastors of all the churches which used to be Mount Zion Ministries, come in force this time to beard the lion in his den. And this time, they weren't crashing the party either. Every one of them had a blue admittance badge plastered to his chest. This was definitely going to get interesting.

As the clutch of clergymen formed a tight muttering knot at the foot of the stairs, the wives peeled off in my direction, whispering among themselves as they waited for the next act to unfold.

Mrs. Highsmith caught sight of me and smiled. I smiled back and gave a little wave. I watched as she excused herself from the other women and began walking my way. "How nice to see you again, Mr. Waterman," she said.

"Just couldn't stay away," I said. "Nice to see your husband's not going it alone this time."

"They've sworn not to interrupt. They're calling it a silent vigil of protest."

"I notice he's not calling these things sermons anymore. The ad for this one called it a speech."

"For the sake of the church," she said. "That way they can charge admission. They'll make more tonight than a month's worth of donations."

Out in the street, the cops were checking the pastors' badges.

"Is that that poor Mr. Stone?" she asked.

She was looking through the window into the backseat of my car, where a streetlight lit up my collection of postmortem photos and other paperwork spread all over the seat.

"You know him?" I asked.

"He used to be part of Pastor Townsend's congregation," she replied. "As I understand it, he suffered some sort of mental breakdown and left the fold."

I opened the car door and gathered up all the stuff that was scattered around.

I thumbed through it, found the picture of Blaine Peterson, and showed it to her.

"What about him?"

"His wife was a member, I think. As I understand it, he wasn't a believer and wasn't particularly happy that his wife was either."

I reached into my pocket, pulled out my phone, and thumbed my way to the photo I'd taken of Biggs and Bostick at the church building on West Woodland.

"What about these two?" I asked.

She blanched and brought a hand to her throat. "Oh . . . those two," she said.

"You know them?"

"Unfortunately." She tapped the screen with her finger. "Nate Tuttle—he's the man who left all the properties to Aaron Townsend. A good-hearted soul if ever there was one—he used to take in foster children. Something like thirty of them. Rescued lots of children over the years. Created quite a few good, successful Christian souls. But these two . . ." Her finger shook. "These two were the last boys he took in, and I'm afraid they were beyond Nate's help. All they were interested in was the money."

"What money?"

She heaved a sigh. "Nate was a little eccentric, I'm afraid. He didn't trust banks, so, back in his younger days, he used to keep quite a bit of cash around the house all the time. Those two idiots were just convinced that the money still had to be around one of his properties somewhere. They badgered the church council about it, disrupted meetings and services, injured a man who tried to make them leave, and constantly harassed Pastor Townsend and his family, when the truth was that, by the time Nate passed away, all the cash had long since gone toward his medical expenses." She shook her head. "But those two just wouldn't listen. It was really quite awful."

She made a disgusted face. "I know we're all God's children," she said. "But people like those two give one pause to wonder."

A rumble began to ripple over the assembled multitude as two lines of uniformed officers began parting the mob like the Red Sea. We watched as they pushed the crowd back, using their batons to force open a corridor. Shouts began to fill the air in the moment before Aaron and Alice Townsend came into view. They linked arms and held their ground as the corridor directly in front of them collapsed in a melee of churning arms and legs. As the cops began to clear the way, one body at a time, I decided to go with my lead-in.

"Did you know the first Mrs. Townsend?" I asked.

Mrs. Highsmith nodded. "Tracy was a kind soul, but not very strong," she said. "Not really prepared for the kind of life she found herself in."

"How so?" I asked.

"Poor thing was just overwhelmed by Aaron's level of success. She never wanted anything like that. All that notoriety was just too much for her. It was like she was smothered by it all."

I cast a glance over at the crowd scene. "Doesn't seem to bother the present Mrs. Townsend," I said.

She either smiled or grimaced. It was hard to tell. "Alice is a different kettle of fish altogether," she said. "That's a woman who knew what she wanted from day one. She swallowed Aaron Townsend like the whale swallowed Jonah."

The cops had finally cleared the way. Aaron and Alice Townsend were moving forward again. When they reached the top of the stairs,

Pastor Highsmith and the loyal opposition fell in behind them. I watched as the other wives began to follow their husbands up the stairs.

"I have to go," Mrs. Highsmith said.

I reached into my jacket pocket and came out with a note I'd written earlier in the day. "You think maybe you could give this to Alice Townsend for me?"

"I'll do my best," she promised.

I believed her.

I stayed around long enough to hear the rousing cheer Townsend got as he walked to the microphone, then walked down to Broadway for a cup of coffee.

The Grind House was a classic Seattle coffee shop. All fancy-ass coffees, dried-out pastries, and people pecking at laptops. I weathered the usual *poor bastard* look from the barista when I ordered regular coffee with cream and sugar, found myself a table along the wall, and sipped at the java while I tried to figure out why in hell Aaron and Alice Townsend had lied to me about not knowing Stone, Peterson, Biggs, and Bostick. No matter which way I turned it, I couldn't come up with a good reason for them to lie about it.

The door tinkled. I looked up and she was coming down the aisle, slowly, carefully, as if she were approaching the edge of a cliff. I gestured toward the other chair.

She just stood there, glaring at me. I figured she was thinking about turning around and walking out in the ten seconds before she finally took a seat.

"Can I get you something?" I asked.

"What do you want?"

"To apologize."

"If you're looking for money, my husband knows about my past," she said. "So if you think—"

I cut her off. "I'm not. Nothing like that."

Now that I really studied her, I realized that her face didn't move much. Big things like her smile and the frown she was wearing now appeared natural enough, but the subtler movements were missing, as if her face had been created in place and designed to operate only within certain narrow limits.

"Then what do you want?" she asked again.

"I told you I want to apologize."

"For what?"

"For sticking my nose into your life, when it wasn't any of my business."

"And that's how you got the name Tuesday Jo."

"I was investigating something else and I . . . I seemed to have opened a can of worms."

"What can of worms?"

I told her. About sending her prints to IAFIS and my little adventure in Las Vegas. It took a while. She sat in stunned silence for the better part of thirty seconds after I'd finished.

"Do they know who . . . I mean, about me? About Alice Townsend?"

"No," I said. "There's no way they know who you are now."

She huffed. "Then why tell me about it? I've left that life behind me."

"Because there's a couple of bananas from Vegas in town, nosing around."

She rolled her eyes. "Those goombas never give up."

"We're working on a plan."

"Who's we?"

"I can't tell you that."

"What's the plan?"

"Theresa Calder is about to be dead and buried."

"How's that going to happen?"

"Can't tell you that either."

Another strained silence.

"Is there anything I can do?" she asked finally.

"You might consider keeping a lower profile for the next week or so, if that's possible."

She was shaking her head before I finished the sentence. "Believe me, I've tried," she said in a low voice. "My husband . . ." She paused, as if choosing her words carefully.

"My husband is transformed by his work," she said after a moment. "It's like he becomes someone else when he preaches. Someone who lights up a room. Someone who knows what the rest of us don't." She shook her head again. "He can't stop. He doesn't feel alive unless he's got an audience." She got to her feet. "He says he becomes filled with the Lord," she said. "But sometimes I think he's just full of himself." Her eyes narrowed. "Men are like that."

I stood up.

"I've got to get back. I hope you know what you're doing," she said.

"Me too."

"Why didn't you just mind your own damn business?"

"I really wish I knew the answer to that."

■   ■   ■

According to the following morning's *Seattle Times*, Aaron Townsend's speech had been a rather contentious affair, punctuated by a series of outbursts from the audience, which had resulted in a number of people being forcibly removed from the building. The rest of the article rehashed the rise and fall of his career as leader of Mount Zion Ministries and speculated on precisely how he had become such a polarizing figure within the local religious community.

I was on my second cup of coffee when Rebecca called. "I've got one," she said.

"A body?"

"From Pierce County. A Jane Doe. Perfect for our purposes. Been dead for more than a week, most of it spent in Commencement Bay. There's a problem though."

"What's that?"

"We have to go get it. Harry Downes, the Pierce County ME, is the cheapest SOB alive. Which means I'd need to provide a van, which I can manage, and a transportation crew, which I can't."

"You can't use your regular guys," I said. "'Cause that would create a paper trail with the union that you might have to explain later."

"Right."

"I could—"

"No. It can't be you. I can turn off the CCTV system in our garage when I leave tonight, but whoever picks up the body will be on TV the whole time they're in the Pierce County building. We need a couple of guys from off the grid."

"Oh . . . I know twenty or thirty of those."

"Maybe George and somebody else. Not Norman or Ralphie."

"I'll find somebody."

"They need to be sober."

I laughed out loud.

"And you need to clean them up. They need to look like county employees. I can provide a couple sets of scrubs so they look official."

"When?"

"Tomorrow afternoon."

"Tomorrow's Saturday."

"Which is perfect. We've got crews on call, but nobody's actually on site."

"What if they get a call?"

"That's a chance we're just going to have to take."

"I'll get on it."

"I need to find her a burial plot."

"I've got a few," I said.

"Where?"

"Up at Lakeside."

"How'd you end up with those?"

"They were supposed to be for my father's sisters, but they all ended up moving down to Scottsdale and Palm Springs and getting buried down there, so I ended up with four extra plots."

"There's something terribly ironic about an unclaimed Jane Doe ending up on top of Capitol Hill, spending her eternity with the city's movers and shakers."

"I kinda like it."

"The beef brothers came around again this morning. Filed an official request to see the body. They're saying they think it's someone they know, using another name. I explained that only family members were allowed to view the remains, but that I'd check with my boss to see if maybe we couldn't make an exception."

"You don't have a boss."

"Yeah, but they don't know that."

"Can we let 'em look?" I asked.

"I'm thinking it might be the fastest way to get rid of them. I've seen the postmortems. About the time I pull back that sheet those two are going to wish they were doing something else. Ms. Doe is pretty far gone."

"You'd have made a great criminal," I said.

"I'll take that as a compliment."

"I'll find us some volunteers."

"I'll call Pierce County. Tell them they'll be down tomorrow for the remains."

■ ■ ■

Whoever it was who said there wasn't much point in putting lipstick on a pig was right. George Paris and Red Lopez were as clean and sanitary as they'd been in years, but, even to the casual observer, something about them was still a bit off-kilter, as if living on the streets for long enough robbed a man of his tribal affiliation, like some piece of his soul was forever lost . . . something that couldn't be replaced by a haircut and a new pair of shoes.

I thought back to that kid living under the freeway, a kid who could never be a part of regular society again, 'cause once the light of belonging is extinguished, you're in the dark forever. Always on the outside looking in.

I'd often thought that was why George had kept his driver's license current, as if being entitled to drive was a link with better times he wasn't willing to sever, even though he didn't own a car, and didn't know anybody but me who did. The license was a filament to his better days, a link that, in his mind, separated him from the truly lost.

It was one thirty on Saturday afternoon. The boys were stomping around in their crinkly new scrubs when Rebecca pulled into my driveway driving a white King County Coroner's van and got out.

"Georgie," she said. "You look very official."

"Damn things are drafty," he groused.

"Hey," said Red Lopez. "Do I look medical?"

"Ready for surgery," she assured him.

She walked to the back of the van and opened the doors. "Come over here, fellas," she said. "I'll show you how to use the gurney and how to tie it down for the ride."

I kept out of it. Standing over by the shrubbery, I watched as she showed them how to get the gurney out, raise it up, roll it around, and then lift it back into the van, lock the wheels, and connect the safety straps so the stiff would stay still.

She slammed the door, dusted off her hands, and asked, "You got it?"

They said they did.

She handed George the paperwork. "Make sure you get a signature," she reminded. "This van doesn't have a built-in radio, so I got two handhelds. One for you guys and one for us. We'll be right behind you all the way."

George's driving was a little shaky at first, but, by the time we made the freeway, he'd gotten the hang of it again and was tooling right along.

Traffic was like it always was, like the city was being evacuated. I was hanging back a couple of cars as we blew past Southcenter and started up the hill.

"I can't believe we're doing this," I said. "It'll be a miracle if we pull this off."

She chuckled. "If we don't . . . we all get arrested; I get fired; you and I move somewhere where nobody's ever heard of either of us, somewhere the sun shines all the time, and then you and your old man's money support me in a style to which I shall soon become accustomed."

● ● ●

"Left at the stop sign," Rebecca said into the radio.

George turned left onto Pacific Avenue.

"It's the second building on your right," Rebecca said. "Pull up to the gate. Red, you get out and push the intercom button. When somebody answers, you just say, 'King County. We're here for the remains.'"

I hung back, keeping a full block between us and the van. We pulled over onto the shoulder and watched as Red got out and used the intercom. Ten seconds passed before the gate began to roll open. "Over to the left side of the building, George," Rebecca said.

"There's a garage door down at the far end. Back right up to it."

She pointed through the windshield. "Go up a ways," she said to me. "So we can see what's going on."

I rolled two blocks up the street and pulled back onto the shoulder. The King County van was backed up to a green garage door. The boys were wrestling the gurney out of the back doors. A third guy in a pair of blue coveralls was standing nearby watching them. No prompting from the radio now. The boys were on their own.

When they finally got the gurney out and standing on its wheels, all three of them disappeared inside the building.

Rebecca was gnawing at her thumbnail, trying to look confident. The dashboard clock said they'd been inside for the better part of ten minutes when they finally reappeared. A black rubber body bag was belted onto the gurney in three places.

Took two tries, but they managed to hoist the gurney up into the van. Red climbed up inside to tie things down. George gave Blue Coveralls a two-fingered salute and headed back to the driver's seat. Red reappeared, closed the doors, and climbed in next to George.

"They did it," Rebecca whispered.

I waited for an eighteen-wheeler and a city bus to pass, then did a K-turn and pulled back onto the shoulder, facing in the opposite direction.

George gave us a jaunty toot of the horn as he drove by. "Left at the stop sign," Rebecca said into the radio. George growled something back about knowing the damn way back. I had to wait for a FedEx truck to pass before I could pull out. Unfortunately, FedEx was going the same way we were, so we lost our visual on George and Red.

When we hit the freeway north ramp, I could see the King County van about four cars in front of me. Rebecca suddenly sat forward in the seat, nearly pressing her nose to the glass. "Is the back door ajar?"

"I can't see. The damn truck's in the way."

"I think it is," she said. "We've got to get up there."

"George," she said into the radio. "George."

No response.

She tried again with the same result. And then again.

"It's not working," she said, as much to herself as to me.

"Hang on," I said as I whipped the wheel to the left, put my foot into it, and began passing people on the shoulder of the on-ramp. The

FedEx driver leaned on the horn as we went flying by. The Asian couple in the Smartcar were, quite literally, cowering as we roared by them and then swerved back onto the pavement.

George was two cars up and in the process of merging onto the freeway. That's when I clearly saw the right-hand door bouncing. "I think you're right," I said.

"We've gotta get him to pull over."

She tried the radio again. Nothing.

The minute my front tires hit the interstate, I floored it and roared out into the center lane, only to find a big pulsating arrow dominating the road ahead. Merge Right . . . Construction Next 6 Miles . . . 40 mph . . . Fines Double in Construction Zones . . . 40 mph. The road signs strobed by like a picket fence.

I heard Rebecca's breath catch in her throat as I veered back the other way, jamming myself into the slot directly behind George, missing the first orange barrier by about an inch as we narrowed to a single lane of traffic.

I had to stand on the brakes to keep from piling into the back of them. Just as my heart was climbing back into my chest, we had one of those *and then everything seemed to go into slow motion* moments of song and story.

The van hit a big pothole. The back doors flew open, and the gurney bounced out onto the highway. The second and a half it hovered in the air was sufficient for the spring-loaded wheels to deploy. Like a cat, the gurney landed on its feet, just in time for me to plow into it, sending it rocketing back from whence it had come.

When the gurney's wheeled undercarriage collided with the back of the van, it folded up, sending the gurney and the last mortal remains sliding into the interior of the van, at considerably greater speed than was ever intended by the manufacturer.

I watched in horror as the gurney shattered the Plexiglas shield that separated the driving compartment from the dead body compartment.

Apparently we now had George's attention. He'd slowed down to about ten miles an hour by the time we came to an area where the orange barriers ended and rubber cones were being used to mark the edges of the roadway.

Up ahead was a deserted area the construction crews had leveled off and were using to store equipment. George angled the van in that direction, ran over several cones, and slid to a stop immediately behind a paving machine.

George and Red came tumbling out of the van, swatting at the air around them like it was full of bees. Rebecca opened her door and stepped out. I stayed put, trying to tamp my nervous system back into place.

From twenty yards away, through the open car door I suddenly could smell it. A decaying body has an odor like no other. Stepping out the door was like running into a wall. The stench was truly overpowering as I haltingly approached the back of the van.

Red looked like he was about to puke. George had both hands clamped over his face.

I was still crabbing my way in that direction when Rebecca sprinted back to the car, rummaged around in her purse, found a tube of something, and hustled back. I watched as she squirted something onto her finger and then smeared it beneath her nose.

I stayed where I was, swallowing hard, trying to hold on to my cookies as she did the same thing for both George and Red. She turned and crooked a finger in my direction.

I walked over. The smell was making my eyes water. She applied a finger full of something to my upper lip. The unmistakable smell of Vicks VapoRub suddenly filled my head.

"It's what the homicide cops use." She grabbed me by the shoulder. "I need you to help me," she said as she hurried over to the van. I followed along like a recalcitrant puppy. Took us a full five minutes to get the gurney secured. The body bag had ripped halfway down one side.

We loosened the yellow belts and rolled the remains over, trying to get her weight to help seal the rubber. It got a little better, but not much.

We closed and fastened the doors, by which time George and Red had sidled about fifty yards away. "Come on," I yelled.

At first, neither of them moved. Eventually they short-stepped it back over to us.

"Goddamn that's ripe," George growled.

"Ooooweee," Red howled.

"You're just going to have to live with it," Rebecca said. She handed the Vicks tube to Red. "If it gets bad, put more of the Vicks on yourself."

She reached out, grabbed George by the shoulders, and turned him around. "You know how to get back to my yard," she said. "We're going to go on ahead and make sure everything is ready. Go!"

They moved at glacial speed.

Rebecca and I got back in the car, waited for a break in the traffic, and then headed north. I watched in the mirror as the boys navigated their way back onto the roadway.

"What are you going to do about the damage to the van?" I asked as we got up to speed.

"Call the cops," she said. "The van and the gurney were taken out of service a couple years back. They've been sitting out in the corner of the yard ever since. Apparently some vandal broke in over the weekend."

"The world's going to hell in a handbasket," I said.

"The end of civilization as we know it."

A couple of miles later, I asked, "How do you work around that smell?"

"You get used to it," she said. "It's just a couple of diamines. Putrescine and cadaverine. They show up in the body when the amino acids begin to break down. Individually, they smell pretty bad. Together they really stink."

"Okay. I feel better now."

• • •

Next time I saw the dearly departed was right after 7:00 that evening, from behind a one-way glass partition in the basement of the King County Medical Examiner's Office. Rebecca was dressed in her full Doctor Death scrubs, mask, hat, and all.

The Vegas contingent was milling around the far corner of the room. The older of the two was going gray around the temples and pudgy around the waist. The younger guy had buzzed his head since the last time I'd seen him. They both had the kind of eyes generally only seen on the Discovery Chanel, during Shark Week.

"Gentlemen," Rebecca began. "I want to reiterate that what you're about to see is rather unpleasant. I know you feel it's possible that the remains might be those of a woman who you, at one time, knew under another name, so I've arranged this special viewing to help you put your minds at ease. I want to assure you, however, that the Integrated Automated Fingerprint Identification System makes very few mistakes and that these are indeed the remains of one Tuesday Jo Hollister. Born, Elko, Nevada . . ." She read the vital statistics from a clipboard. "Ms. Hollister was found floating in Commencement Bay five days ago. It's estimated she'd been deceased anywhere from seven to ten days at the time she was found. The state of her decomposition makes it impossible to determine the cause of death." She looked over at the deadly duo. "The remains will be interred in Lakeview Cemetery at three thirty tomorrow afternoon."

She paused. "Are you gentlemen ready?" she asked.

They sauntered over to her side. The very picture of studied nonchalance. Rebecca looked from one to the other and pulled down the zipper. Before she'd even pulled the rubber back, the diamines began to work their olfactory magic. Both men took an involuntary step backward, as if shoved by an unseen hand.

Rebecca reached down and parted the black rubber bag. The older of the two began a slow backpedal. The younger guy turned his back to the corpse and puked all over the floor.

"Yeah okay," the older guy choked out. "That's her. Thanks."

Rebecca handed Buzz Cut a paper towel. He was still wiping his chin as they wobbled from the room. Rebecca walked over and looked down at the puddle on the floor. She pulled the mask down over her chin and looked over at me.

"Either penne or ziti, it's hard to tell," she said with a grin.

■　　■　　■

I'm not much of a believer. The way I see it, you're here on earth for an indeterminate period of time, and then the lights go out. End o' story. Fade to black. Could be I'm wrong. Lord knew a lot of people felt otherwise, but that's the way I see it.

And I'm not much for formal good-byes either. I'd rather remember the person as they were in life. So, funerals had always seemed a bit beside the point and overly melodramatic to me.

Didn't matter though. Sometimes you just gotta do what you gotta do. At three forty-five on the following afternoon, I was standing by an open grave in the Lakewood Cemetery, looking out over Portage Bay, while a Lutheran minister droned on about eternity and the Almighty.

"Who shall separate Tuesday Jo from the love of Christ? Shall trouble or hardship or persecution or famine or nakedness or danger or sword?"

If indeed there was some omnipotent being watching over the proceedings, He or She had evidently decided that this afternoon's theme was going to be WET. What had started out this morning as an intermittent drizzle had morphed into a full-fledged downpour of biblical proportions. The kind where you have to shout to be heard by the person standing next to you.

"Listen again to the words that we heard earlier, but this time with Tuesday Jo's name. Hear the word of the Lord Almighty."

I'd recruited Ralph Batista and Harold Green, Margie, and Shorty from the Zoo to act as mourners. Red Lopez refused to be parted from his new set of scrubs and George claimed his sinus cavities were never going to be the same, so neither of them were putting in a guest appearance.

On my right, Rebecca was doing yeoman's duty, standing tall under a black umbrella as the rivers of retribution fell from the sky. On my left, Sergeant Roscoe Templeton was beginning to look as if maybe he'd never seen this much water at one time in all his life.

I'd called him yesterday. Asked him if maybe he couldn't fly out from Vegas and lend a further air of authenticity to today's proceedings, just in case the Braciole Brothers hadn't given up the ghost. Which they hadn't.

They were huddled together about three graves down, not too far from my grandparents. I got the impression that whoever they worked for wanted to know that they'd followed their assignment through to the soggy end.

"No, in all these things are more than conquerors through him who loves Tuesday Jo. For I am convinced that neither death nor life, neither angels nor demons, neither the present nor the future, nor any powers, neither height nor depth, nor anything else in all creation, will be able to separate Tuesday Jo from the love of God that is in Christ Jesus our Lord."

I was doing my best to ignore the torrent of water dripping from the end of my nose.

Most everybody I'd ever been related to was buried right around here somewhere. My mother and father rested side by side just over the crest of the hill. My father's brother Frank was marked by a weeping marble angel, which, if you'd known Frank Waterman, could only be taken as a final irony. His oldest sister, Anne, was remembered by an ornate garland of chiseled flowers.

Mercifully, the preacher was winding down.

"Eternal God, your love is stronger than death, and your passion more fierce than the grave. We rejoice in the lives of those whom you have drawn into your eternal embrace. Keep us in joyful communion with them until we join the saints of every people and nation gathered before your throne in your ceaseless praise, through your Son, Jesus Christ our Lord. Amen."

The preacher made the rounds, shaking everybody's hand, telling them how Tuesday Jo was in a better place now, which seemed a bit overly optimistic to me, having recently returned from my near-death experience in Vegas.

The Vegas crew didn't stick around for the pleasantries. By the time the preacher had finished, they'd already made it to their rental Buick and were headed up Fifteenth inside a moving cloud of rainwater.

I slipped Margie a fifty and told her to buy everybody a stiff one on me. By the time the Zoo crew had shambled out to the street, only Rebecca, Roscoe Templeton, and I remained. Templeton nudged me with an elbow. "I don't know how in hell you pulled this off," he said with a wink, "but nice work."

"Thank her," I said, nodding Rebecca's way.

Templeton smiled and gave Rebecca an admiring nod.

"Let's hope that's the end of it," I said.

"Those two bananas are booked on the six twenty-five to Vegas."

Rebecca took my arm. We started down the hill. Behind us, a cemetery worker started up the backhoe. The wind was rising. The trees were whipping in all directions at once. The diesel smoke rode the wind southward like a black arrow.

"Give you a ride somewhere?" I asked Templeton.

He shook his head. "Got me a rental," he said.

"Thanks again for coming."

"It was the least I could do for her."

Rebecca and I stood and watched Templeton short-step it down the hill and disappear from sight. Rebecca pulled at my arm. "Come on," she said, pulling me up the hill instead of down.

The backhoe operator already had the grave filled in and was folding up the big blue tarp that we'd all been standing on.

We walked to the top of the hill and then started down the other side. She pulled me over to the left and then stopped. There they were. My parents. William H. Waterman. The day of his birth and the day of his death. That was it.

Mary Catherine Waterman. Same thing with the dates. *The fairest rose fallen far too soon.*

We stood there for a long time.

"He was just a man, Leo," she said finally. "Bigger, meaner, and smarter than most, but just a man."

"He's always been hard for me to separate," I said after a long moment.

"From what?"

"From the stories that are told about him. From the way he's still portrayed, whenever his name comes up in the media. From the guy who never approved of a single thing I ever did."

"Maybe you'd feel better if you took all that money that he supposedly squeezed out of the city coffers and gave it back."

"Fat fucking chance."

We both laughed out loud.

"Have you still got that enormous bathtub with the jets?"

"Yeah."

"Let's go back to your house and roll around in it together."

"Best idea I've heard this week."

. . .

She's naked. She smiles at me, shy and a little uncertain, as she steps back into the tub. The tub is only half full of water because we've sloshed the rest of it all over the floor. I stand up, put my hands on her shoulders, and turn her around. It's always been amazing to me that this power-ful woman becomes so compliant with all her clothes off. She's quite beautiful. Tall, slim. A tangle of dark hair between her legs. I pull her to me and nestle against the crack of her ass. Makes me feel paralyzed, like I'll never be able to move again, which, under the circumstances, would be just fine by me.

I find the soap and begin to soap her breasts. Then I scrub her back. I run my fingers over the vertebrae. She emits a low groan. The movement of the water is reflected on the ceiling as I rinse the soap from her body.

I've got a hard-on that feels like forever. I pick her up and set her on the floor beside the tub, then I get out, wrap her in an enormous white towel, and carry her to the bedroom. We lie across the bed diago-nally, and I begin to draw the towel apart, slowly, as if I'm removing a bandage. Her flesh still smells of soap. My hands find her wet flesh. She raises her legs and pulls me down. I feel myself enter her. Her breath suddenly leaves her. She arches her back as I bury my face in her white throat.

When it's over, we fall asleep without a word.

I came off the bed like a rocket. Sitting there, not sure of anything, until the house phone rang again. Second time in five years. I checked the clock. Only 9:30. Rebecca groaned and rolled over. I stretched out, reaching for the receiver. I brought it to my ear and lay back against the damp sheets. "Yeah," I said.

"Dis you, Leo?" a familiar voice asked.

"Who's this?" I ask.

"Charity, mon. It's Charity."

"How'd you get this number?" was all I could think to say.

"Got it from Mr. Carl's number book. But listen, mon. He's hurt real bad. I stopped by to help him get to bed. Somebody done kicked down the door and beat the bloody shit out of him. Done beat him like a dog."

I found myself sitting up, jamming the phone into my ear, like I was trying to push it through my head. Rebecca picked up the vibe. She leaned against my back and put a comforting hand on my shoulder.

"Call 911," I said.

"Already done it, mon. Cops too. Ambulance come and took him away. I don't think he gonna make it, mon. His head's all stove in."

"Where'd they take him?"

"Northwest Hospital. 'Bout five minutes ago."

"I'm on the way."

. . .

Hospitals make my skin crawl. Breathing that recycled air makes my lungs feel like somebody punched holes in them, but tonight it didn't matter.

It was a little after ten when I roared into the Northwest Hospital parking lot. Rebecca'd been in my ear all the way from home. "Take it easy. For God's sake, slow down. He's in good hands. I'm sure they're doing everything possible for him."

We sprinted into the ER hand in hand. Little redheaded nurse took one look at me and held up a restraining hand.

"Carl Cradduck," I growled.

She checked her clipboard and pointed down the hall. I dropped Rebecca's hand and ran in that direction. The sight of half a dozen green-clad personnel huddled around a gurney in a room to my right brought me to a stop. Blood was all over the place. I watched as they worked feverishly. Hooking up multiple intravenous bags. My heart

threatened to jump out of my chest as I watched them wheel in a ven-
tilator. I don't know much about medicine, but I knew that meant he'd
stopped breathing. So did I.

Rebecca was back at my side. "Nurse didn't know anything," she
said. "She just came on shift." She read my mind and threw an arm
around my waist. I shrugged her arm and started into the room. The
nearest doctor stepped away from the others and blocked my path.

"No," he said through his mask. He was an East Indian, or a
Pakistani, something like that. "You can't come in here. If you want to
help this man, please just let us work." He turned and hurried back into
the room. Someone called for a vessel clamp. A voice droned. "Blood
pressure one seventy-three over forty-seven." Somebody called for forty
CCs of something.

Two nurses moved to the far side, and for the first time I saw Carl.
He looked like a child lying there, except that even through the mound
of bandages, I could see that his head wasn't round anymore. I turned
away and stifled a sob. Rebecca pulled me away, down the hall toward
the nurses' station.

"Come on, come on," she chanted as I reluctantly backpedaled.
"He's in the best possible hands. Come on. We'll wait over here."

They were at it for nearly an hour before two nurses and an orderly
wheeled the gurney out into the hall, rolled it into an elevator, and
disappeared from view.

A couple minutes later, the doctor who'd barred my way stepped
out into the hall, dropped his mask, and began to pull off his gloves.
I started to get up. But Rebecca threw an arm across my lap. "Let me
handle this," she said.

I watched as she walked down, introduced herself, and then showed
him her King County ID. They had a nice, long, doctor-to-doctor
confab before he disappeared into the elevator and Rebecca came back
my way.

"So?" I said after she plopped down next to me.

"They've taken Carl down to the ICU. He's hypercritical."

"Which means what?"

She hesitated, took a deep breath. "It means they're not at all sure he's going to make it." I put my hands over my face and bent low over my lap. She patted my back. "He's got a severe depressed skull fracture. A broken jaw. Two basal fractures of the eye orbits, several broken ribs, and at least four missing teeth. He stopped breathing in the ambulance, but the techs were Johnny-on-the-spot and auto-ventilated him."

"Can I see him?" I asked.

She shook her head and began rubbing my back.

"No," she said. "All we can do now is wait. If he makes it through the night . . . maybe we'll know more in the morning."

"I'll wait," I said.

"There's nothing you can—"

"I'll wait anyway." I pulled my car keys out of my pocket. "Take the car," I said. "I know you need to be at work tomorrow. I'll just hang around here. I'll leave my phone on. Anything changes, I'll let you know."

She tried a couple more times to talk me out of staying, then kissed me on the cheek and headed for the door.

I spent the next couple hours wondering who would do such a thing to a little guy in a wheelchair. Was it something random? Was Carl working on something that brought the wolf to his door? There was just no way to tell.

I was nodding at 2:30 A.M. when the sound of my name jerked me back to reality. Charity. It was Charity sitting in the seat beside me.

"How's my man doing?" he asked.

"Not so good."

"He gonna make it . . . right?"

"It's still up in the air," I said.

Nobody said anything for a while, then Charity said, "Had to get my cousin Zag Boy to come over wid some plywood . . . you know, board up the door. Mr. Carl wouldn't like nobody messing with his stuff. Zag Boy staying in de odda bedroom till we get somebody to come out and put on a new door."

"Thanks."

"No need to thank me, Leo. He be my friend too."

"I know."

He slid a long arm across my shoulders. "Cops thinkin' it was a home invasion. Dey done tore the place all up. Everything scattered all over. Cops want to know what's missing, but how in hell anybody but Carl know dat?"

"Yeah," I said. "And Carl's never gonna get the Betty Crocker housecleaning award. I doubt if even he knows what was in there."

"We be hea when he wake up in the morning."

"Yeah."

Next thing I remember, it was 5:50 A.M. A hand was shaking my shoulder. When I opened my eyes, Charity was spread out over three chairs, snoring lightly. The doctor from last night was saying, "Sir . . . sir . . . sir . . ."

"You're Mister Cradduck's friend?" he asked.

"Ahhh . . . yes," I managed to stammer out.

"We've put your friend into a medically induced coma," he said.

"Why? I mean, why would you do that?"

"We're going to give his brain a rest," he said. "For the next forty hours or so." He handed me a slip of paper. "That's my cell phone number. Give me a call Wednesday morning. At that point—" He stopped himself. I could tell . . . he didn't want to make any promises he couldn't keep. He shrugged and walked off.

I sat there and collected my wits for a few minutes.

Charity came awake with a start. I told him what the doctor had told me.

"No point in bein' hea den," he said.

"No . . . I guess not."

Charity headed for the door. I went over to the restroom, brushed my teeth with my finger, and washed my face. Wasn't till I got outside and the freshening breeze slapped me wide awake that I remembered Rebecca had taken the car.

◦   ◦   ◦

Took most of the towels I owned to wipe up the water on the bathroom floor. I was on my second load, throwing the towels in the dryer and the sheets in the washer, when someone began pounding on my front door. And I mean pounding.

I dropped the laundry and hot-footed it out to the front of the house. I was reaching for my shotgun when a voice boomed through the door. "Seattle Police Department. Open the door. Open the door, now."

I looked out through the peephole. Sure enough . . . cops. Tactical cops with ballistic shields and a battering ram. A bunch of them.

"I'm coming out," I shouted. "I'm not armed."

"Open the door," the voice boomed.

I pulled back both bolts, opened the door, and then laced my fingers together on top of my head and stepped out.

In the movies this is where the snappy dialogue always happens. Where our hero flogs his tormentors with withering repartee. In reality, at this point, doing anything other than exactly what you're told will, almost certainly, get you killed. Before another word was spoken, a pair of enormous cops were on me like ants at a picnic. One behemoth was kneeling in the middle of my back, grinding my face into the concrete porch while his buddy was busy handcuffing my hands somewhere up behind my neck. As they hoisted me to my feet, I could feel my nose bleeding.

"One of you guys wanna give me some idea as to what's happening?" I asked.

The two of them grabbed my elbows and nearly lifted me off the ground. Felt like both arms were going to break.

"You're being arrested for suspicion of capital murder," a voice behind me said.

"Anything you say can and will be . . ."

. . .

Only thing worse than hospitals are jails. At least in hospitals, excrement isn't considered a means of expression. I didn't know who wrote "JESUS LOVES ME" on the rear wall, but I had a pretty good idea what it was written in.

Other than that, I didn't know any more than I did when I'd opened my front door to the cops about four hours ago. I had the cell to myself, and had deduced from the fact that a jailer walked by every five minutes that they thought I might harm myself and were taking precautions.

I'd made my one phone call. Called my longtime lawyer and friend, Jed James, on his private number. Jed was a judge these days and therefore not able to directly advise me. He was also still the principal partner in Seattle's most prestigious law firm. He recused himself whenever the firm was involved in a case. He'd reminded me that he was no longer my attorney and then assured me he'd be sending the cavalry forthwith.

I had no doubt that, by this time, his minion was already working at it, so I wasn't surprised when my private jailer escorted a studious-looking young African American woman to the corridor outside my cell and set up a folding chair for her.

He was hanging around like he was planning to stay for the party. She had other ideas. She poked her nose right up in his face. "I remind you that, according to the U.S. Supreme Court, my client and I have an expectation of complete privacy here. No recordings of any kind are permitted. So if you'd excuse us."

She waited until he'd shuffled off to Buffalo before she sat down.

"I'm Laurie Thatcher," she said. "Mr. James sent me."

"Good to see you," I said.

"What have they told you?"

"Not a thing."

"What have you told them?"

"Absolutely nothing."

"Good."

"I don't even know who I'm supposed to have murdered."

"Someone named Richard Seigal."

"He's a neighbor of mine."

"I don't know what they have. They're playing it extremely close to the vest until your arraignment first thing tomorrow morning, but I get the distinct feeling they're almost giddy about their case against you."

"I didn't kill anybody."

She raised a stiff finger to her lips and shook her head. "Don't say anything," she whispered. "I don't trust these people one bit. This place is probably wired for sound." She got to her feet. "They've got you on suicide watch, so you should be fine until morning. Mr. James asked me to assure you he'd be making some calls for you."

I nodded that I understood. He meant he'd call Rebecca.

"I'll see you in the morning," she said.

* * *

The only words I uttered at my arraignment were "Not guilty, Your Honor." Like Ms. Thatcher had so astutely noted, the DA's people were snarky confident about their case. Richard Seigal had been found in the street early yesterday morning, just outside my wall, with a single bullet hole where his right eye used to be. Not only that, but they'd found my fingerprints on both the gun and the magazine. In a brief statement to police, Janet Seigal had confirmed a certain amount of bad blood between her husband and me, including a tidbit about how

I'd threatened to kill him a few days before he was killed. To top things off, my neighbor Wilson Harvey had given the SPD a statement to the effect that he'd witnessed an altercation between Richard Seigal and me the previous Tuesday evening.

The only ace I was holding was that I hadn't been alone much on Sunday, the day Richard Seigal had been killed. I'd picked Rebecca up for the funeral at two thirty and wasn't alone until I got home from the hospital yesterday morning, so determining a precise time of death was going to be crucial to my future freedom. The real eyebrow-raiser of the proceeding was when it was announced that an autopsy was presently being performed by Snohomish County medical examiner Peter Nance, as the King County medical examiner, Rebecca Duval, had recused her office from the case because of what she described as a *personal relationship* with the defendant. Results were expected later in the afternoon.

Things didn't get contentious until the matter of bail arose. The charge of murder is a non-bailable offense in the state of Washington. However, as Ms. Thatcher so ably pointed out, I hadn't yet been charged with anything. I was merely being held on suspicion. Thatcher was all over them about how I was deeply rooted in the community, had never been convicted of a violent crime, how I would be willing to turn in my passport, and pay any reasonable bail.

The judge just sat there doing her impression of Mount Rushmore. I was remanded to custody until further notice. The only point we won was my right to meet with my lawyer after the arraignment.

They took off my cuffs and shepherded me into a room two doors down from the courtroom. Ten minutes later, Thatcher showed up looking a bit ashen.

She sat down across from me. "It's not good at all," she said. "If we went to trial tomorrow, we'd lose. The jury'd be out about ten minutes."

"You don't have to sugarcoat it for me."

"This isn't funny," she snapped. "They have physical evidence and two eyewitnesses. Ninety percent of the people in prison are there on a lot less than that."

"What are we going to do?"

"We're going to make no statements while we wait for the autopsy results. They're very likely going to give you somebody to talk to, in hopes you'll say something incriminating." She got to her feet. "I'm going to file an appeal on the matter of bail. I need to get it filed by noon, so it will be on the docket for tomorrow . . . so if you'll excuse me."

I waved a good-bye. Next time the door opened, a pair of King County mounties came in, shackled me hand and foot, and shuffled me back over the sky bridge to my cell.

That Thatcher woman was right on the money. Suddenly I had a cellmate. Guy about thirty with Celtic rune tattoos on his forearms and a fashionable five o'clock shadow.

I turned to the jailer. "Get this guy out of here," I said.

He ignored me, walked down the corridor, and disappeared.

"That ain't real friendly," my new cellmate said.

I walked over and stood in front of him. "Listen, asshole," I said. "You're either a cop or some kind of jailhouse rat trying to get your sentence reduced by making up some shit I supposedly said. Either way, this is the last conversation we're ever gonna have. You start running your mouth or come over to my side of the cell, and you're gonna become the world's foremost expert on dental implants. You hear me?"

He didn't say anything. Just stood there, chewing a piece of gum, trying to look tough.

I walked over to the bunk on the far side of the cell and sat down. He must have had a pager in his pocket, because ten minutes later the jailer showed up and took him away. No shackles either, which made him a cop rather than a snitch.

I'd never really thought about the possibility of doing hard time before. Sure, I'd done a day here and two days there, for stuff like withholding information or interfering with an investigation, but nothing life-changing like this.

I started running scenarios in my head. You know . . . the kind of thing a person does when facing the unknown. Cellblocks and sliding doors. Mess halls. Walled yards and bad tattoos. Every prison movie I'd ever seen flashed through my mind as I sat there in that rancid cell, imagining how I was going to survive in that hell we call the American prison system. The place where we lock up anybody who doesn't fit the mold—the criminal, the crazy, the poor, the disenfranchised, the wretched refuse of our teeming shores. Anybody who threatens to interfere with shopping.

It wasn't till I heard the voice that I realized someone was standing outside the door of my cell. "You ready to confess?" he said.

In the window on the other side of the corridor, light was fading from the sky.

Lieutenant Timothy Eagen. Come to smirk, I guessed. To revel in the fact that he finally had me where he wanted me.

"You want to talk to me, call my lawyer," I said, without looking his way.

"Hey," he said.

I looked over. He was holding a bunch of papers in his hand.

"You know what this is?" he asked.

"Why don't you enlighten me."

"It's the autopsy report on Richard Seigal."

I kept my mouth shut.

"Says Mr. Seigal was killed between eight and ten Sunday night."

I turned his way, trying not to look like a kid on his birthday. "I've got an alibi for that time period."

"I know," he said. He peeled several pages off the back of the bundle. "This is a statement taken earlier today from Dr. Rebecca Duval. Says you two were together doin' the horizontal bop during those hours. Also says she was asleep during part of the time period in question. Enough time for you to go outside and knock off Mr. Seigal and come back in. So it don't necessarily get you off the hook." He gave an exaggerated shrug. "Now normally I'd figure an alibi from the suspect's girlfriend was about worth wiping my ass with, but . . ." He paused. "But I've worked with that woman for the better part of fifteen years now." He shook his head. "For the life of me, I never could figure out what the fuck she saw in you, but . . . you know . . . notwithstanding her appalling taste in men, that woman's as straight as an arrow. She's not alibiing anybody for murder. Not even you." He rocked back on his heels. "So why don't you tell me how your fingerprints got all over the murder weapon."

I gave it some serious thought. Trying to decide whether Eagen had an angle I couldn't figure, and was simply looking to put the final nail in my coffin. In my mind's ear, I could hear Ms. Thatcher telling me to keep my mouth shut.

I decided to take a chance.

"I took it away from him some night early last week," I said finally. "He was drunk and waving it around."

"Tell me about it."

I did. At great length. Leaving out nothing.

"What's Mrs. Seigal saying about it?" I asked at the end.

"Not much," Eagen said. "She gave us a brief statement and then lawyered up. Supposedly she's under heavy sedation and won't be making any further statements in the foreseeable future. And you know what?"

"What?"

"I can't find any doctor anywhere who's diagnosed her with MS."

That's when it finally dawned on me. Like a cloud lifting. What I should have picked up on from the very beginning. "She set me up," I said, as much to myself as to Eagen. "She saw me coming from a mile away. Captain Magnolia to the rescue. I couldn't figure out why that idiot was so sure I was messing with his wife. But . . . it was her! She was feeding him that crap. Fanning the flames."

Eagen made a dubious face. "If what you're telling me is true, she took one hell of a chance assuming you'd be alone."

I shook my head. "She had every reason to assume I'd be alone in the house last night. Since they moved in, I've always been alone. If my car was in the drive, I was there by myself. Rebecca and I just got back together a couple days ago." I threw an angry hand in the air. "She walks that damn dog out in front of my house several times a day. Nobody was more familiar with my comings and goings than she was."

He didn't say anything. Just stood there mulling it over.

"Be interesting to know whether the Seigals had a prenup," I said after a while.

"Is that what you steely-eyed private dicks would do?"

I ignored the sniping. "And I'd like to know how much he was insured for, and who ends up with the dough."

"Sam Spade on the case," he said.

I watched as he folded the paperwork and slid it into the inside pocket of his suit coat.

"One more thing," I said as he began to walk away.

"What's that, hotshot?"

"Like I told you, when I took that gun away from him, I removed the magazine and jacked one out of the chamber. The one from the chamber's probably still on my neighbor's lawn. Up front near the driveway."

"You don't say."

• • •

The cuisine left a great deal to be desired. I felt pretty certain that the pile of yellow stuff they were calling scrambled eggs had never been anywhere near a chicken. The toast was so over-toasted you could snap it in two like a cracker. I smeared it with the little packet of grape jelly and choked it down anyway.

Just after noon, a pair of beefy jailers came in, chained me up hand and foot, and waddled me over to my bail hearing. As we turned the final corner, I found myself staring into a bank of TV cameras. My first instinct was to raise my hands, to cover my face Mafia-style, but I thought better of it and lifted my boyish chin instead.

The minute I walked in the door, I could tell something was up. The crew from the DA's office was welded chest to chest out in front of the prosecution table. Looked like they were having either a collective stroke or an argument in pantomime.

Jed and Rebecca were sitting side by side in the back row. Half a dozen reporters were huddled together behind the defense table. The jailers deposited me in the chair next to Ms. Thatcher and lumbered to the back of the room.

The judge entered the courtroom, the bailiff began to drone, everyone scurried for a seat except for an assistant DA whose face I recognized but whose name escaped me. Walton or Waltman, something like that. He walked to the front of the courtroom and began whispering into the judge's ear. The expression on the judge's face suggested either she'd slipped a disk on the way in, or she didn't like what she was hearing at all.

A minute later she lifted a hand and made a "scat" motion with her fingers.

The assistant DA slogged back to the defense table and sat down.

At which point the judge noticed Jed sitting in the back of the room. She looked out over her half glasses. "To what do we owe the honor of a visit from the most honorable Jedediah James?" she inquired.

Jed got to his feet. "Your Honor, I am present purely as a private citizen. Mr. Waterman is a former client and one of my oldest friends."

"Ah," she said. "Moral support."

Thatcher jumped to her feet. "Your Honor, if I may, I would like to protest, in the strongest terms, my client being dragged into this court-room chained up like an animal. It's prejudicial in the extreme. I—"

The judge raised a stop sign hand. "Save it, Ms. Thatcher," she said and then looked over to the prosecution table. "Mr. Wagner, I am given to understand that the district attorney's office is not prepared to charge Mr. Waterman at this time."

Wagner stood up. Coughed into his hand. "No, Your Honor. We are not, but . . . to reiterate what Your Honor said, we are declining to press charges . . . *at this time*. We reserve the right to reinstitute these charges at any time in the future."

"So noted," she said, then turned to me. "Mr. Waterman, you are hereby released on your own recognizance. You are ordered to surrender your passport and not leave the friendly confines of King County without this court's expressed written permission. As an additional aid, we're going to issue you an Omnilink monitoring device for your ankle. We'll send someone over to your house in the morning to install it and collect your passport. Be home. Do you understand?"

I said I did.

BANG. She slammed the gavel down and then waved the little hammer angrily at the back of the room. "Get Mr. Waterman out of those damn manacles," she said.

My babysitters hustled up and relieved me of the hardware. They sounded like the Ghost of Christmas Past as they clanked off. The bailiff began to drone again. Everybody stood up. The judge nodded curtly and strode out the side door.

Thatcher was staring at the side of my head. "What just happened?" she asked.

"It was a miracle," I said.

"My butt."

I was rescued by the arrival of Jed and Rebecca. Hugs and hand-shakes all around.

"You had me more than a little worried there, big fella," Jed said.

"Me too. Believe me, I've spent the last two days running George Raft movies in my head."

He patted me on the arm and inclined his head toward the side door. "I'm going to leave through the judge's room," he said. "There's quite a few cameras out in the hall. It just wouldn't look right to . . . you know."

I told him I understood. We shook hands. "Nice work, Ms. Thatcher" was his final utterance before exiting stage left.

Rebecca hooked her arm in mine. Thatcher rounded up her papers and stuffed them into her briefcase. "You must have somebody watching over you, Mr. Waterman."

"Two of 'em," I said. "My best friend"—I jostled Rebecca with my shoulder—"and my worst enemy."

"I don't understand," Thatcher said.

"I think it's probably best we leave it that way."

We waited for the building to clear and then walked down to Cherry Street and devoured a couple of first-rate turkey sandwiches at Bakeman's. "Eagen came to see me in my office yesterday afternoon," Rebecca said as we were finishing up.

"Came to see me in jail too."

"Had a forensics team go over your car. Asked me if I was sure about the times I'd given in my statement. I told him I was."

"You're always sure of everything."

"You know what he also told me?"

"What?"

"He had this bullet he said he'd found on your neighbor's lawn. Said he didn't think you'd killed Seigal. Said it just wasn't your style."

"He's a good cop. Knows shit from shoe polish."

"He's asked me out a few times, you know."

"I figured he had," I said.

"No cops," she said.

"Figured that too."

"You owe him a thanks."

"Not sure I could choke it out," I said.

"Work on it."

I promised I'd try.

．　．　．

They'd left the search warrant standing up on my kitchen table. From the look of it, SPD'd been through my house from top to bottom. Every door and drawer was open. All my guns and ammo were laid out on the living room floor. They'd been looking for anything that matched the peashooter that killed Richard Seigal. If they'd found anything, I'd still be downtown, staring at those dodgy scrambled eggs.

What hospital and jails have in common is that both of them are the worst places on earth to try to get a night's sleep. I put my arsenal back where it belonged, except for the Mossberg and a Smith & Wesson M&P 9mm. I carried those two and enough ammo to start a war in the Balkans into the bedroom with me. Cold comfort, but comfort nonetheless.

Naturally, the cops had trashed the bed. Just in case I'd stashed a howitzer under the box spring, I guessed. I grabbed the comforter from the floor, found a couple of pillows at large beneath the wing chair, and threw myself into bed fully dressed.

I slept for fourteen hours. With me, that much sleep is both a blessing and a curse.

For reasons I've never understood, sleeping more than seven or eight hours gives me nightmares. The kind where Dracula swoops down and eats your liver, with a side of fava beans. Always happens in the morning, when I've slept too long.

When I finally opened my eyes, I was in a partial panic and a full sweat. I felt like I'd been running for my life but couldn't recall why. Only the flow of the cool air over my clammy skin made me certain it was true.

I rolled over onto my back and dug around in my pocket for my phone. Found it.

Pushed the button. Nothing. Pushed the button on top. Likewise nada. Thing was deader than a herring.

I swung my feet over the edge, grabbed my weaponry, and headed for the kitchen by way of the bathroom. By the time I'd scrubbed the moss off my teeth, brewed up a pot of coffee, and swallowed most of it, my phone had collected enough of a charge to check my messages.

Two from Rebecca telling me that a date we'd made for later this evening was going to have to wait, as she had three victims of an auto accident who were going to require her services even more than I did. One from my insurance agent that I didn't listen to for long enough to find out what he wanted, and finally, one that came in about an hour ago, from Northwest Hospital, wanting to know if I had any information regarding Carl's medical insurance or next of kin.

I called Carl's home number. Zag Boy answered. "Cradduck place," he said.

"You Charity's cousin?" I asked.

"That be me."

"I'm his friend Leo."

"Heard 'bout you, mon."

"I need you to do something for me."

"What be that?"

"Carl keeps his wallet in the junk drawer in the kitchen. Last little drawer, over by the window. I need you to go over there, find his medical insurance card, and read me the company and the number."

"Hang on, mon," he said.

I found an old golf pencil and a piece of an envelope to write on.

"Premera Blue Cross," Zag Boy said.

He read me a thirty-seven-digit number. I wrote it down.

"Thanks," I said. "I gotta go."

■   ■   ■

"He's got no next of kin," I said for the third time. "Years ago he had an older brother who died in some kind of industrial accident. That was it. He never married. Never had any children. Lived by himself. Anything you need signed, I'll sign. You need somebody to be financially responsible for whatever his insurance doesn't cover, just show me the dotted line."

"You do realize the degree of legal liability involved in the—"

"Where do I sign?" I said a little louder than necessary.

His name was Paul Edlund. Chief of the Neurosurgery Department. A stout-looking fellow who looked like he'd spent a lot of time in the weight room.

He bent over and had a whispered conversation with the hospital administrator, whose name I hadn't caught. She pulled some paperwork from the top drawer of her desk and slid it over to me. Somebody'd thoughtfully pasted bright yellow arrows, pointing at the places I needed to sign. I went through it and signed them all.

When I'd finished, I looked up at Dr. Edlund. "I thought you guys were going to try to bring him out of his coma today," I said.

"I'm afraid that won't be possible," he said. "Now that the swelling has gone down marginally, we can see quite clearly that his skull is touching his brain, in two places. That has to be remedied before we have any hope of him regaining consciousness."

"How do you do that?" I asked.

"We drill holes in his skull. Outside the fractured area. We save the bone fragments and bone dust for later reconstruction of the holes."

Just the sound of it made me wince.

He went on. "The fractured segments are then removed. If the fragments are interlocked, a routine craniotomy is performed, including the depressed fracture."

I was sucking air through my teeth. He stopped talking and gave me a chance to regain my composure and then went on. "The bone flap is then turned upside down and the fragments are reduced using a mallet." He waited to see how I would react.

I looked away. Closed my eyes. "And then . . . ?"

"The bone flap is returned to the skull and fixed in place. At which point the bone dust from the burr holes is used to refill the openings."

"What's the prognosis for something like this?"

He waggled a noncommittal hand. "Quite frankly, it's a miracle that he's still alive at all. His vital signs are actually improving, and God knows he's got a hell of a will to live, but none of that's going to matter even a little bit if we can't take the pressure off of his brain."

"You know what Carl would say?" I asked.

"What's that?"

"He'd want to know why we're standing here running our mouths about it, instead of getting the damn job done."

"You're sure?"

"I knew him before he lost the use of his legs. That man took being paralyzed with a grace that was hard to believe. He never blamed anybody and never asked anybody for help. He just sat his skinny little ass in that wheelchair and made a life for himself like nothing had happened. So . . . yeah, I'm sure."

He nodded solemnly and then checked his watch. "I can have the team ready in two hours."

"Let's do it," I said.

· 171 ·

They were at it for four and a half hours. When Edlund came out of the operating room, he looked like he'd just run a marathon. He checked the waiting room, making sure we were alone. "That's the toughest little son of a bitch I've ever seen," he said.

"He made it?"

"He's alive. For now, that's all I can say."

"When will we know?"

"The next forty-eight hours are critical. If he's still alive on Friday, anything's possible."

■   ■   ■

His name was Timothy Prichert. He was a King County court officer. I handed over my passport, at which point we had one of those conversations you can only have with a true bureaucrat.

"This is expired," he said disgustedly.

"So what?"

"It's no longer valid."

"I was ordered by the judge to turn it over to you."

"But it's expired."

"Since I'm also ordered not to leave the county, and you're about to slap an ankle monitor on me, that shouldn't be a problem, should it?"

"It's also a means of identification," he snapped.

"The expiration date has very little to do with my identity."

He punished me by taking his sweet-ass time connecting my ankle monitor, and by running his mouth the whole damn time.

"This is a GPS tracking device. Should you remove it from your person, or exceed the twenty-five-mile limit to which it has been set, you will be returned to the King County jail, where you will be held without bail until the disposition of your case. Do you understand?"

I said I did. He went on babbling.

"You will be tracked indoors and out, 24/7, by both satellite and wireless technologies. The device is waterproof. The strap contains a tamper detection system utilizing fiber optics. If an individual cuts the ankle strap, removes the battery, or tampers with the transmitter, an alert signal is sent and the violation is reported. You will be given a warning should you exceed your boundaries. The monitor will begin to blink red. At that point, you have four minutes before it begins to beep. Should that happen, you will immediately be taken into custody. Do you understand?"

It was a little black gizmo about the size of two flip phones, connected to my ankle by a wide plastic strap. When he'd finished, he stood there like he was waiting for me to thank him. Instead, I showed him the door.

I'd just poured my second cup of coffee when the doorbell sounded. I figured he'd forgotten something, so I took my time answering.

Wasn't him though. It was a pair of cops.

"You Waterman?" one of them asked.

"Yup," I said.

The other one reached out and handed me a business card. SPD North Precinct. "I'm Detective Sanchez. This is my partner, Detective Gomes. We're working your friend Carl Cradduck's case."

We shook hands all around. "You guys making any progress?" I asked.

"We've had a rash of home invasions in that part of the city," Gomes said.

"Eleven in the last thirty days or so," Sanchez added.

"You know any reason why anybody'd want to hurt Mr. Cradduck?"

"I can't think of any reason why anyone would do that to another human being."

Gomes asked, "You familiar enough with Mr. Cradduck to tell if anything was missing?"

"Nobody but Carl could tell you that, and I'm betting he couldn't either. The guy isn't very domestic. His world is that wheelchair. As long it can still roll around his place, he's happy. When it gets so bad he can't get around, we take him out to lunch and a movie and send in the Maid Brigade. He goes crazy when we get back. Claiming we've ruined his whole filing system. That's just how he is."

"Got a big heroin problem up there in North City," Gomes said. "Those tweekers will do whatever it takes to stay high. We're kicking in shooting gallery doors, but we haven't come up with anything worth talking about."

We tossed it around for another ten minutes. "If there's anything I can do to help," I said finally.

"We'll get back to you," Gomes assured.

I closed the door and went back to my coffee.

■   ■   ■

The Seigal house was buttoned up tight. Curtains drawn, lights out. About thirty yards up the street a black SUV with midnight-black windows was cozied up against the curb. Looked to me like the boys in blue were keeping an eye on Janet Seigal.

I'd thought about Richard Seigal's death at some length and had come to the conclusion that all she had to do was keep her mouth shut and she was pretty much guaranteed to get away with murder. Without a handful of "probable cause" the cops can't actually compel anybody to talk to them. As most of the evidence had pointed at me, it was safe to assume that they had little or nothing on her. The only possible link was if they found her fingerprints on the gun . . . but *I* was her alibi for that. I'd dropped the gun into her raincoat pocket after I took it away from him. No traction for the cops there. Yeah . . . this was one of those times when, if she was smart, and she was, silence was truly going to turn out to be golden.

I was on my way up the back stairs when my phone began to buzz.
"Yeah," I said.

"Mr. Waterman?"

"Who's this?"

"Paul Edlund at Northwest Hospital."

"Oh no man, don't tell me . . ."

"Quite the contrary," he said. "I think you ought to come up here."

"Twenty minutes," I said.

▪   ▪   ▪

His head was bandaged like the Mummy and about the size of the noggin on the Jack in the Box guy. All they'd left open was the area around his left eye. And it followed me, bright and blue, as I tiptoed into the room. Felt like a car had been lifted from my back.

"Jesus," I whispered. "You scared the shit out of me, you little fuck."

He blinked.

"The doc says I can't stay long."

He blinked again, which told me for sure he knew what I was talking about. Then his right hand twitched. The hand was connected to the bed frame by a piece of surgical gauze so he couldn't pull out any of the IVs.

"Take it easy," I said. "You just get better."

His hand moved again. But it wasn't twitching. He was making a back-and-forth motion. I walked over next to him. He did it again.

"What do you want?" I asked.

Back and forth. Back and forth. And then I got it. He was making a scribbling motion. "You want to write something?"

He blinked.

I patted myself down. Came up with my notepad and that same green golf pencil.

I reached down and carefully slid the pencil between his fingers and then slipped the pad beneath the pencil. He took a deep breath before his hand started to move. He lost his grip on the pencil. It rolled across the pad and down onto the sheet.

I picked it up and started to put it back in my pocket. He began tapping his finger on the pad. The feral look in his eye told me everything I needed to know.

I slipped the pencil back into his fingers and stepped back. Took him the better part of five minutes that felt like an hour and a half. By the time he finished he was about out of gas. He closed his eye. The pencil slipped from his fingers again. His chest was heaving as he sucked oxygen from his mask.

I walked back and retrieved the pencil and the pad.

The letters were crooked, and there were only five of them, but I knew right away what it said.

When I looked up he had me fixed with that bright blue eye.

"Biggs?" I said.

He blinked.

"Why?"

One shaky finger rose slowly off the bed, and it was pointing right at me.

Chapter 4

I wrapped the shotgun in a navy-blue blanket and laid it on the floor behind the driver's seat, then carried the U-Dub duffle bag of ammo around to the back, lifted the carpet, and put it where the spare tire used to rest.

The Smith & Wesson M&P was riding in the passenger seat today, where I could reach over and pet it. Carl had been right from the very beginning. He'd warned me that we were running blind, and that when that happened, things had a tendency to go to shit in the blink of an eye. And, of course, I'd listened. Oh yeah . . . just like I always do.

All I'd managed to accomplish thus far was to endanger the lives of any number of innocent people, get myself beat up, kidnapped, and dumped in the trunk of a car, then arrested and charged with capital murder, and now for my grand finale, I'd caused one of my best friends to very nearly get beaten to death.

And the thing was . . . I still didn't know how or why. I had no idea how Biggs and Bostick had connected Carl to me, or how they'd found out where he lived, or why they'd want to hurt him.

Neither did I have the faintest idea how Chuck Stone and Blaine Peterson had ended up dead, what Biggs and Bostick had to do with any of this, or how my father's ugly tweed coat played into the whole damn thing.

I only knew one thing for sure, and that was that Aaron and Alice Townsend had both denied knowing any of them, and, for the life of me, I still couldn't figure out why. Why not just tell me Stone and Peterson had been former parishioners, and that Biggs and Bostick were a couple of ne'er-do-well jerk-offs who used to be foster kids of their parishioner Nathaniel Tuttle, and who now spent their time trying to muscle some of Tuttle's estate from anybody they could. That, in all probability, would have been the end of it. Why lie?

The other thing I knew for sure was that I was damn well going to find out. The minute I'd walked in the door from the hospital, I sat down at my computer and navigated my way to Aaron Townsend's website, looking to find out where he was speaking this week, see if maybe he didn't have a gig tonight. And what did I find? A notice stating that all his speaking engagements for the near future were cancelled while Pastor Townsend went into a period of deep meditation and soul-searching. He thanked everyone for their prayers and patience, and wished them peace with the Lord. How nice.

You know what they say about Mohammed and the mountain . . . if Aaron Townsend wasn't coming to Seattle, that meant I was going to Salvation Lake.

I don't drive much during rush hour. Today I remembered why. If I had to fight my way through the masses twice a day, they'd find me hanging in the basement within two weeks.

I figured it to be something like twenty-five miles from downtown Seattle to Duvall. I just had to hope that the distance from downtown didn't set off my ankle monitor. Took me the better part of an hour and a half. By the time I turned north onto Retribution Road it was damn near six thirty and the hazy sun was sliding low over the trees. The box on my ankle was quiet as a mouse.

The ASCENSION ACRES sign was still standing. The rain had cleaned it off, leaving the colors more vivid than I remembered. I pulled over. The promised model home looked a lot like Tara. Columns and all. Some kind of idealized vision of simpler times. Sometimes I think that the most revealing question one can ask another human being is whether they think things are getting better or getting worse. No equivocation allowed. Better or worse?

The people who make me nervous are those retro souls who long for those thrilling days of yesteryear. Whether it be Evangelical Christians or the Khmer Rouge insurgents, the results are always disastrous, because time, quite simply, doesn't move in that direction. Time is a forced march forward. A one-way street. You don't have to like it, you just have to keep walking. It's like Satchel Paige said: *Don't look back. Something may be gaining on you.*

What with my recent penchant for walking into hornet's nests, I doused the lights as I rolled up the last hundred yards of the Townsends' driveway. And it was a good thing too, because the white Range Rover was sitting right in the middle of the yard.

I braked to a halt, picked up the Smith & Wesson, and waited to see if I'd attracted any unwanted attention. When a couple of minutes passed and it seemed I hadn't, I threw the car into reverse and began to ease back out of the yard, rolling slowly on the dark, rutted track, until I found a small turnout nearly back at the main road.

I got out, pulled the Mossberg Slugster out of the blanket, and then walked to the back and retrieved my bag of ammo. I had eight rounds in the S&W 9mm, four in the Mossberg's belly and another one in the chamber. I filled one side pocket with 9mm cartridges and the other with shotgun shells.

I threw the ammo bag on the backseat and locked the car. The air was heavy and wet. Took me five minutes to creep back to the house. The brass carriage lights on either side of the front door were glowing fuzzy in the misty darkness. The lights were on in the back of the house.

I was about to knock on the door when I heard a high-pitched yelp of pain. And then another. Then a man's guttural grunt and an anguished scream.

I stepped off the porch and began to make my way around the north side of the house. A voice was shouting something. Something about hands. And then another scream. I flattened myself against the house and peeked into the nearest window. Looked like an office. It was empty.

I stepped back out of the shrubbery and kept going. The voices were louder now, the agony more distinct. "Hands on your head, bitch!" someone screamed.

Then a loud, flat crack and another scream. I slipped in among the rhododendron bushes, flattened my back against the bricks, and peeped into the corner of the window.

I jerked my head back in disbelief. Someone was groaning now. I took several deep breaths and then peeped again. The family room. Four people in sight.

Aaron Townsend was slouched in a red leather chair. He was naked and bleeding from several places on his face. Brother Biggs had him by the shoulders, forcing him to sit and watch what Bostick was doing to his wife.

Alice Townsend was over in the back corner of the room. Squatting. Naked. Her arms protecting her chest. "Get up," Bostick screamed.

She slowly pushed herself up the wall. Her eyes were wide and wet.

"Hands on your head, bitch," Bostick ordered.

"Please," she begged, cringing back into the corner.

"On top of your head," he bellowed.

I watched as she laced her fingers together atop her head and squeezed her eyes shut. The whole front of her was red as a lobster.

Bostick stepped forward and began slapping her breasts. First one, and then the other. Hard. Left and right. Back and forth, until she couldn't take it anymore and slid back down the wall onto her haunches, weeping uncontrollably now.

Bostick turned to Aaron Townsend. "You like that, do ya?" he asked. "Like watchin' those big titties of hers bounce around?"

Townsend tried to get up, to come to her defense, but Biggs slammed him back into the seat. When Townsend began to fight, Biggs clubbed him in the right eye and then began to choke him.

"You ready to tell us yet?" he screamed.

Townsend's mouth was bloody. "I told you," he whimpered. "I already told you. For the love of God, believe me."

Biggs hit him again. Townsend slid down onto the carpet. His mouth wide open, his eyes rolling in his head like a spooked horse.

"Guess we're gonna have to get serious with her," Biggs said to Bostick.

I pulled back until I was out in the middle of the yard where the house lights didn't reach, and then hurried around to the back of the house. I hadn't seen any sign of their little girl, Lila. I'd have felt a lot better if I'd known where she was, but I just didn't have the time to make sure she was safe.

I duck-walked under the big window that overlooked Salvation Lake and up onto the back porch. "Bend over," I heard Bostick say in the second before I kicked in the back door.

Looked like a game of freeze tag. Everybody glued in place. I swung the shotgun back and forth between Biggs and Bostick.

"Just give me an excuse," I said. "Either of you assholes, just give me an excuse and I'll blow you back to wherever hellhole you came from."

Apparently, they caught my drift. Neither of them so much as twitched.

Townsend had come to his senses and was pulling himself to his feet.

"Call 911," I told him.

He looked at me like I'd lost my mind.

From behind me, Alice Townsend said, "No . . . no . . . no police."

I threw a quick glance over my shoulder. She was squatting against the wall, panting, covering her chest with her elbows.

Townsend began to stagger in my direction.

"No," he gargled around a mouthful of blood. "No police."

Biggs and Bostick were inching toward the center of the room, hoping to put Townsend between themselves and the shotgun.

"Get out of the way," I shouted at Townsend, but he kept tottering forward, until he was directly in the line of fire.

That's when Biggs and Bostick saw their chance and made a run for the door.

I shoved Townsend aside. He reached out and grabbed my shirt-front, throwing me off balance. I straight-armed him to the floor and brought the Mossberg back up to my shoulder, but they were around the corner by then.

I could hear the pounding of their feet as they ran for the front door. I started after them, but Townsend was back on his feet now, barring my way. "No . . . No . . ."

I threw him aside and ran after them. I could feel the monitoring device slapping against my ankle as I sprinted for the front door.

I heard the Range Rover start, heard the roar of the engine and the tires spewing gravel as I got to the doorway. I brought the shotgun up, squinted out over the bead, and squeezed off a round. The back window exploded. The car fishtailed wildly, then righted itself and disappeared into the darkness.

My head felt as if it was going to explode. My hands were shaking as I walked to the back of the house. Aaron Townsend was crawling around looking for his clothes. Alice had pulled a throw from one of the chairs and had it wrapped around herself.

I told myself to stay calm, but I was so pissed off, I lost it anyway.

"What the fuck is the matter with you people?" I screamed. "Somebody comes in here, beats your ass, sexually assaults your wife, and you don't want to call the cops? Have you lost your goddamn minds?"

Townsend looked up at me from the floor, and then over at his wife.

"They've got Lila," he said.

"They said they'd kill her," Alice whispered.

"You ought to be more afraid of what will happen to her if they don't kill her," I said, and then immediately wished I hadn't.

They both looked away. Alice began to cry again.

"Get dressed," I said. "Both of you get dressed."

I waited until they were gone, then pulled out my phone. I'd made a mistake with Richard Seigal by not calling the cops. I wasn't about to make that mistake again.

NO SERVICE, the screen read. No bars on top either. This was God's country. I cursed and hurried out to the kitchen, grabbed the receiver for the landline. No dial tone.

·   ·   ·

She'd dressed quickly. A pair of jeans and a thick green sweater that looked like it probably belonged to her husband. Her face was flushed and streaked with makeup, but otherwise she seemed to have recovered her wits, which, considering what she'd been through tonight, was pretty damn remarkable. I could see what it was that Roscoe Templeton had found admirable in her. She did, indeed, have a certain kind of tough-minded pluck.

"Where'd they take Lila?"

"If they see the police, they'll kill her," she said.

"Where'd they take her, damn it?"

She looked toward the bedroom. The door remained closed. "There's another house here on the property," she said after a moment. "It's where Nathaniel lived until he went into hospice care. They've been living there ever since they came back."

"When was that?"

"Two weeks ago."

"What do they want?"

"First . . . it was a place to stay, then it was Nate's car, then it was the money. They're convinced Nate left a bag of money around here someplace." Her eyes filled up. "We tried to tell them . . . they wouldn't . . . they . . ." She began to sniffle, but held it together.

"Tell them what?"

"That there wasn't any money and that Aaron had already signed Nathaniel's properties back over to the church council. Day before yesterday. That there wasn't any money, just the properties. And that now, this house and land was all we had left."

"How do I get to this other house?"

I could hear water running in the other room. She looked for her missing husband again. The running water stopped.

"We're not getting any help from in there, honey," I said. "That one's all talk and no action. If we can't call the cops, then I'm the only hope Lila's got. So . . . where is it?"

"Half a mile north," she said. "There's a driveway on the other side of the road."

As I started for the door, Aaron Townsend came lurching out of the bedroom. He was holding a bloody washcloth to his face. It was like he'd been listening at the door, waiting for this moment. "Wait," he said. "I'll come."

I could tell he didn't mean it. He reeked of fear and self-pity. He was only offering to come along because he felt he had to.

"You're the last thing I need," I said. "See if you can't figure out where they cut the phone lines. See if you can splice them back together. Call for help."

The front door was hanging open. I jogged through and kept on running, across the grassy yard and then up the rutted track of a driveway. Jogging at half speed, making sure they hadn't doubled back to ambush anyone who followed.

Apparently losing the back window to a shotgun blast had proved sufficient motivation to keep on driving. I was panting like a racehorse and drenched with sweat by the time I got back to my car.

I left the headlights off and drove blind, my head on a swivel as I moved along. The gravel drive was right where she said it would be. I eased in and rolled ahead slowly, then thought better of it.

Instead, I staged a quick K-turn in the middle of the road. Back and forth three times until my car was perpendicular to the roadway, at which point I took a deep breath, threw it into reverse, and floored it, crashing into the undergrowth backwards, bouncing over the uneven ground until something stout enough to stop the big car's momentum rocked me to a neck-snapping halt. I forced open the door and then fought my way through the twisted thicket to the back of the car. I yanked open the rear passenger door and grabbed as much ammo as I could carry. My pockets bulged like saddlebags as I started forcing my way back to the roadway.

I crawled up onto the gravel track and looked back. The car was rammed so far into the undergrowth that it was invisible. Whether I'd be able to get it back out was a bridge I'd have to cross later.

I carried the shotgun in front of me like an infantryman as I trotted along. There was no wind. Overhead, the moon was moving in and out of a thick bank of clouds.

Seemed like Nate Tuttle hadn't exactly looked to encourage visitors. The road was narrow and serpentine, twisting among the enormous, first-growth trees, seemingly with no rhyme or reason, as if it had been laid out without a particular destination in mind.

My eyes were beginning to adjust to the darkness when a sudden rustle in the undergrowth jerked at my attention. I raised the shotgun and slid my finger under the guard. I waited, eyes straining, breath caught in my throat, trigger finger quivering in anticipation. Two black-tailed deer stepped into view. The sound of my relief sent them bounding off into the blackness. I stood still for a minute, waiting for my heart to stop hammering, and then forced myself on.

Quarter mile later, I thought I saw an eye shining in the darkness. Maybe another deer. A glimmer of light that winked out before I could be certain it was there. I took another step forward and it glimmered again. It was the house, intermittently visible through the thick underbrush. I kept moving, slower now.

Another hundred yards and the clearing flashed into view. I stepped off the road and worked my way into the thick tangle of the forest. I could see the back of the Range Rover now. Its rear window a jagged mouth of broken glass. Beyond the car, a Greek Revival mansion looked completely out of place, as if it had fallen from the sky on the way to somewhere else.

I made my way around the house, trying to find a natural line of approach, but Nate Tuttle had been smart enough to keep a fifty-yard fire lane all the way around the place. No matter which direction I approached from, I was going to be faced by fifty yards of coverless no-man's-land, so I retraced my steps back to the only cover I had, at the rear of the Range Rover.

I crept forward until I was resting my back on the rear bumper. The ground behind the car was littered with beads of shattered safety glass. The moon peeked out from under the clouds, casting an eerie glow over the forest.

I heard raised voices coming from inside the house. Then heard the front door slam open, and the voices get louder. "Come on, C-Man," Biggs yelled. "I'll get the damn kid. Meet me at the car." I shivered at the possibility of Lila being driven off into the night by these two maniacs, and I knew, without a doubt, that there was no way I could let that happen.

So I did the only thing I could think of. I moved all the way over to the passenger side, reached over, and put the barrel of the Mossberg on the driver's-side rear tire and pulled the trigger. The tire disintegrated.

I then repeated the process on the other rear tire. Whatever was going to come down was going to happen right here, right now. They weren't taking Lila anywhere.

I pumped another shell into the chamber, fumbled around in my pocket, found some more shells, and fed them into the Mossberg's belly.

They'd turned off the house lights. Biggs's voice rattled through the trees.

"Throw out that gun, or I'll kill her," he yelled.

I trained the shotgun on the front door and waited. The way I saw things, Lila was their only ace in the hole, and I was betting both our lives that even those two bozos were smart enough to figure it out.

"Let the girl go," I yelled, "and I'll let you two walk out of here."

They came out the front door in single file, Biggs holding Lila in front of him like a shield. Bostick ducked to the left, throwing himself behind one of the big fluted columns that held up the portico. Biggs just stood on the porch, squeezing Lila hard against his chest, daring me to take a shot.

He brought his other hand out from behind his back. He was holding a big silver automatic. He put the muzzle on Lila's head. "Throw that goddamn gun out or I'll blow her fucking brains out," he yelled. Lila began to squirm and kick her legs.

What I *was* certain of was that giving up my gun would get both Lila and me killed instantly, so there was no way I was gonna do that. Biggs pointed the automatic in my direction and touched off a round. The slug ricocheted off the side of the Range Rover, throwing sparks into the night. He fired again. I rolled over to the other side of the car.

In my peripheral vision I saw Bostick dash from the porch into the woods. He was going to flank me, and there wasn't a damn thing I could do about it. A cold ball bearing rolled down my spine.

Biggs was taking the aggressive approach. He was coming straight at me, gun in one hand, Lila in the other. The girl was struggling for all she was worth. Kicking, arching her back, squirming as only kids can do, but Biggs held on like a vise.

He was half a dozen steps closer when her gyrations nearly wrested her from his grasp. Biggs made the mistake of hitching her up higher on his chest, finally giving me a field of fire. He was out at the edge of shotgun range, but I allowed for the drop, flattened myself on the ground, and let one go. He screamed like a panther and dropped to one knee. Lila fell from his grasp with a resounding thump.

"Run, Lila!" I screamed. Didn't have to tell that girl twice either. She rolled to her feet and began running awkwardly in my direction. They'd duct-taped her hands behind her back and sealed her mouth, but the kid was game.

Enraged now, Biggs took a shot at the fleeing girl and missed. He cursed and began scrambling back toward the house; I stood up, sighted out over the roof of the car, and emptied the gun at his fleeing shadow, hoping I'd get lucky. I didn't.

What I got was a bullet from the bushes that came within an inch of burying itself in my skull. In the excitement, I'd forgotten about Bostick. He wasn't quite behind me yet, but it wouldn't be long. I had to move.

I crawled around to the passenger side. Found the 9mm at the small of my back and let loose three rounds in the general direction of where I imagined Bostick to be, hoping like hell I could buy enough time to reload the shotgun.

The sound of running feet jerked my head around. My breath froze in my chest. I raised the 9mm, certain that Biggs had reversed his field and was coming at me with that big silver automatic. Instead, Lila came staggering up to the car. I grabbed her and pulled her down to my side. For reasons I can't explain, getting that tape off of that little girl seemed more important than reloading the Mossberg.

I held a stiff finger over my lips as I found an edge and ripped the tape from her mouth. The hands were more difficult. I couldn't find the end and had to tear it with my teeth before I was able to rip it the rest of the way.

Another slug slammed into the car. And then another. I saw the muzzle flash of the second round, picked up the 9mm and aimed at the spot and fired twice. By my count, I only had four rounds left in the pistol. I needed to get somewhere and reload.

"We've gotta get out of here," I whispered.

She nodded that she understood. I stowed the 9mm in my belt, grabbed the shotgun, and put my face right up into hers. "Ready?"

She nodded again. I took her hand and we made a dash for the woods. Muzzle flashes spewed from the front door of the house. The sound of high-caliber bullets crashing through the trees and undergrowth surrounded us as we picked our way through the dense underbrush. She tripped and fell. I pulled her back up. I kept telling myself that the deeper we got into the forest, the better off we were. They had to be careful that we weren't lying in wait for them. We didn't have that problem. There was nothing in front of Lila and me but trees. All we needed was to put enough distance between us and them to allow me a minute or two to reload. After that, I was willing to take my chances.

We kept stumbling on, tripping over roots, finding our way blocked by fallen trees and impenetrable thickets. Always moving west, toward the road.

Above the sound of my own labored breathing, I could hear Biggs and Bostick crashing through the underbrush behind us, shouting back and forth as they forced their way through the tangled forest. I heard Biggs shout, "Stay left. Stay left. Make sure they don't get to the damn road."

Something huge loomed in front of us. I tripped and fell, taking Lila down with me. We struggled back to our feet. The sounds of our pursuers were closer now. Her breath was coming harder. Her face was covered with a sheen of sweat. She looked like she was just about out of gas.

I took her hand and hurried forward. A massive old cedar tree blocked the way ahead. One of those first-growth monsters that pioneers used to fell and then discover they couldn't move, even if they cut it up to firewood length.

My peripheral vision caught the jagged outline of the stump, and I veered in that direction. Hand in hand, we wheeled around the butt end of the ancient tree and threw ourselves to the ground behind the massive trunk.

The ground was uneven; the trunk was straight. Several dark hollows offered sanctuary and cover. I leaned the shotgun against the fallen tree and lifted Lila up on top of the trunk. "Watch," I whispered. "Tell me when you see them coming."

I went to one knee as I reached for the box of shotgun shells in my pocket. It was gone. I stifled a groan. Must have fallen out one of the times I'd tripped and fallen. I cursed silently and pushed my hand deeper into the pocket. All that remained were three loose shells. I thumbed them into the Mossberg's belly and then jacked one into the chamber. I told myself, three was better than none.

Took me another thirty seconds to reload the 9mm and jam it back into my belt.

Lila came sliding down from her perch. Her eyes were huge. She pointed back out into the forest. She opened her mouth to speak, but I covered it with my hand.

I threw my hand around her shoulder and pulled her down into a big loamy hollow beneath the fallen tree. I could hear them now. They were close. We waited.

They were skirting the downed cedar at both ends, trying to squeeze us between them. I could hear the nearest one's breathing. I flexed my hands around the shotgun, trying to stay loose, and then out of nowhere, Lila began jerking on my pants leg.

One of them was parallel with our position now. Trying to peek over the stump but finding it too tall and then inching forward again. Lila grabbed my leg.

I looked down, and my heart did a backflip. My head felt like it might blow up.

My ankle monitor was blinking. Red and insistent.

I poked a frightened finger at the blinking red eye. Lila got the message. She grabbed my pant leg, pulled it down over the monitor, and then held on with both hands.

They were past us now. Down at the far end, I caught the reflection of moonlight off Bostick's glasses as he crept through the woods. Biggs was no more than twenty feet away, his eyes rolling back and forth over the terrain as he limped silently forward.

Had I been alone, I would have blown Biggs away right there and taken my chances one-on-one with Bostick. But with an eight-year-old girl clinging to my leg like a life preserver, it seemed a better idea to let them creep out of sight and then disappear into the forest behind them. I put the shotgun sight on Biggs's broad back and left the bead there until he melted into the darkness.

That's the moment when the ankle monitor's little electronic brain sent a message to its little electronic lips and it began to beep, just like that idiot Prichert had told me it would.

I grabbed Lila by the back of her sweater and lobbed her out from under the tree, and then crawled out after her. I had no idea how long the monitor would continue to beep. Maybe forever. What I did know, however, was that as long as it kept beeping we didn't have a chance in hell of getting out of there alive.

"Come over here," I whispered to her.

I reversed the shotgun, putting the business end down next to my ankle, then angled the gun in such a way that, if we got lucky, it might not blow off my foot. Finally, I reached down and held the plastic monitor strap directly over the bore. I turned to Lila. She was slack-jawed with fear.

"Pull the trigger," I said.

She put both hands over her ears and looked at me. I reached out and gently pulled one of her hands down. "Trust me, baby. Pull the trigger."

She dropped to her belly, put two fingers inside the trigger guard, and looked up at me once again. "Do it," I said in a low voice.

She sobbed once and gave it a yank.

The boom nearly broke my eardrums. For a moment, I was blinded by the fog of dirt thrown into the air by the blast. Lila was snuffling and trying to wipe the dirt from her eyes. I could hear Biggs and Bostick in the near distance, shouting back and forth, trying to make sure they were both all right.

I looked down. The monitor was still on my ankle and still beeping. I pulled the foot up onto the other knee so I could see better. All that was left of the security strap was about the thickness of a pencil.

That's when I noticed that the blast had blown off part of my shoe. I bent and looked closer. I could see the bloody mess that used to be my little toe and feel warm blood seeping into my shoe. Inexplicably, I felt no pain at all.

I got up on one knee, squeezed my fingers under the remnant strap, got a good grip, and pulled for everything I was worth. About the time I was sure my heart was about to burst, the plastic snapped and I was thrown back against the ground, panting and dazed by my own momentum.

I struggled to my feet, grabbed the Mossberg in one hand and Lila in the other, and took off running. Every step seemed to awaken the pain in my foot a little more. By the time we were fifty yards from where we'd started, the foot was beginning to throb, and I was having trouble putting my full weight onto it.

We kept moving forward. Heading in what I hoped was the direction of the road.

Lila tripped and fell again. I pulled her back to her feet. The ground was getting boggy. Most of the trees were snags now, gray and bare in the moonlight. The moss was thicker here and more iridescent. On our left, swamp grass was poking up through a foot of water. Another hundred yards and the ground on our right was gone too.

I went down to one knee and looked around. My foot burned like somebody was holding a blowtorch to it. From what I could see, the recent rains had filled in the low areas of the forest with water, leaving a single tongue of dry land running down the center. I looked up at Lila. One of her braids had come undone. Somewhere along the line, she'd torn the buttons from her sweater. She had a nasty-looking scratch on one of her cheeks. She gave me a wan smile.

"Let's go," I whispered.

She took my hand again and we staggered forward for what seemed like an hour, but was probably no more than ten minutes. The narrow isthmus of dry land got thinner and thinner, until it disappeared altogether and our feet began to slap water.

My foot was dragging now, catching on everything. Seemed like I just couldn't lift it high enough to keep it out of the tangles. I pulled us to a stop, put one knee in the water, and listened. Nothing. Either they'd given up the chase or they were circling around us through the flooded forest. At that point it didn't much matter. All we could do was keep moving forward.

Ahead in the darkness, I began to make out a long straight line. The kind of thing that doesn't exist in nature. Something man-made.

"There." I pointed. Lila turned her gaze. "The road," I whispered.

We joined hands again and stumbled the last seventy-five yards. I boosted her up onto the raised roadway and crawled up beside her. We sat there hip to hip, trying to catch our breath, when the sudden faraway roar of an internal combustion engine shattered the wet stillness of the night.

Back in the direction of Nathaniel Tuttle's former home, headlights swung back and forth across the landscape, like a prison break. We heard the unmistakable sound of a car moving in our direction, the engine straining, the headlights bouncing up and down erratically as it closed the distance.

Lila and I slid back to the bottom of the berm, found the nearest stump, and squatted in the cold, dank-smelling water. She was shivering. I hugged her close to me.

As the roaring engine grew nearer, Lila pressed herself harder into my side. The blinding white spear of halogen headlights pierced the forest. I peeked out.

The square roofline told me the Range Rover was coming. I pulled Lila deeper into the shadows as the SUV limped by, dragging its flattened rear tires with its front-wheel drive, weaving all over the road as it fought for traction.

We squatted in that squalid bog, Lila and I, shivering in the darkness, listening to the sound of the car receding into the distance.

Any momentary sense of relief evaporated the second I considered where they might be going. Had to be back to Townsend's place. Back to finish what they'd started, and then wait for us to arrive.

Nothing else made any sense. No way they could drag those flat tires all the way back to town. The paved road would flay the rubber from them in a couple of miles, leaving then dragging steel rims down the road in a rooster tail of sparks. No way . . . it was back to the Townsend house for sure. They had no place else to go.

"Come on," I said. "Let's get out of here."

We scrambled up onto the gravel roadway and began limping along as fast as I was able. Lila must have had some innate sense of the danger her parents were in. She kept pulling on my arm, trying to get me to move faster. I did the best I could.

"Come on, Leo, you can do it," she whispered as we trudged along.

Took us ten minutes to get back to where I'd stashed the car. I picked her up, told her to cover her face, and began to force my way through the dense thicket. My foot screamed at me and slipped around inside what was left of my shoe.

The brush was almost too stout for me to force us through, but I kept pushing, one slide-step at a time, until I quite literally crashed into the front bumper of my car.

My breath was coming in ragged gasps as I slid us along the fender, muscled open the driver's door, and set Lila on the seat.

"Climb over," I told her. "Buckle yourself up."

Took everything I had left to climb up onto the driver's seat and close the door. I belted myself in and looked over at Lila.

"You ready?" I asked.

"I wanna go home," she said.

"Hang on," I told her as I dropped the car into low and punched it. We shot forward about ten feet and then stopped dead. I backed up as far as I was able, dropped it back into low gear again, and floored it.

We bounced forward, bending the thicket before us, hidden rocks pinballing us left and right, things slamming into the undercarriage so hard I could feel the impact in my feet as the car lurched forward.

And then the road was right in front of us, and the windshield was filled with nothing but the night sky. I cut the wheel hard right as we blew out into the moonlight. The car began to drift, threatening to shoot off the other side. I held my breath as the passenger-side wheels came off the ground. Lila squealed in the second before the drive wheel found purchase and sent us rocketing down the road.

I braked to a stop, put the car in park, and slouched behind the wheel, dazed, glazed, and mouth-breathing as I sucked air and tried to reassemble my parts. Out in front of the car, I could make out two deep furrows where the Rover's back tires had been dragged along the length of the grade.

I moved the transmission down to drive and started rolling down the road. We were dragging something. I could hear it, scraping along with us. Halfway back to the paved road, I noticed that the temperature gauge was way above its normal range and rising. I was betting that, somewhere along the line, we'd poked a hole in the radiator and were leaking coolant.

The good news was that we probably weren't going far enough for it to be a problem. The bad news was that I didn't have a plan of any sort. What I needed most was a safe place to stash Lila while I checked on the Townsends.

I looked over at Lila. "Is there any way into your daddy's place other than the road where you and I met?"

"There's the road to the barn," she said.

"What barn?"

"It's over on the other side of the lake," she said.

"How do we get there?"

"I'll show you."

Two minutes later, we reached the pavement of Retribution Road.

Lila pointed to the right, back in the direction of her house. I followed instructions. As I'd suspected, the pavement had been murder on the Rover's flat tires. Every few yards a piece of shredded radial littered the road.

We were approaching the Townsend driveway. "Keep going," Lila said.

Just before the entrance to the drive, one of the Rover's tires had come completely off the rim and lay on the shoulder like steel-belted roadkill. I could see where the rim had gouged a furrow in the pavement, once the tire was gone.

"Keep going," she said again.

We were almost back to the ASCENSION ACRES sign when Lila pointed.

"There," she said.

I crossed the center line and pulled into a narrow indentation in the scrub oak. A massive rusted chain was stretched across the opening. I got out and had a closer look.

The chain was big enough to anchor a freighter and the lock looked brand new, but the two wooden posts that held the ends of the chain had obviously been in the ground for a while, and in the wet Pacific Northwest that meant they'd probably seen better days.

I got back in the seat and buckled my seat belt.

"I'm gonna need to hang on again, huh?" Lila asked.

"Good idea," I said.

I put the front bumper on the chain and fed it some gas. The wooden posts splintered almost instantly. Rather than drag the chain all over creation, I backed up, got out, and pulled the rotted, rusted mess out from under the car. Steam was seeping out from under the hood, and the air was tinged with the acrid smell of boiling coolant. I climbed back into the driver's seat. The temperature gauge was maxed out. A small red light was blinking in the dash.

"How far?" I asked Lila as I buckled up again.

She pointed out ahead. "Just past those trees."

"What's in the barn?"

"Boxes and boxes and boxes," she said.

The barn turned out to be a big metal prefab. Looked brand new. Regular steel walk-through door on the left, three big roll-up garage doors on the right.

I turned off the car and got out. The engine shuddered hard enough to rock the big car on its springs, and then, with a noise remarkably like a death rattle, it conked out. I had a feeling that whatever happened next wasn't going to include driving my car.

I pulled open the rear door, found the ammo bag on the seat, loaded everything to the hilt, and stuffed my pockets with as much firepower as I could carry. When I turned around, Lila was standing behind me.

"I know how to get in," she said. "Buster and I come here sometimes when we want to be alone."

"Show me," I said.

She ran around to the side of the building. About a third of the way down the west wall, she stopped and pointed. I hobbled over. She grabbed a piece of metal siding and pried it out about a foot. Looked like the workmen had left out a couple of bolts when they'd put it up. Just the kind of thing kids will find every time.

She looked up at me. "I'll let you in the front," she said as she squeezed herself through the opening and disappeared.

As I limped back around to the front of the building, I could hear shouts rolling across Salvation Lake, coming from the area of the house. I didn't like the sound of it at all, but first, I needed to get Lila out of harm's way. After that . . .

The door rattled as she fumbled with the lock from the inside, and then it opened a crack. I grabbed the knob and ducked inside.

It was like she'd said. Boxes and boxes, damn near floor to ceiling. Guiding Light Publishing. All of them. I laid the shotgun on the nearest carton and ripped open the top of another. *The Christian Couple.* Townsend's supposed bestseller. Twenty-five copies per box. I looked around. Must have been a couple hundred thousand copies in here. I shook my head in angry disbelief, wondering what, if anything, about Aaron Townsend was on the up-and-up.

I swallowed my righteous indignation and turned to Lila.

"I need you to stay here, honey," I said.

"I wanna go with you, Leo," she said right away. "Those men will hurt my daddy."

"I won't let them," I promised. "But you gotta stay here."

"I wanna go with you," she said stubbornly.

I went down on one knee and gave her a hug. "No. You stay here," I said. "If I don't come back, wait till it's light out and then walk back in the direction of town. Keep walking till you get there. If anybody comes by in a car, tell them you need to call the cops. You understand?"

She turned away from me in the darkness. Her little shoulders began to shake.

"I gotta go now, honey," I said. "I'll be back."

She didn't say anything.

I picked up the shotgun, walked back to the door, locked it from the inside, and pulled it shut behind me.

I got one step in the direction of the house, when I was jerked to a halt. The sky was bright orange. I could see the yellow blades of flame stabbing above the trees. I groaned out loud and began to stumble forward as fast as my foot would allow.

The lake was close; I could smell it. A minute later, I burst out of a scrub oak thicket and found myself standing on the shore of Salvation Lake, directly across the water from the Townsend house. The rear of the house was engulfed in flames. Glowing cinders rose like fireworks into the night sky.

I hurried left, the short way around the water. As I rounded the east end of the lake, I could see the Range Rover crouched on its rims out in the middle of the drive, its headlights pointed at the sky like supermarket searchlights. The closer I got, the louder the roar of the flames became. An anguished cry tore through the air.

The front door burst open and slammed back against the house. Biggs came out backwards, crouched low, dragging Alice Townsend by the hair, waving the big automatic in an arc, looking for a target . . . any target.

Unlike his wife, Aaron Townsend was on his feet when he stepped outside. Bostick had the barrel of his gun wedged in the hollow at the back of Townsend's head. He kept stiff-arming Townsend forward as they stutter-stepped out into the yard.

Biggs lifted Alice Townsend to her feet by the hair. He screamed something unintelligible into her face and slapped her with the gun. Her knees buckled, but she managed to keep her feet. She lashed out at Biggs, trying to pluck his eyes from the sockets. Biggs snarled and hit her with the gun again. This time she went down in a pile and stayed there. He let go of her hair and started limping toward Bostick and Townsend. "Open it up, goddamnit," he screamed.

Bostick shoved Aaron Townsend forward. I got it then. They were going for Townsend's car in the attached garage, and the reason they'd come outside was that the inside entrance to the garage was in the kitchen, which was presently on fire.

Two seconds later, they turned away from me and headed for the garage. That's when I made my move. The pain in my foot was incredible. I ground my teeth as I scrambled for the cover of the Rover.

Much as it pained me, I couldn't let Biggs and Bostick drive off with these two either. The Rover wasn't going anywhere. Neither was my car. It was probably a two-hour walk back to Duvall. If they got out of this yard, they were pretty much home free.

Townsend was down on one knee trying to unlock the garage door. His hands were shaking so badly, he couldn't stick the key in the hole.

I stood up, thumbed the Mossberg's safety off, and blew Bostick into the middle of next week. The force of the shotgun blast lifted him from his feet and threw him face-first into the garage door. He bounced off and managed two bug-eyed steps back in my direction before I gave him another dose. This time he landed flat on his back, his left arm pointing to the sky and twitching, like he was signaling to eternity.

I pumped the slide and swung the gun the other way. Biggs was waving his automatic back and forth like a baton, not sure whether he wanted to point it at Alice Townsend or at me. I'd already made up my mind. Either way, I was going to kill him. If for nothing else, then for Carl. At least that was the plan, until I heard the sound of little feet slapping the ground behind me and then heard the high-pitched, plaintive wail. "Buster," Lila screamed as she ran into the yard. "Daddy. Buster's in the basement. Daddy—"

My heart nearly stopped when I saw Biggs swing his gun in Lila's direction. Without thinking, I made a desperate lunge for her, caught her around the waist, and pulled her to the ground. A slug plowed a furrow right in front of my face, sending a spray of mud into my eyes. I held on to Lila and began rolling. The next shot hit the Mossberg's walnut stock, nearly tearing the gun from my hand. I was pawing at my face trying to clear the dirt from my eyes as two more shots whistled by my head.

I picked the girl up and ran for the front door, shoulder-rolling us inside onto the stone floor. I pushed Lila deeper into the entranceway and then poked my head out. Biggs was on the move, firing over his shoulder as he limped for the woods. I raised the shotgun, put the sight in the middle of his back . . . and then Lila, for the first time all night, lost her cool. She came clawing and scratching over me, a whirlwind of crazed kiddie arms and legs, screaming about Buster burning. All I could do was fire a round in the general direction of the fleeing Biggs while I held the girl at bay with my other hand. When I looked out again, Biggs was gone.

Five seconds passed before the crackling roar of the fire found its way into my consciousness again. Lila was wailing at a pitch available only to girls of tender age and garage door openers. Out in the driveway, Alice Townsend was bruised up pretty good but was sitting up now, trying to clear the cobwebs. Over by the garage door, Aaron Townsend sat with his back against the door, his hands hanging loosely in his lap, his face a mask of broken bewilderment.

"Where's the cellar door?" I asked Lila.

She stopped wailing for long enough to point back over her shoulder.

"Please, Leo," she sniffled.

I mean . . . what was I gonna do, let Buster braise?

"Go to your mom," I said, pointing at Alice out in the driveway. "Run."

She scrambled over me and was gone. I leaned the shotgun in the corner of the entranceway, grabbed the door handle, and instantly wished I hadn't. The knob was hot enough to fry bacon. I cursed and jerked my hand away.

I used my sleeve like a pot holder and managed to pull the door open. A wall of hot smoke poured up from the basement. I waited until the worst of the smoke blew by, got down on my belly, and bodysurfed down the stairs.

Mercifully, Buster must have heard me coming. He was right there at the bottom step, filthy with soot and pissing all over the floor, but otherwise okay. I grabbed him by the scruff of the neck and crawled back up the stairs, through smoke so thick you could chew it.

I sat in the corner of the entranceway for a couple of minutes, trying to get my shit together and coughing my lungs out. When I felt as good as I figured I was gonna, I grabbed the shotgun from the corner and lurched outside.

The Townsends were huddled together in the driveway, dog and all, arms loosely thrown around each other, while Aaron Townsend prayed. To what? For what? I couldn't possibly imagine.

Much as I hated to interrupt, I limped over and held out my hand. "Gimme the keys," I said to him. When he kept right on praying, I reached down and pulled the ring of keys from his fingers.

He looked up at me. "No police," he said.

I would have laughed in his face, except that my ears picked up the wail of the siren in the distance. I held my breath and listened harder. Several sirens, actually. A veritable chorus of electronic wailing. Two minutes later, pulsing red and blue lights were bouncing around the treetops, and I could hear the deep roar of the fire truck as it raced in our direction. I dropped the keys back in Aaron Townsend's lap and walked over to what was left of the Rover. I put the Mossberg, the 9mm, and all the ammo on the hood of the car, then sat down on the ground and waited for the second coming.

■   ■   ■

King County had been kind enough to hold my cell for me. The "JESUS LOVES ME" suite, as I liked to call it, was exactly as I'd left it. Disgusting.

Like I'd figured, a pair of King County mounties had roared up right behind the fire truck. They'd taken one look at the late Chauncey

Bostick and immediately jumped my bones. I spent the next hour and a half chained in the back of a county cruiser, getting my foot tended to by county EMTs and watching fire trucks and aid units come and go, before a couple of Seattle uniforms finally showed up in an SPD van and transported me back downtown.

I'd been in the "JESUS LOVES ME" suite all night. I knew something was up when the jailer showed up, unlocked my cell door, handed me the artisanal scrambled eggs and toast, and then walked away without locking the door.

I was choking down the last piece of roofing material toast when I heard footsteps coming down the corridor. I didn't need to look up; I knew who it was.

"Twice in one week," Eagen said.

"Yeah. But this time I *did* shoot the guy."

"You could play ping-pong through the hole in that fella's chest."

"I'm not much with a gun," I admitted with a shrug. "I need something you can just point and pull the trigger."

"Speaking of your last supposed victim," he segued.

"Seigal?"

"Turns out you had some interesting ideas last time we chatted."

"Like?"

"Seems they did have a prenup. According to that, she walks away with four hundred grand and half the community property."

"Not a bad day's work."

"But . . ." He gave it a long pause. "With the demise of Mr. Seigal at the hands of person or persons unknown, she now comes into his insurance, which is good for two mil, and another two mil from a policy his firm kept on him, plus whatever she gets out of the house and other property. We figure, even allowing a cool million for lawyers' fees, she'll end up walking with about seven and a half mil by the time the whole thing is settled."

"What does she say about it?"

"Absolutely nothing," Eagen said. "Her attorneys have informed us that she won't be making any further statements. Now or ever. They're practically daring us to charge her with something."

"You gonna?"

He spread his hands. "We haven't got squat. We charge her, she sues us for malicious prosecution and walks away with another coupla mil."

"They find Biggs yet?" I asked.

Eagen shook his head. "Nope," he said. "We've got everybody and his brother looking for him, but he's still at large out there someplace."

I stood up. "Am I free to go?"

He nodded. "Everybody seems to agree that you saved the day. The little girl thinks you're Captain America, for Christ's sake." He pulled open the cell door. "The shotgun's evidence. We'll be keeping that. I'll send a cruiser round with the rest of your gear later in the week."

I moseyed out into the corridor. "What's going on with the Townsend family?" I asked. "They okay?"

"Stayin' over at the W until we get through taking formal statements from them. From what they tell me, the house is a total loss. What wasn't burned up was so smoke and water damaged it ain't worth talking about."

We walked down the corridor side by side.

"Any idea what happened to my car?" I asked.

"We had it towed up to the SPD garage on Twelfth." He patted me on the shoulder. "You're gonna be needin' a rental for quite a while."

Eagen and I parted ways at the property room. I collected my belongings and mamboed out onto Fifth Avenue, where it looked a lot like spring had finally shown up. The city felt light and bright and clean. To the west, sunlight glittered on the patch of Puget Sound visible at the bottom of Seneca Street. I pulled my collar up around my neck and walked a block downhill to Fourth Avenue. Whatever those EMTs had given me for my foot was wearing off. One downhill block and it was starting to throb like a bad tooth.

The desk clerk at the W made a valiant effort not to notice that half my shoe was missing, but couldn't manage to pull his eyes from the hunk of bloody gauze so close to defiling his Berber carpet. I asked for Aaron Townsend. The clerk made a hushed call and informed me somebody would be down. I limped over to the nearest chair and took a load off.

Ten minutes later, Alice Townsend stepped from the elevator, caught sight of me, and wandered over and sat down in the chair next to me. We made quite a pair. The whole left side of her face was swollen. One side of her jaw was turning the color of an eggplant and I was even worse. Virtually no square inch of me wasn't scratched, scraped, bruised, or blackened.

"How's everybody?" I asked.

She looked down at the carpet and sighed. "Rough night," she muttered.

"Lila okay?"

"Kids are resilient," she said. "They just shake it off and go on."

"That what you did?" I asked. "Just shook it off and went on?"

She pinned me with an angry glare. "You know, Leo, the self-righteous thing really doesn't become you. I appreciate what you did for us. I really do. But, you gotta understand. I did what I needed to do. Believe me when I tell you, you had to be in *my* shoes to get it." She straightened herself in the chair. "I've got no apologies for any of it. If you've come here looking for some kind of contrition from me . . ."

"I'm just looking for a couple answers is all."

"Some things are best left alone," she said. She started to get out of the chair, changed her mind, and plopped back onto the seat, with anger in her eyes. "Why are you so damn nosey?"

"Not knowing things wears on me," I said. "They stick in the back of my mind and drive me nuts. It's just how I am."

"What do you want to know?" she asked.

"I want to know how come two of your ex-husbands came out to your new house, walked into your new life, and then ended up dead in the trunk of a car. Let's start there."

"I can't talk about that."

"Can't or won't?" I asked.

"Doesn't really make much difference, does it?"

"Must have given you quite a start when they showed up on your doorstep."

"They were looking for . . . Theresa Calder. Blaine managed to find Chuck. I don't know how, but he did. They both knew she'd been one of Aaron's parishioners; they were hoping Aaron knew where they could find her."

"Little did they know, you were standing right next to them."

"Blaine was relentless that way. The golden boy wasn't used to losing. Nobody was going to walk out on him."

"Especially with a pile of his cash."

"I only took what was coming to me. In case you've forgotten, this is a community property state. That money was going to end up in my pocket either way."

"And neither of them had the faintest idea they were standing right next to the woman they were looking for."

She made a face. "I think Blaine may have . . . right there at the end."

"How so?"

"My voice. I think he may have picked up on my voice."

"And then?"

"And then Chuck started losing his mind. I mean . . . he just went berserk, screaming at Aaron, screaming at Blaine, throwing himself around the yard."

"And?"

"I told you. I can't talk about that."

"Why not?"

Another voice piped in, "'Causa me."

Lila stepped out from behind a potted palm.

"Lila, go back to—"

"I gotta tell him what I did, Momma. Leo saved Buster."

"Do as I tell you."

Lila backed into the shelter of Alice's legs and leaned back against the chair.

"I pushed the shaggy man in the lake," she said.

I looked over at Alice. "Chuck Stone," she said.

"He was yelling at my daddy. He wouldn't stop. So I pushed him off the dock."

Alice pulled Lila close. "It wasn't her fault," she said in a low voice. "He was wearing this huge coat. It just pulled him right to the bottom."

"And then the other man jumped in to save him," Lila said.

"Blaine went in the lake after him?"

Alice nodded. "Blaine the hero," she said bitterly.

"And they both drowned?"

"No," Alice said. "That's the strange part. Blaine got him out. They were both laying there on the grass, spitting water, and then, all of a sudden, they both stopped breathing and fell over dead."

I reached over and patted Lila on the cheek. "Wasn't your fault, honey. Things like that just happen sometimes."

"He was yelling at my daddy," she said again.

"I know," I said. I raised my eyes to Alice. "I'll bet I can guess the rest of it."

She turned her face away.

"About the time you're trying to figure out what to do with a couple of dead bodies, Biggs and Bostick show up and offered to get rid of them for you."

"They thought we'd tell them where Nate Tuttle hid his cash if they did—and we let them think that. We needed those bodies gone."

"And so you made a deal with the devil."

Alice nodded again. "We had no choice. When they came back, we told them the truth. But they didn't believe us. They thought we were playing games with them. So they searched the church and everywhere else they could think of. They just waltzed in and out of our house whenever they felt like it," she said. "Took anything they wanted. Walked off with whatever they could sell."

"So that's why you and your husband were so dead set against calling the police. You were afraid that Biggs and Bostick would implicate Lila."

"It wasn't her fault," Alice insisted.

"Nobody has to know but us," I said.

She took a moment to read my face. "You're serious."

"Nobody'll hear it from me," I said. "Not now. Not ever."

She opened her mouth to speak, but I cut her off.

"But I've got a couple more questions. When I showed you the pictures of your exes, they had little stickers in the corner of them. Something my friend Carl puts on everything he touches. That's how Biggs and Bostick found out about him, wasn't it?"

She nodded. "They wanted to know about you. What your part in all of this was. Aaron tried to appease them. They were slapping him around." She looked over at me now. "What else was he going to do? They're animals. They hurt people for fun."

I swallowed my rage and bent over and got close to Lila. "Would you do me a favor, Lila?" I asked.

"Sure, Leo."

"Would you go upstairs and see how your daddy's doing and maybe give Buster a hug for me while you're there?"

She looked back over her shoulder at Alice. "Go ahead," Alice said.

"See ya later, Leo," she said as she skipped off.

When she was gone I said, "One last thing."

"Yeah."

"Where's the real Alice Brooks?"

She sighed and looked away. "Alice and I used to work the same motels in North Vegas for a while." She shrugged. "Real low-budget shit. She was a sweet kid with a two-hundred-dollar-a-day heroin habit. She OD'd one night and the motel manager . . . guy namea Cliff . . ." She took a deep breath. "Motherfucker just put her out with the trash."

She got to her feet. "My whole life has been about making sure I don't go out like that, Leo. You can think what you want, but I'm not ending up in a landfill."

I watched her as she crossed the lobby and got into the elevator, then I walked outside and asked the parking attendant to call me a cab.

■　　■　　■

The rental car beeps. It beeps when you open the door. It beeps if it senses something in front of you. It beeps if it thinks you're about to back over something. It's like riding in a car with your friggin' grandmother.

Eagen had heard right. The Townsend house was a goner. Only the entranceway and the garage were still standing. The rest of it had burned to cinders and collapsed into the basement. The acrid smell of fire hung in the air like a damp shroud as I retrieved the bag from the backseat and started around the side of the house.

I stood for a minute looking out over the obsidian sheen of Salvation Lake. Thinking about how, somewhere in my heathen mind, salvation was linked to the notion of atonement. Of somehow making up for all the bad shit you'd done, and wiping the slate clean so you were ready for whatever came next. For the life of me, I couldn't see anybody who'd come out of this mess with clean hands, except maybe Buster, and I wasn't sure he counted.

I unpackaged the gloves, put them on, and then walked out onto the dock, knelt down, and filled the jar with water. I set the jar on the dock and screwed the lid on. Then I put the jar and the gloves into a white plastic Bartell Drugs bag that I'd brought from home for that purpose.

I threw the Townsend place a final look over my shoulder, aimed beeping Betty between the trees, and headed back for the city.

. . .

"Anatoxin-a," Rebecca said. "I'm going to have to notify the Department of Ecology and the EPA. They're going to want to know about this." She looked over the lab table at me. "Jed called and said you were back in jail, but not to worry. How'd you come up with the sample?"

"They cut me loose early this morning. I rented a car and drove back out to the Townsend place," I said. "I figured if Stone and Peterson hadn't drowned, then it had to be something about the water."

"It's a cyanobacteria. It attacks the central nervous systems of mammals."

"How'd it get in the lake?"

"Believe it or not, it's a natural occurrence. Rare but completely natural. Happens every spring about the time the skunk cabbage blooms. It's a blue-green algae. It only shows up in truly toxic levels once in a great while. Mostly in man-made bodies of water, where the water transfer rate is fairly low. Green Lake's been closed three or four times in the past decade because of the same thing. Not anywhere near this level of toxicity, but enough to make you wish you'd stayed away from it. When the toxicity gets this high, bacteriologists used to refer to it as a 'VFDF'—short for 'Very Fast Death Factor.' Depending on the dose, its potency, and the size of the victim, anatoxin-a can kill a person in less than three minutes."

"I don't know why, but somehow I feel better that my old man's coat didn't drown the poor guy."

She wagged a finger at me. "I told you back when this started. There was no water in their lungs."

"Because they didn't breathe it in, they swallowed it."

"Right . . . so by the time the bodies got to me, they'd been drying out in the trunk for a couple of days, during which time, they'd absorbed the lake water, which left no sign of the cyanobacteria in the bodies."

"From what I'm told, the Stone guy got crazy and jumped in the lake and then Peterson jumped in to save him."

I was taking a big chance here. First off, there was no way she was going to let me tell her how to do her job, and secondly she always knew when I was lying. Always.

"I'll be sure to include that in my report," she said, without looking my way.

"I'm betting the Peterson family will feel a little better knowing their son was doing the right thing when he died."

"No doubt," she said as she turned off the lights. "You ever find out how they got in the trunk of that car?"

"Nope," I lied.

"You going to buy me dinner?" she asked as we headed for the door.

"I heard the Sorrento Hotel did a major overhaul of everything, including the menu. Maybe we ought to try it out."

She looked down at my foot. "Can you make the walk?" she asked.

"Long as we go slow."

"Not too slow," she said. "I've got a seven o'clock budget meeting at city hall."

"And here I was hoping for a bit of late-night tea and sympathy."

"This weekend," she said.

"I'm not big on deferred gratification," I groused as we walked along Ninth Avenue.

She patted my arm. "I know," she said. "I'll make it up to you."

. . .

As I drove up Magnolia Boulevard, I finally found a song on the radio I recognized. The sound of Lloyd Price singing about how the night was clear and the moon was yellow, set my little heart aflutter, ". . . and the leaves came tumbling down."

I was bopping along, alternately singing and using a Sorrento Hotel matchbook to pick the last of the short ribs from my teeth, when I rounded the corner to my house and saw the moving truck.

White truck. Big green letters. BEKINS. Sitting right there in the Seigals' driveway. Looked to be about half a dozen guys pulling stuff out of the house and packing it into the truck. The silver Lexus was parked over on my side of the street in front of the Morrisons' place. The blacked-out SUV was sitting half a block north. Obviously, Eagen still had a couple of his men keeping an eye on the proceedings.

I drove by, keeping my eyes straight ahead as I pulled up to my gate and got out to fetch the mail. Usually, as long as it wasn't raining too hard, I'd sort through it before I got back into the car, but not tonight. Tonight, I tucked the pile under my arm and walked straight back to the car. That's when it hit me: I didn't have the remote for the gate. It was still in my car someplace. I was going to have to do it manually.

I leaned over the seat, found the envelope I'd gotten from the police property room, and shook out my key ring.

I got out and started for the gate, when I was stopped dead by a voice from behind.

"How's Captain Magnolia tonight?"

I took a deep breath and turned around.

The widow Seigal and her dog.

"I was told you're not talking," I said.

"I'm moving instead," she said.

"So it would seem."

"The house has so many memories," she said.

I couldn't help it. I had to laugh out loud.

"Sometimes things just work out for the best," she said with an ironic shrug.

"Sometimes they get a little help."

She turned and walked away. No cane. No limp. No nothing.

"You seem to have staged quite a recovery," I said to her back.

She stopped out in the middle of the street, and looked back at me. I ambled in her direction.

"Misdiagnosis," she said with an unctuous smile.

"A miracle perhaps," I offered.

"More like a great weight's been lifted from my shoulders," she said.

I walked over and scratched Poco behind the ear. I was working on something pithy to say when I first heard the sound of an engine. A tenth of a second later the cop behind the wheel of the parked SUV laid on the horn. I turned that way in time to see both its doors fly open.

The passenger-side cop shouted something as he scrambled out of the vehicle, pointing out over my head with one hand and reaching for his gun with the other. The engine roar was louder now; I turned toward the sound.

A white XFINITY van with a ladder on top was bearing down at us at about twice the speed limit. I reached for Janet Seigal, reached to pull her to safety, but she'd already bolted in the other direction, trying to get to the far side of the street.

The van hit her flush, sending her pinwheeling up and over the top, like a broken doll, before it abruptly veered right and came screaming at me. In the second before I dove for the ditch, I caught sight of Brother Biggs's grinning face behind the wheel, and heard the crack of gunshots again tearing through the night.

The rear of the van passed so close to my head that the tailpipe nearly parted my hair. I covered my head with my hands as more gunfire rang through the trees.

I got to my knees in time to see both cops pouring fire into the windshield of the van as it headed their way. I watched, slack-jawed, as the van veered right, bounced off one of the stone pillars that held up my gate, and then careened back the other way, the momentum shift so sudden that the van began to roll, tearing loose the ladder, bursting open the back doors, puking its contents all over the street in the second before it completed its roll and disappeared over the edge of the bluff.

I could hear the van tearing itself to pieces as it bounced off the cliff face on its journey down to the beach. I turned and ran in the direction of Janet Seigal, but I didn't run very far. Her red shoes were standing there in the street like she was still wearing them, but, even from a distance, I knew Janet Seigal was dead. Looked like the impact had broken every bone in her body. I looked around for Poco, but didn't see him.

I whistled and called his name. I was thinking maybe he was under her body, and I was going to have to go over there and make sure, when he poked his little white head out of the Morrisons' hedge and barked.

I looked back up the street. One of the cops was standing at the edge of the cliff looking down. The other was yelling into the SUV's radio. I sat down on the shoulder, violently shaking from spilled-over adrenaline. Poco climbed into my lap.

. . .

"What are you going to do with the dog?" Rebecca asked.

I was standing at the stove watching bubbles form in the tops of blueberry pancakes. Rebecca was sitting at my kitchen table with Poco curled contentedly in her lap. She was drinking Irish coffee with one hand and scratching Poco's ears with the other.

"I'll find somebody in the neighborhood who wants him," I said. "Animal Rescue was going to take him to a shelter, but . . . I don't know . . . seemed like he'd already had a tough enough day. I didn't see any reason he had to go through that too, so I brought him home with me."

"Maybe you should keep him."

"I'm not responsible enough for pets."

"It takes a big man to walk a small dog."

Before I could respond, the doorbell rang.

"I'll get it," she said. Rebecca took the coffee and the dog along with her as she disappeared into the hall.

I heard the low mutter of voices from the front door as I flipped the cakes.

A minute later she came back into the kitchen and nodded back toward the door.

"I think you probably ought to handle this," she said. She set her coffee on the table and held out her hand. I gave her the spatula, wiped my hands on a dish towel, and headed for the front door.

Lieutenant Timothy Eagen. Standing on my front porch holding a standard-issue cardboard box and a black garment bag.

"I brought you your gear back," he said.

And then Poco was at my heels, barking like crazy at Eagen. I picked him up.

"That the Seigal dog?" Eagen wanted to know.

"He's just visiting."

"You should keep him," he said.

I reached out with my free hand and took the box from him. It was heavy enough for me to tell it held the Smith & Wesson and the rest of the ammo.

"Come in for a second," I said. "We're making pancakes."

"Aw, no. I've got to—"

"Blueberry. Come on."

Shrugged. "Okay. But really, I'm gonna have to head out pretty quick."

I stepped aside and let him walk down the hall past me. I left the box on the table in the hall and padded back into the kitchen.

I pointed at the garment bag. "What's that?" I asked.

Instead of answering, he stuck out his arm and handed it to me.

The pure heft of the thing told me what it was. I peeled off the plastic and there it was. My old man's tweed overcoat. All forty pounds of it. I don't know why, but I leaned over and gave it a sniff.

"I had it cleaned," Eagen said. "Thing stunk to high heaven."

I didn't know what to say, so I walked over and hung it from one of the knobs on the kitchen cabinets. "You want coffee?" I asked Eagen.

"I mean . . . if you got some made . . . no trouble."

"No trouble at all," I assured him.

As I was pouring him a cup, he said, "I went out to the Townsend house last night. Hell of a spread they had out there . . . except that the place was crawling with EPA guys in nuke suits."

"The lake's contaminated with anatoxin-a," Rebecca said.

He took a sip of coffee. "I guess sometimes Mother Nature takes her own brand of retribution," he said.

"Amen," I said.

About the Author

Photo © Skye Moody

G.M. Ford is the author of eight other novels in the Leo Waterman series: *Who in Hell Is Wanda Fuca?*, *Cast in Stone*, *The Bum's Rush*, *Slow Burn*, *Last Ditch*, *The Deader the Better*, *Thicker Than Water*, and *Chump Change*. He has also penned the Frank Corso mystery series and the stand-alone thrillers *Threshold* and *Nameless Night*. He has been nominated for the Shamus, Anthony, and Lefty Awards, among others. He lives and writes in Seattle, Washington.